"Have you thou
you?"

Bethany nodded. "D~~o you~~
good marriage, even in these circumstances?"

"You and I have always made a good team. I'm
asking you to give up a lot, though. If there's
someone you've been wanting to marry, you'll lose
your chance if you marry me."

She shook her head. "There is no one else."

"Then you'll do it?"

Andrew made their marriage sound like a business
arrangement. Bethany couldn't tie herself to a man
who would never love her, could she?

Just then, Mari lifted her head, roused by her
uncomfortable position and the noise around
them. She turned in Andrew's arms and reached
for Bethany. When Bethany took her, the little girl
settled in her arms with a sigh and went back to
sleep.

If Bethany didn't accept Andrew's proposal, Mari's
grandmother would take her back to Iowa, and
she would never see her again. She swallowed, her
throat tight. And if she didn't accept Andrew's
proposal, she would never know the joys of being
a mother. Because if she didn't marry Andrew, she
would never marry anyone.

"*Ja*, Andrew. I'll do it. I'll marry you."

Jan Drexler enjoys living in the Black Hills of South Dakota with her husband of more than thirty years and their four adult children. Intrigued by history and stories from an early age, she loves delving into the world of "what if?" with her characters. If she isn't at her computer giving life to imaginary people, she's probably hiking in the Hills or the Badlands, enjoying the spectacular scenery.

Books by Jan Drexler

Love Inspired Historical

The Prodigal Son Returns
A Mother for His Children
A Home for His Family
Convenient Amish Proposal

Amish Country Brides

An Amish Courtship
The Amish Nanny's Sweetheart

JAN DREXLER

Convenient Amish Proposal

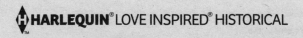

Recycling programs
for this product may
not exist in your area.

LOVE INSPIRED BOOKS

ISBN-13: 978-1-335-00521-2

Convenient Amish Proposal

www.Harlequin.com

Printed in U.S.A.

For my thoughts are not your thoughts,
neither are your ways my ways, saith the Lord.
—*Isaiah* 55:8

To Brooklyn

"I have loved thee with an everlasting love…"
—*Jeremiah* 31:3

Soli Deo Gloria

Chapter One

LaGrange County, Indiana
May 1934

Bethany Zook paused and stood at the top of the porch steps, the rag rug still quivering in her hands from the hard shake she had given it. What was that sound? Turning her head, she tried to catch it again. There! Was it a cat's cry? She turned again and heard something like a bird call.

Draping the rug over the porch rail, Bethany followed the sound and stopped when she reached the gravel road, dusty in the late May sunshine. When she heard the sound this time, it was laughter. A child's laughter. And the sound was coming from the Yoders' farm. Bethany crossed the hot road quickly, trying not to step on any sharp stones, and picked her way along the shady edge toward the Yoders' farm lane. The family had moved to Iowa four years ago, and the place had been empty ever since.

Bethany paused. Squatters often took over abandoned houses, she had heard. Ever since the hard times began a few years ago, men had gone on the road to find work. Even whole families. She glanced toward the safety of the house she had just left. *Daed* and the boys were working out in the fields, too far away to hear her call for help if she ran into a stranger. But then the laugh came again. A child wasn't dangerous.

The giggling child came closer, as if she was running down the lane toward the road. Right toward Bethany.

"Mari!" a man's voice called. "Where are you!"

Bethany reached the end of the lane at the same time as the little girl, who collided with her skirts. Bethany caught the sight of deep blue eyes rimmed by long dark eyelashes, and then the toddler turned and ran back toward the house. A man came rushing from the back of the long-empty farmhouse and swooped the girl into his arms, nearly crushing her as he clasped her to him.

Taking a step back, Bethany couldn't believe her eyes. Andrew Yoder. The last time she had seen him, she had watched the wagon disappear as his family left Indiana behind four years ago. Four years. It might as well have been a lifetime.

Squirming in his arms, Mari pointed a finger in Bethany's direction. "Who's that? *Daed*, who's that?"

Too late, Bethany thought of hiding, but Andrew's sky-blue eyes had already followed Mari's finger. "Bethany?"

She swallowed. He was still as handsome as ever, with his beard giving him a maturity he had never had during the years they had been neighbors, friends and rivals. The only thing missing was his smile. He shifted Mari onto one hip and headed in her direction.

"Bethany? It is you, isn't it?"

She nodded.

"I didn't think I would see you."

She forced a smile. "I didn't think I'd ever see you again, either." *But then I wasn't the one who moved away.* Shifting her gaze to the child in his arms, she took in the girl's light brown curls covering her head. She wore an apron…but no dress. The child's mother was certainly lax in the care of her daughter. The child's mother…

Bethany forced her smile to continue, ignoring the possessive way Andrew held Mari. "When did you get home?"

He stopped at least ten feet away from her, his eyes shuttered. "I…we just arrived today."

Bethany had always been able to tell when Andrew didn't want to tell her something, but if she pushed, he would never reveal what she needed to know. This time she wanted to know where Mari's mother was. She looked past him toward the house. All was quiet.

"You're moving back here?"

He nodded. "*Daed* never sold the farm. He couldn't, even after we had moved to Iowa. I think he always planned on coming back here." He ran one hand over his face. "He never got the chance. And the rest of the family is settled out there."

Andrew's father had passed away? Bethany drew closer. "I'm sorry about your *daed*. You must miss him."

Andrew nodded again.

"So, what brings you back to Indiana?" Bethany bit her lower lip. Did she really want to know?

Lifting his eyebrows, Andrew looked at her. "Things... changed. I wanted to make a new start."

Things changed? She watched Mari squirm in Andrew's arms. They certainly had.

Andrew shifted the little girl to his other hip. "How is Peter?"

"Peter who?"

Andrew frowned. "Peter Schwartzendruber. Your husband."

Bethany took a step closer. Now she was only a few feet away from him. "Why do you think I'm married to Peter?"

"Dave Zimmer and I have been keeping in touch. A few months after we had arrived in Iowa, he wrote that you and Peter were getting married."

She would have laughed at the idea if it hadn't been so ridiculous.

"You know I would never marry Peter."

His face went white as he set the restless girl on the ground and took a step toward Bethany. "Dave said—"

"Peter asked me, and then he spread the news around that we were planning a wedding before I had the opportunity to say no." Bethany moved another step closer to Andrew. His face was pale. "Did you really think I was married all this time?"

He nodded.

Bethany glanced at Mari, digging in the soft dirt with a stick. "So that's why you never wrote to me." Now it was her turn to feel sick. Then her queasy stomach stilled. The evidence of Andrew's rejection looked like she was almost three years old. "How long did you wait before—before you got married?"

Andrew rubbed at the back of his neck. "When I found out about you and Peter, I reckoned there was no reason to come back to Indiana, and when I met Lily, well..." His voice trailed off as his shoulders shrugged the end of his thought.

In a recent sermon, Bethany had been struck by a phrase Preacher John had used. Something about girding up your mind to face the trials to come. She lifted her chin and straightened her shoulders, bracing herself for the reality of meeting this Lily. The woman Andrew had chosen to be his wife.

"I would like to meet her." She managed a smile. "I'm sure we'll be good friends, since we're to be neighbors."

His eyes shuttered once more before he shifted his gaze to his daughter. "I...we lost her. Just a few weeks ago. There was an accident—"

Bethany leaned forward and placed a hand on his arm. "Andrew. I'm so sorry."

He lifted his gaze to meet her eyes, and for the first time, Bethany felt like she was seeing the real Andrew. Then his expression grew hard once more.

"Denki." The reply was automatic. He bent down to pick up his daughter again, closing out Bethany. "I have to get back to work. I'm glad you stopped by."

Bethany chewed on her lower lip. She should be neighborly, even if the neighbor was Andrew Yoder. And if he had just moved from Iowa, he couldn't have

brought much with him. What was he planning to prepare for his meals?

"Would you like to have supper with us tonight? *Daed*
and the boys would be happy to see you."

Andrew brushed some dust off of Mari's apron. "Not
today. It's been a long day already, and Mari will need to
get to bed early." He half turned. "Another time, though.
Maybe in a few days, after we get settled."

"*Ja*, for sure." Bethany spoke the words as he carried
Mari back to the house. "Another time."

Andrew kept his wiggling daughter in his arms until
he reached the washtub behind the house. He didn't
blame her for wanting to get down and run through the
soft grass. Lily wouldn't let her play in the sparse, dusty
grass in Iowa, and Mari's grandmother didn't let her go
outside at all, in case another dust storm blew up.

For the first week, Lily's mother had cared for her
while Andrew was still coming to grips with the fact that
his wife was gone and had left him behind to raise their
daughter. Before long, though, Andrew could tell that
Rose's clean, orderly farmhouse was the wrong place for
Mari. Rose Bontrager had her own regimented way of
raising children and thought her way was the only way.
But when Andrew had caught a glimpse of his daughter at the church meeting the week after the funeral, he
hardly recognized her. She had stared at him with sad
eyes, looking lost and abandoned, even though she was
safe in her grandmother's arms.

He had gone to bring Mari home that afternoon, with
Rose's protests ringing in his ears. And while he had

been thinking of returning to Indiana for months, it was Rose's threat to send the bishop to talk to him that cemented his decision to bring Mari home, out of Rose's reach.

Now that he was back on the family farm, though, he still couldn't let her run free. She had disappeared so quickly a few minutes ago! How far would she have gone if Bethany hadn't been there to stop her at the end of the lane?

Bethany. Before his mind could dwell on what it meant to see her again, Mari pushed against his chest.

"*Daed*, let me down. I want to play." Mari patted his cheek to get his attention, then grinned when he looked at her. She had started talking at an early age, according to Lily, and hadn't stopped since. She also had a stubborn streak that he knew very well. It ran in the Yoder family without fail.

"I need to wash our clothes and I can't risk you running away again."

She squirmed. "Won't run away. I see flowers. I want to smell them."

Andrew glanced at the bed of lilies *Mamm* had nurtured while they had lived here. Now, after being neglected for four years, the orange flowers had spread to cover half the old garden space. Lily would have loved them. But the bed trailed away toward the stream and the old springhouse, a spot that would prove irresistible to his curious daughter. How did parents with several children keep them safe? How had Lily gotten any work done with Mari to take care of? Then he spied the length of clothesline he had found in the house. He set Mari down and tied the end of the rope around her waist. It might not be what Lily would have done, but at least she couldn't get into too much trouble.

"You can go smell the flowers, but when you feel the rope get tight, then you know it's time to come back toward me."

Mari fingered the rope. "So I won't get lost?"

"That's right." Andrew tied the other end of the rope to his own waist. "And I can wash our clothes and not worry about you."

He watched her run to the first flower, bury her little nose in it and then sneeze.

"Be careful, there might be bees in the flowers."

Mari grinned at him, then looked carefully into the next deep blossom. Her profile, so much like Lily's, made his breath catch. How could he hope to raise Mari alone? He had so much work to do to bring the farm back to what it had been, and he would never get that work done and take care of Mari at the same time. But he couldn't give her to Rose, either. Lily had told him how stifled she had felt growing up under her overbearing mother, and he couldn't let his bright, happy daughter grow up the same way.

He turned back to his washing, scrubbing the stain on Mari's only dress. With his mother-in-law pressuring him to let her raise Mari, he'd had to leave Iowa before he could make arrangements for someone to make new dresses for her. A two-year-old grew faster than a long-legged colt, and she needed new clothes for the warm months ahead.

As he scrubbed the fabric, he noticed a small tear in

the front of the little dress. Holding it up, he could tell that the tear was just the beginning. The entire skirt was threadbare and nearly transparent in places. He dropped the dress into the rinse water and leaned heavily on the washtub. Sighing, he glanced at Mari as she pulled one of the flowers from its stem.

Before Lily died, he hadn't had any worries. He worked the fields, hoping that the drought they were experiencing would pass soon. Lily took care of the house and Mari, and each evening they thanked the Good Lord for their life together. That last morning Lily had told him that she suspected another little one might make his appearance in the winter. They had talked of adding a room onto the house, and Andrew had gone to the barn with dreams of a blessed future. But in one instant, everything had changed. A dark, boiling line had appeared on the horizon, pushing dry thunder ahead of it. Lily had run to gather the eggs before the dust storm came…but she hadn't reached the chicken coop. A stray bolt of lightning had destroyed her and their dreams. A single instant, and Lily was gone.

He bowed his head, not even trying to form his questions into words. He had prayed himself dry over the past few weeks, and he was exhausted. No one could tell him why it had happened. No one could give him any hope for the future. If it wasn't for Mari, he would have nothing to pull him out of bed in the morning.

Andrew shook his head to clear his vision. He had to keep Mari with him. Living here in Indiana was the only way to keep her safe and out of Rose's clutches.

The next morning, just after Andrew finished his

breakfast of lumpy oatmeal, a knock sounded at the door. Through the dusty window, Bethany's face appeared. She held up a basket as he approached the door.

"I thought you might need some clothes for Mari," she said. Walking into the kitchen, she put the basket on the table and held up a small dress and apron. "I had some dresses left from *Mamm*, so I used the skirt fabric to make a dress. I hope it fits her."

Mari stood on her chair and reached a sticky hand toward the blue dress. "Pretty?"

"Wait, Mari." Andrew took the damp dishrag and wiped her hands. Then he dared to look at Bethany. Her smile as she showed the dress to Mari lit up the room.

"Are you done with your breakfast?" Bethany looked at Mari's bowl still partly filled with cold oatmeal.

"*Ja*, I'm done. It's cold."

"But are you still hungry?"

Mari nodded, rubbing her stomach. "I want some bacon." She grinned at Bethany. "And hotcakes."

Bethany took Mari's bowl and stirred the oatmeal. "We don't have any bacon or hotcakes, but I can warm up your cereal for you."

As Andrew watched, ignored by both of them, Bethany took some hot water from the kettle on the stove and stirred it into the pasty oats until the cereal was warm and smooth. Then she reached into her basket and took out a package of raisins, putting a few in the cereal.

"What's that?" Mari asked as Bethany set the bowl in front of her again and helped her sit down.

"Raisins help make the oatmeal sweet. I thought you would like them." Bethany took a jar of cream from her basket and poured some over the cereal. "There. Now try it."

Mari took a small bite, then nodded her head as she dug her spoon in for another bite.

"Did you bring your whole kitchen over in that basket?" Andrew couldn't keep from smiling as he watched Mari eat.

"*Ne*, but I brought some things I knew you wouldn't have been able to get yet." She took more items out and set them on the table as she named them. "Butter, eggs, some potatoes and a slice of ham for your dinner."

Mari's eyes brightened when she saw the ham.

"I appreciate it. But you don't need to take care of us."

She didn't meet his gaze. "Just think of it as neighbor helping neighbor. I have my own work to do, but before I go I'll put a potato casserole in the oven." She took a paring knife out of her basket and started peeling the potatoes while Mari finished her cereal.

Andrew sat next to her at the table. "You said you had some dresses left from your mother. Dave mentioned her passing in one of his letters."

Bethany nodded. "A few years ago. It sounds like it might have been around the same time as your *daed*."

"So, you take care of the house for the family? Your *daed* and your brothers?"

"It isn't hard, just busy."

"Too busy to keep company with anyone?"

She shrugged, keeping her attention on the potatoes. "There's really no one to keep company with. The fellows our age are married."

Andrew grinned. Actually grinned. Talking with

Bethany had always been easy. "So, no one has his eye on you?"

She blushed. "Only Hiram Plank."

She pressed her lips together in a tight line. He could have some fun with her now. He picked up a raisin and dropped it in his mouth as he planned his attack.

"Hiram would make a good husband for anyone."

"Not for me." Her face grew even redder. He had hit his target.

"I don't know. He's mature, experienced, has his own farm."

He popped another raisin in his mouth as she slammed the knife handle on the table and faced him.

"He's fifty years old if he's a day, and—" Bethany broke off and glanced at Mari, who was watching them with interest. "And he...has a distinct aroma." She wrinkled her nose.

Andrew stifled a laugh, then he couldn't hold it back any longer. "Then he isn't improving with age?"

Bethany glared at him, picked up the knife and the potatoes and took them to the sink to finish peeling them. Andrew kept laughing as he cleaned up Mari's hands and put her new dress and apron on. A chuckle or two slipped out as he ran a comb through Mari's curls.

"I need to work in the barn today," he said, talking mostly to Mari, but knowing that Bethany was listening to every word. "You can come with me, but you must obey me, and not wander off."

"She can spend the day with me today, if you like," Bethany said, her back still turned toward him. "I'm going to be planting the garden and she can help."

The laughter gone, Andrew stared at Bethany. Could he impose on her this way? But then, the barn could be dangerous for a little girl. He hadn't looked inside yesterday, but he could imagine the dirt and vermin that filled the place since *Daed* had closed those doors four years ago. He wouldn't get much work done if he had to watch Mari the whole day.

"Are you sure?"

Bethany turned to him with a soft look on her face that he couldn't interpret. "For sure. We'll have a good time together. I spend every day taking care of my brothers and my *daed*, so Mari will be a *wonderful-gut* change." She smiled. "A breath of fresh air." She started slicing the potatoes. "I'll take her to our house after I put your dinner in the oven, and you can come to get her when you've finished your work."

Andrew found himself agreeing. After all, he knew Bethany better than he knew anyone else, and he could trust her with his daughter.

By the middle of the morning, Bethany was exhausted. She loved children and enjoyed spending time with Rachel, her friend Lovina's daughter, but she hadn't realized how energetic a two-year-old could be. Mari never stopped moving or talking.

"You have a *daed*?" Mari asked as Bethany set the table for dinner.

"*Ja*, I have a *daed* and four brothers."

She counted out two forks, then gave them to Mari one at a time as the little girl set them on each plate.

"Where are they?" Mari turned her sweet face toward Bethany.

"They went to a sale today, so they won't be home until suppertime."

"My *daed* eat with us?"

"He'll eat his dinner at home."

"With *Mamm*?"

Too late, Bethany realized her carelessness. Of course, Mari would think of her home in Iowa, not the house here in Indiana. Bethany kneeled on the floor and stroked Mari's curls.

"Not with your mother. He's here, at your new house."

Mari's eyebrows knit together. "That house smells bad. Don't like it."

"It only smells that way because no one has lived in it for a long time." Bethany stood again and checked the potatoes boiling on the stove. They weren't quite done, so she pulled a chair out from the table and sat down, lifting Mari into her lap. "Let me tell you about that house."

As Mari leaned against her, Bethany told her how the house was so old that many little children had lived in it. "Your *daed* was one of those little children. He grew up in that house."

Mari shook her head. "*Daed* is a big man."

"He is now, but once he was little, just like you." Bethany closed her eyes, remembering Andrew as a little boy. His blue eyes throwing challenges to her from the tops of fence rails, or from the top of the chicken house. He was always climbing, doing, going...and wanting her to come along with him. As Mari wiggled on her lap, she almost laughed. His daughter wasn't much different than he had been.

"I want *Mamm* to come back."

Bethany swallowed the sudden lump that appeared in her throat. "I'm sorry, but she can't. She's in the Blessed Land."

"*Mammi* Rose said that. She cried."

Blinking back her tears, Bethany nodded. Mari's grandmother Rose must be Lily's mother. "The Blessed Land is a beautiful place. We miss people when they are there, but we don't need to feel sad for them."

"Is *Mamm* happy?"

"I'm sure she is. Our Lord Jesus is there."

Mari leaned against her again. "*Daed* talks to Jesus. He cries."

Bethany leaned her cheek on Mari's soft curls. Of course, Andrew would grieve over his wife. He must have loved her very much. When the tears welled up again, she rose to her feet, setting Mari on the chair.

"The potatoes are done, and it's time to put dinner on the table."

By the time the meal was finished, Mari was nearly asleep in her chair. Bethany washed her face and hands, then carried her to the little bedroom off the kitchen that was Bethany's own. She laid her on the bed and covered her with a light flannel blanket. Mari turned over, closing her eyes as the door latch clicked into place. Bethany paused, her fingertips on the smooth wood, listening to make sure Mari was settling in for her nap.

The little girl's sweet softness had tugged on a dream Bethany thought she had buried months ago. Years ago. After Andrew's family had moved away, and after *Mamm* had passed on, leaving Bethany to care for her father and brothers.

She went back to the sink and started scraping the dishes left from dinner. But dreams didn't die, even if you buried them under a mountain of dirty dishes and laundry. Andrew had moved on with his life, but what had she done? Nothing. Her life had changed very little from the day she watched the Yoder family drive away with all their household goods piled in their wagon.

After dipping hot water from the stove's reservoir into the dishpan, she carried it to the sink and swirled soap shavings until they disappeared in the warm water. She washed dishes the way *Mamm* had taught her, cleaning the glasses and silverware first, then moving to the plates and serving bowls. The pots and pans would be last.

As she dried the last pan, Bethany's thoughts went back to the past four years. She had turned down two suitors, both of whom had gone on to marry and start families. She had even turned down an opportunity to travel to Ohio to be a nanny for her cousin. Sarah had thought it would be the perfect opportunity for Bethany to meet someone new…but she didn't go. And then *Mamm* had passed on, and she couldn't leave *Daed* and her brothers to fend for themselves.

But that had only been an excuse. Bethany rinsed the dishrag and wiped off the kitchen table. When it came right down to it, she had to admit that she hadn't gone to Ohio because she didn't want to risk loving another man.

She had made a fool of herself over Andrew once, and she wasn't going to make that mistake again. She dropped the dishrag in the washtub as that embarrassing day passed through her mind. Why had she thought she liked him so much? She had thought she knew how he felt about her, but then she tried to kiss him on the cheek. Right there at the fishing hole, while he was busy taking a fish off his hook. He had dropped the fish and, losing her balance, she had slid off the grassy bank and into the water. She could still hear his laugh, and that stupid name he had called her for months afterward.

"Fishbait." She shuddered.

They had never gone fishing again. And their friendship had never been as easy as it had been before that.

But now Andrew had made a life for himself without her. While she had waited for her life to begin, he had fallen in love with someone else.

Bethany rinsed the dish towels in a pan of clean water, then took them outside to dry on the line. She was there with a clothespin in her mouth when Andrew showed up, walking around the corner of the house.

"This place hasn't changed much," he said, taking in the house, the yard and the garden.

Bethany stuck the clothespin on the line, fastening the towels. "You're right. Things have pretty much stayed the same."

She tugged at her sleeves to pull them back over her elbows as she watched him. When they were children, he had spent as much time here as she had at his house. Today he looked around as if he couldn't get enough of the familiar sights. He fingered an envelope, then lifted it up to show her.

"I got a letter from my mother-in-law. I don't know how she found me so quickly."

"She probably asked your mother where you were."

"*Ja*, you're right." He tapped the envelope with an absent gesture. "I hadn't told anyone, even *Mamm*. I didn't want her to know we had come here."

Bethany led the way to the chairs in the shade on the east side of the house, where *Daed* liked to sit in the evenings. "Why didn't you tell her your plans? She's Mari's grandmother, isn't she? Wouldn't she want to know where you are living?"

Andrew lowered himself into a chair with a sigh. "She's one of the reasons why I came back to Indiana. She wants to take Mari from me and raise her as her own daughter."

"Wouldn't that be all right? A lot of fathers let their young children live with someone else if they don't have a mother."

He glared at her. "*Ne*, it isn't all right. You don't know Rose. Whenever she's involved in something, she takes over. Mari wouldn't be my daughter anymore, she'd be Rose's daughter."

"What does the letter say?"

Andrew stared at the envelope. "Rose is coming here to visit. She says she only wants to help us get settled, but I know she intends to take Mari back to Iowa with her."

Bethany's stomach clenched. "What does her husband say?"

"Rose has been a widow for years, and that's part of the problem. If Lily's father was still alive, Rose would have someone to take care of. But now she's alone and has nothing else to do but think of ways to interfere with people's lives."

Bethany folded her hands in her lap to keep from reaching out to take Andrew's hand. "And she misses her daughter."

He nodded. "She can't have Lily back, so she wants Mari."

"Why does she think you can't take care of her?"

"Rose says Mari needs a mother." Andrew leaned his elbows on his knees and ran a hand over his face. "I know she's right."

"What will you do?"

Andrew turned his head toward her and some of the old gleam returned to his eyes. "We could pretend that you're Mari's mother."

Bethany held up a hand to stop his scheming. "I won't have any part of lying to your mother-in-law, or to anyone else. Besides, she'd never believe you came back to Indiana one day and got married the next." She shook her head. "It won't work."

He sat up. "What if we only said we were getting married? We can set a date and announce it to everyone. Then when Rose gets here and sees that plans are already made, she'll have to be satisfied."

"It's still lying, Andrew. You can't tell her you're getting married when you have no intention of following through with it."

Andrew stared at the ground while Bethany watched a pair of ducks fly overhead.

His voice broke through the afternoon heat, soft and hesitant. "What if we did follow through with it?"

Bethany stared at him, her heart pounding. "What do you mean?"

He shrugged. "We like each other, don't we? Even after not seeing you for so long, here we are, talking like no time has passed at all. We're still friends, aren't we?"

Bethany's fingers grew cold. "What does that have to do with anything?"

"We could get married. Mari needs a mother, and after only one day at the house, I can tell I'm not cut out to be a bachelor. I need someone to watch after Mari, cook my meals and take care of the house. You can do that, can't you?"

"You want me to be your housekeeper?"

He looked at her, his eyes unreadable. "It's the perfect solution. You don't have any other prospects, do you? You couldn't have been serious about old Hiram."

"You want me to marry you…and be your house-keeper."

"And Mari's mother."

Bethany had to turn away from him. He wanted her to be everything a wife would be, except she would never be his wife. Not really his wife. Not as long as he still loved Lily, and that would be forever. He was crazy to even suggest that they marry. Friendship was one thing, but marriage required love, didn't it?

"We could make it work." Andrew's voice was insistent, holding a note of excitement. This was just another one of his schemes.

"This isn't a game you're talking about, Andrew." She turned to face him again. "Marriage is forever."

His blue eyes dimmed. "Until death parts us." He

picked up a twig and started breaking off pieces. "I was only thinking of Mari, I guess."

Bethany let her memories play through the morning she had spent with Andrew's daughter. She could step into the emptiness of Mari's life. The tug she had felt earlier returned and strengthened until her chest ached. As busy as she was with her home and family, she hadn't realized how hollow her heart had been until Mari came into her life. And now Andrew was offering her a chance she might not ever see again—the chance to be a child's mother.

She cleared her throat, hoping her voice was steady. "This is a big step, Andrew. I have to think about it."

Andrew took her hand and she looked into his eyes. "Don't think too long. Rose said her train arrives on Saturday."

Chapter Two

~~~

Whit the afternoon sun shimmered in waves off the wooden shingles of the barn roof, Andrew kept a close eye on the line of clouds in the southwest. Something had torn a hole over the haymow, probably a raccoon, and he needed to get it patched before the weather could do any more damage to the interior of the barn. *Daed* had always said a barn was only as good as its roof.

Andrew glanced over his shoulder at the line of clouds again and wiped the beaded sweat off his upper lip. Lightning could travel for miles, and he couldn't risk staying on the roof for much longer. He pounded in the last nail and slipped his hammer into his tool belt. He glanced toward the southwest again. The clouds hadn't come any closer, but he scrambled down the roof to the safety of the ladder, anyway. Once on the ground, he pulled off his straw hat and wiped his brow, leaning against the barn wall. He had never been fearful of lightning before. He rubbed his quivering knees. But now he knew how deadly it was. Swift and deadly.

He went to the pump and worked the handle until cool water gushed out. Leaning over, he stuck his sweating head under the stream until it stopped, then shook like a dog to keep drops from running into his eyes. As he wiped the last of the water away on his shirttail, Lily's face appeared in his imagination, as it often did. He kept his eyes closed, savoring the memory of her sweet smile. Then the smile turned to a frown and his eyes opened. What would Lily think of his proposal to Bethany?

He hadn't meant for it to happen. But once he had said the words, it had felt right. There wasn't anyone else he would trust more to raise Lily's daughter than Bethany. There wasn't anyone else he could imagine living with. Andrew ran his fingers through his damp hair. And Mari needed a mother. Lily would have seen the sense in that. It was convenient for both of them.

That was all, though. Mari needed a mother, but he didn't need a wife. He still loved Lily. He would always love Lily.

Ja, for sure, once he thought he had loved Bethany, too. But his love for her had faded when he learned she had married Peter. And when he met Lily, his love for Bethany had died. Lily had driven the thought of any other woman from his mind, and she still did. He couldn't think of being truly married to Bethany, and she understood that, for sure. A marriage in name only, so that Mari would have a mother to care for her.

Andrew thrust his shirttail back in his waistband and headed for the barn, ignoring the uncomfortable thought that if he hadn't believed Bethany had married Peter, he never would have looked at Lily. He had thought Bethany would wait for him…and when he heard that she hadn't, he had pushed aside any thought of coming back to Indiana until last year, the second year of drought. And until he needed a home for Mari far away from Rose's clutches.

The sound of buggy wheels on gravel made him turn toward the road. When Dave Zimmer jumped out of the buggy, Andrew couldn't keep from grinning.

"Andrew Yoder, I was sure you wouldn't be here." Dave shook his hand, then pulled him close for a hug. "I ran into Aaron Zook at a sale east of Shipshewana this morning, and he said you were back, but I didn't believe him." Dave held him at arm's length. "You don't look too bad. Iowa must have agreed with you. What brings you back here?"

Seeing Dave felt good, as if time hadn't passed at all. He was grateful that Bethany's brother had spread the news of his return. "What did Aaron tell you?"

Dave shrugged. "Nothing. Just that you were here."

"Come on into the barn. We can talk while I work." He glanced toward the southwest, but the clouds had moved on. "It's a long story."

"First of all," Andrew said, motioning for Dave to grab a hammer from the workbench. "Your letter changed everything."

"Which letter?" Dave followed him to the horse stalls. Almost every board needed to be replaced after rats had chewed away the wood in their quest for salt.

"The letter you sent just after we moved, telling me that Bethany was marrying Peter Schwartzendruber."

Andrew knocked a board loose with his hammer while Dave worked on the other end.

Andrew started on the next board, but Dave stood and stared at him. "I wrote to you about that?"

"It was four years ago, just a month or so after we moved. You told me your brother was getting married and so was Peter."

"For sure, I remember now. It turned out that Peter had spoken out of turn. He hadn't even asked Bethany yet." Dave helped him remove another board and they tossed it on top of the first one. "She turned him down, just like she turned me down."

Heat flared somewhere in Andrew's middle. "You asked Bethany to marry you?"

Dave shrugged again. "She's a nice girl. I thought we'd get along pretty well, but I guess she didn't think so. I got the feeling she knew who she wanted to marry, and I wasn't the one."

"Who do you think it was?"

"I don't know. Whoever it was, she never did marry him. She's still taking care of her *daed* and brothers."

"*Ja*, I know."

"You've seen her, then?" Dave tossed the next board onto the growing pile. "Has she met your wife and daughter yet?"

"Lily was killed in an accident a few weeks ago." Andrew swallowed. Every time he told someone of Lily's passing, it was as if he relived that day over again.

"*Ach*, Andrew. I'm sorry. What about your daughter? Where is she?"

"Bethany is taking care of her today."

Dave leaned an arm on the supporting post at the end of the stall. "There's more to the story, isn't there? Something happened to make you bring a two-year-old all the way back here, away from your family."

"Lily's mother wants to raise her. To keep her for her own. I can't let that happen." Andrew tapped at the next board with his hammer, but his thoughts were with Mari. "I need to find someone to take care of her."

Dave rubbed at his beard. "I wish I could help, but my Dorcas just had twins. They're only a few months old, and she still has her mother staying with us to help her."

"Twins are a blessing. Boys or girls?"

"One of each." Dave grinned. "I guess both of our lives have changed since we last saw each other."

Tossing another board on the growing pile, Andrew rubbed his own beard. "I wasn't asking if you could take care of Mari. I already have someone in mind."

Dave nodded. "Bethany."

Andrew knocked the next board loose. He needed advice, and Dave had always been a good friend.

"What would you think if I married Bethany?"

"I'm surprised you're thinking of marrying again already."

"I hadn't even thought of it until today. I received a letter from my mother-in-law. She's coming on Saturday to visit, and I'm sure she wants to take Mari back to Iowa with her." Andrew's hammer hit the last board harder than he intended and split it in two. "She says Mari needs a mother, and she has appointed herself."

"What are you going to do?"

Andrew leveled his gaze at his friend, watching for

his reaction. "I asked Bethany to marry me, to be Mari's mother and to take care of the house."

Dave frowned. "And she agreed to that?"

"Not yet. I'm waiting for her answer."

"How long were you and Lily married?"

Andrew swallowed as Dave's words reminded him that his marriage to Lily had ended. "A little more than three years."

"And in all that time you didn't learn the first thing about women."

"What do you mean?"

"No woman, especially one like Bethany, will be happy stepping into a marriage the way you described it. She might agree for your daughter's sake, but she'll want your love, too."

"I can't give her that." Andrew shook his head, the image of Lily's smile in his mind once more. "I can't."

Dave tackled the first board in the next stall. "Then you had better make sure Bethany knows that before you go any further with this idea."

After supper was finished and the kitchen was ready for morning, Bethany took a glass of cold tea to *Daed*. He sat on the shady side of the house, enjoying the evening air.

Reaching to take the glass from her, he motioned to the chair next to him and took a sip of the tea. "*Denki*, Bethany. This is the perfect end to a long day."

"I thought you'd like some refreshment." She leaned back in the chair that had been *Mamm*'s and took a long drink from her own glass. Shouts drifted toward them from the field behind the barn, where her young brothers, eleven-year-old John and nine-year-old James, played a game of catch. "Where are Aaron and Nathaniel tonight?"

"Aaron went to visit a girl, I think. I'm not sure where Nathaniel is, but he caught a ride with Aaron." *Daed* propped his feet on a log he had placed in front of his chair to make a footstool. "Did you see Andrew today?"

Bethany choked as the tea she was swallowing went down the wrong way. *"Ja."* She coughed. "I did. And I took care of his daughter while he worked. She was good company for me." She took another drink. "Andrew asked me something, and I hoped you'd tell me what you thought about it."

Daed settled in his chair, waiting while Bethany ran her finger around the rim of her glass.

"Andrew wants me to marry him."

Running his fingers through his beard as he always did before saying anything, *Daed* stared toward the barn. "This is very sudden, isn't it? He hasn't been back for more than a day or two."

"I thought so, too. But his mother-in-law is coming on Saturday and wants to take Mari back to Iowa with her. He thinks that if he has a wife, or the promise of a wife, then Rose won't feel like Mari is in such desperate need of a mother."

"How long has Andrew's wife been gone?"

"Only a few weeks, he said."

Daed ran his fingers through his beard again as Bethany finished her now lukewarm tea.

Bethany set her empty glass on the arm of her chair. "Tell me what you're thinking."

"The first thought that comes to mind is what kind of woman this mother-in-law must be, if Andrew is afraid that she'll take his daughter from him."

"Andrew said that when she's involved in anything, she takes over. I don't think he wants to argue with her."

A soft chuckle came from *Daed*. "I've known other women like that."

"Who?"

Daed smothered his smile behind his hand. "You."

Bethany pressed her lips together to hold back a protest. She wasn't anything like the way Andrew had described Rose.

"Your mother was like that, too." At this, *Daed*'s smile broadened. "I think it's a good quality in a woman, being able to take charge when she feels she needs to. As long as she has someone who can guide her into making wise decisions rather than relying solely on her womanly emotions."

"You mean a woman always needs a man around?"

Daed shrugged. "It worked well for your *mamm* and me. But it doesn't need to be a man. A good friend, or a relative. Someone who can temper her impulsiveness."

Bethany's face burned. *Daed* often had to tell her to slow down and take a moment to think before she acted. He might not have said her name, but he was talking about her.

"All I know about Rose is what Andrew told me. And that she's a widow."

Daed fingered his beard, his gaze on the barn. Then

he shifted in his seat and looked at Bethany. "My second thought is that there was a time when your *mamm* and I thought you and Andrew would marry someday."

Bethany blinked, her eyes suddenly itching. There had been a time when she had thought that, too.

"Do you still have feelings for him?"

"*Daed*, it's been four years since the last time we saw each other. He's been married and has a child."

"That doesn't answer my question." He took her hand. "Time has passed, and you've both grown into adults rather than young people. You've both known grief and joy, and you've matured. You know that sometimes you have to put your emotions aside so that you can make a decision that is best for all involved."

"You're telling me that I should marry him."

"I'm not going to tell you if you should or you shouldn't. But I am telling you to think carefully and weigh all sides of the decision." *Daed* leaned back in his chair again but didn't release her hand. "Ask yourself what would be the worst thing that would happen, and the best, and ask that about both sides. Then talk to Andrew. Tell him what you think, and don't hold anything back."

"Whatever I decide will affect my life forever."

"Not only your life, but Andrew's life. And that little girl's life. And even Rose's life. It's a big decision, and I will pray for you as you sort through it. But I won't decide for you."

"In a way, I wish you would."

Daed chuckled again and rose to his feet. "I need to

see to the barn and make sure everything is set for the night. I'll send your brothers in, too. It's getting late."

Bethany hadn't noticed the gray and pink streaks in the powder-blue eastern sky, but now she watched them, the barn a dark silhouette against the pale colors. As she had thought about Andrew's proposal this afternoon, she had dreamed about what it would be like to be Mari's mother. The little girl was precious, and a joy to be with. Mari felt the loss of her mother deeply, and Bethany longed to fill that void for her.

But *Daed* had said that she should put aside her emotions and look at the decision from both sides. As far as Mari was concerned, Bethany didn't have any decision to make. She loved her like a daughter already and would happily take her into her arms and her life.

Andrew was a different matter. She had once thought she loved him, but that burning memory of his laughter still rang in her head. They were friends, but she would never trust her heart where he was concerned. His marriage to Lily so soon after he arrived in Iowa proved his lack of romantic feelings for her more than anything else.

But even though love had never blossomed between them, she and Andrew were still friends. Good friends. If they married, they would get along as they always had. She could foresee their evenings together after Mari went to bed, discussing the farm or Mari, or even the weather. They would never run out of things to talk about, and they would enjoy each other's company. They could spend year after year that way, never as lonely as she had been ever since the day when she had watched that wagon carry Andrew to faraway Iowa.

And she would have her own home and her own family. She would care for the Yoder home with its quaint kitchen and the beautiful view from the window that looked over the flat prairies of southern LaGrange County. She would cook and sew for the three of them, and watch Mari grow into a young woman with dreams of her own home and a man to love her...

At that, a sob escaped. She pressed her fist against her lips, closed tight against the other sobs that wanted to force their way out.

With a marriage the way Andrew had described, there would always be only one child. Always only a friendship between her and Andrew.

She had no dreams of any other man to love her—she had never felt drawn to anyone else. So the argument came back to the same place where she had started— could she accept Andrew's proposal, knowing theirs would be a marriage without love?

"Where is our cow?" Mari asked the next morning at breakfast as Andrew set a cup of water on the table.

"We sold our cow because it couldn't make the trip to Indiana with us. Cows don't ride on trains."

Mari giggled at that, covering her mouth with pudgy fingers while Andrew smiled at the joke. But Mari's question had reminded him of his long list of things he needed to get done. With Dave's help yesterday, the barn was now ready to house some horses and a milk cow. Until he found some livestock, though, he'd have to borrow milk from the neighbors, and rely on them for transportation, too. Jonah Zook had always been a good neighbor and would be happy to help out.

"After breakfast," he told Mari, browning toast for her on the stove, "we'll go to Bethany's house and borrow some milk. And then we'll start looking for a cow of our own."

"I want a brown cow." Mari made this announcement as her empty cup thudded on the table. "Like *Mammi* Rose has. With big eyes." Mari pulled her eyelids open with her fingers to show how big a Jersey cow's eyes were.

Andrew couldn't help laughing. "If there is a Jersey cow for sale, I'll try to buy it. But I'll have to wait and see. No promises!"

"And a spot horse, *Daed*. Get a spot horse, like Rascal."

The buggy horse Lily had chosen for him to buy when they got married had been a western mustang with a brown-and-white pattern. Andrew's younger brother had called it a cowboy horse, but Lily didn't care. She had fallen in love with the animal and had pampered it with carrots. Andrew sighed. Rascal had also gone to the sale barn in Iowa.

"I'm not sure they have spotted horses here, Mari, but I'll look for one."

"Bethany likes cows." Mari leaned close to watch him spread a bit of Bethany's butter on her toast. "She likes horses, too. And chickens."

Andrew cut Mari's toast into triangles and put the plate in front of her. "Does she like little girls?"

Mari looked at him, her blue eyes serious. "She likes little girls best of all."

Watching Mari take a bite of her toast, Andrew didn't doubt his daughter's statement. He had seen the attachment between the two of them when he had gone to pick up Mari from the Zook house before supper yesterday. Mari had looked happier than he had seen her since her mother was suddenly taken away from her. And Bethany… He'd had to look away when he had seen the expression on Bethany's face. She loved his daughter already, he didn't doubt that. He hoped that would induce her to accept the idea of marrying him.

With Bethany on his mind, he didn't react right away when he saw her standing in the kitchen doorway, fancying that he only saw her face in his memory.

"Bethany!" Mari waved her toast in the air, and Bethany waved back.

Andrew lurched to his feet, knocking aside his chair. "Come in. I wasn't expecting you."

Bethany's smile brought one of his own. "I was wondering why you were staring at me." She held up a tin pail of rags and brushes. "I thought you might need help cleaning the house if you're having company soon."

Andrew glanced at Mari. He hadn't said anything to his daughter about Rose's pending visit three days from now. When he looked back at Bethany, she nodded to indicate her understanding of the situation.

"I haven't been able to do much with the house." He pushed his chair toward the table for Bethany and sat in the one on the opposite side.

"For sure. You need to get the barn in order, first."

"*Daed* will buy a cow." Mari pushed her eyes open wide again. "A brown cow. With big eyes."

Bethany looked at Andrew and he answered her unspoken question. "A Jersey cow. Rose has a Jersey, and Mari thinks it's pretty."

"What if you can't find a Jersey for sale?"

Andrew shrugged, but Mari already knew the answer. "Then we get a brown spotted one. Or a black-and-white one."

Bethany matched Mari's smile. "Then you'll be content with whichever cow your *daed* thinks is the best?"

Mari nodded. "If it's brown. Or brown-spotted. Or black-and-white."

She picked up her last triangle of toast while Andrew leaned closer to Bethany. "Have you thought about…?"

Nodding, Bethany glanced at Mari. "We can talk later." She looked his way again. "*Daed* said he's going to the sale barn in Shipshewana today. I can take care of Mari if you want to go with him."

"When is he leaving?"

"As soon as he hitches up the wagon. He wants to look for a new cultivator, but if he knows you want to go with him, he'll wait until you're ready."

"Can he wait until I get Mari ready?"

She laughed. "She can stay here with me. It will be hard for you to look for the right animals with a two-year-old underfoot."

Bethany's laughter struck a place deep in his heart, reminding him of a day last fall when he and Lily had taken Mari on a picnic near the stream that ran through their Iowa farm.

He spoke before he could think, before the memory could fade away. "Come with us. Bring Mari. The house can wait another day."

Her smile broadened, reminding him of when they had been children, planning an afternoon of fun adventures. "That sounds like it would be a *wonderful-gut* trip. I don't get to go to town very often."

"If I remember right, sale days are the best days to go."

"I'll get Mari ready while you tell *Daed* that we're going with him. He'll need to put a board in the back of the wagon for another seat."

On his way out the kitchen door, he looked back. The scene looked familiar. Too familiar. As if instead of Bethany bending over Mari, washing her jam-sticky hands, it was Lily. He had to look again. He had never noticed before how much Lily and Bethany looked alike. But Bethany wasn't Lily, and she never would be.

Walking through the sale barn in Shipshewana was something Bethany had done often, but the familiar sights and sounds were fresh as she watched Mari's pleasure. The little girl, safe in Andrew's arms, stared at everything without saying a word.

While *Daed* went to the area where the farm machinery was on display, Bethany followed Andrew as he walked past the cows waiting for their part of the auction to begin. Looking down the row, Bethany saw a brown cow and touched Andrew's shoulder.

"Isn't that a Jersey?"

He leaned down to speak close to her ear in the noisy barn. "*Ja*, it is. Let's get a closer look."

Andrew handed Mari to her and threaded through the crowd until they reached the fawn-colored cow. She was smaller than most of the cows Bethany was familiar with, but she knew that a Jersey's milk was rich with cream. She would be perfect for a small family like Andrew's.

"Cow!" Mari said, wiggling in Bethany's arms. "Look at her eyes!"

The cow turned her head toward Mari and Bethany and reached out with her tongue to lick Mari's toes, making the little girl giggle with delight. The cow's eyes were big and dark, with long lashes framing them. If a cow could be beautiful, then this was the most beautiful cow Bethany had ever seen.

"*Ja*, for sure she's gentle," a middle-aged Amish man said to Andrew. "She gives about six gallons of milk a day, and it's high in butterfat. She's been a good cow for us."

Andrew stroked his beard as he walked around to look at the other side. "Why are you selling her?"

The man chuckled. "Our family is growing so large that we need a better producer. I'm going to be looking for a Holstein today." He glanced at Bethany and Mari. "With your young family, this cow will be all you need for several years."

Andrew stroked his beard again and frowned.

"She's a good investment," the man went on. "She's already bred. I took her to a Jersey bull in Middlebury, and she'll come fresh in the spring."

"I'll have to see how high the price goes in the auction."

"I hope you win her, young man. It looks like you have a nice family. Just the kind I'd want Dinah to go to."

Andrew took Mari again and continued walking down the line of cows. When they got to the end, Bethany followed him outside.

"What did you think of the cow?" Andrew said, stopping in a shady spot between the livestock barn and the horse barn.

"She was very pretty and looked young enough to keep producing milk for a long time."

Andrew shifted Mari in his arms. She had laid her head on his shoulder and her eyes were nearly closed. "I hope you weren't embarrassed by the man thinking that the three of us are a family."

Bethany felt her face heat, but with her bonnet on it was easy to avoid Andrew's gaze. *Ja*, the man's comment had been embarrassing, but only because she felt like they had misled him. Being mistaken for Andrew's wife and Mari's mother made her feel like she was finally where she belonged.

"Not embarrassed as much as ashamed that he thought something that was untrue."

Andrew stepped closer to her. "It doesn't have to be untrue. Have you thought about what I asked you?"

Bethany nodded. She had thought of nothing else since yesterday afternoon. "Do you think we could have a good marriage, even in these circumstances?" She looked into Andrew's eyes. They were open and frank, with no shadows in the depths.

"You and I have always made a good team." Andrew

glanced at the people walking past them, but no one was paying attention to their conversation. "I'm asking you to give up a lot, though. If there's someone you've been wanting to marry, you'll lose your chance if you marry me."

"What makes you say that?"

"Dave Zimmer said that he had proposed to you, and so had a couple other fellows, but you turned them down. He thought you were waiting for someone else."

Bethany tilted her head down so that Andrew couldn't see her face. She couldn't explain what kept her from accepting Dave's proposal a few years ago, other than it just hadn't felt right. Being with any man other than Andrew hadn't felt right. No one else offered the easy camaraderie he did, and she had never felt any love for any other man.

She shook her head. "There is no one else."

"Then you'll do it?"

Bethany pressed her lips together to keep back the retort she wanted to make. He made their marriage sound like a business arrangement. She couldn't tie herself to a man who would never love her, could she?

Just then, Mari lifted her head, roused by her uncomfortable position and the noise around them. She turned in Andrew's arms and reached for Bethany. When Bethany took her, the little girl settled in her arms with a sigh and went back to sleep.

If Bethany didn't accept Andrew's proposal, Mari's grandmother would take her back to Iowa, and she would never see her again. She swallowed, her throat tight. And if she didn't accept Andrew's proposal, she would never know the joys of being a mother. Because if she didn't marry Andrew, she would never marry anyone.

"*Ja*, Andrew. I'll do it. I'll marry you."

Andrew nodded, his gaze on his feet. "That's it, then. I'll talk to the bishop to see when we can arrange the wedding." He motioned to a bench next to the livestock barn. "Do you want to wait there with Mari while I look at the horses? I know she can get heavy."

Bethany nodded, not trusting herself to speak. She sat on the bench while Andrew trotted toward the horse barn without a backward glance.

An older woman sat at the other end of the bench, smiling at Bethany. "That's a lovely baby you have there. How old is she?"

Forcing a smile, Bethany answered. "She's two, almost three."

The woman beamed. "I have a granddaughter the same age. When is this little one's birthday?"

Bethany's smile froze. She had no idea when Mari had been born. She didn't know what she liked to eat, or if she slept through the night. Did she have nightmares? Did she still wear diapers at night? She was going to be this child's mother, and yet she knew nothing about her. What had she gotten herself into?

She looked toward the horse barn where Andrew had disappeared after his cold dismissal of their wedding plans. It looked like she had listened to her emotions, just like *Daed* had warned her not to do. But it was too late. She had given her word.

Chapter Three

The train station platform in Shipshewana was busy on Saturday morning, crowded with folks traveling either east or west, both *Englischers* and Plain. Andrew found a quiet spot to wait for Rose's train from Chicago, and he made it just in time. The whistle in the distance announced the train's imminent arrival.

Andrew shifted from one foot to the other, then adjusted his straw hat and ran his fingers along his suspenders to make certain they were straight. It was too much to hope that Rose would accept the news of his coming marriage easily. She seemed to have her heart set on taking Mari back to Iowa with her.

He straightened his shoulders, taking a deep breath and practicing his speech again in his mind.

I'm getting married, so there is no need for you to worry about Mari. She will have a good mother and a home here in Indiana.

Sweat beaded on his upper lip as the roar of the train drew closer. It was never easy to talk to his mother-in-law.

Bethany loves Mari as much as you do and will be a good mother.

Andrew's stomach clenched as the engine puffed past the platform, followed by the passenger cars. Through one of the open windows he saw Rose gathering her things together. He met her as she stepped off the train and took her largest valise.

"Did you have a good trip?" Andrew smiled. At least he could start the conversation on a pleasant note.

"It was long," Rose said, brushing at the gray soot dusting her black dress. "I don't know why Iowa and Indiana can't be closer together."

As she sighed, Andrew was startled by how old and tired her face looked. "I borrowed a buggy for the trip. It's right over here."

"Mari didn't come with you to meet me?"

Andrew put Rose's valise in the back of Jonah's buggy, along with some smaller bags she carried. "Mari stayed at home."

As Rose settled herself on the buggy seat, she gave him the sharp look he dreaded. "Is she all right? She isn't ill, is she?"

Andrew shook his head as he turned the horse down the state road that would take them home. "She's fine. But I thought it would be easier to leave her at home with Bethany rather than bring her into town."

Rose frowned, her mouth as pinched as if she had taken a bite of a green persimmon. "Who is Bethany?"

Now is the time. Tell her.

Andrew pulled the horse to a stop at the crossroad while he waited for an automobile to drive by.

"She's our neighbor." Andrew's hands shook as he lifted the reins. Jonah's horse was well broken and obeyed every movement Andrew made. It was too bad he couldn't control himself as well.

"A neighbor?"

Andrew cleared his throat. "Not just a neighbor." He searched his mind for the words he had rehearsed, but they were gone. Rose had a way of unsettling him. "She's a friend. A good friend."

Rose didn't say anything, but her eyebrows rose.

"Mari likes her." Andrew pressed his lips together in an effort to keep silent, but Rose's frown demanded an explanation. "She takes care of Mari while I'm working."

"I see." Rose stared through the windscreen. "So she would rather stay with this… Bethany…than see her own *Mammi* Rose."

"I didn't tell her you were coming, in case your train was late or something else happened." Andrew tried to smile. "You'll be a surprise for her."

At that, Rose smiled, and Andrew gripped the reins. She wouldn't be smiling after he broke the news to her.

"Besides, she's helping Bethany get the house ready for the wedding."

Andrew counted the beats of the horse's hooves as he waited. Twenty-two.

"What wedding?" The pitch of Rose's voice heightened with suspicion.

"Mine and Bethany's. We're getting married on Thursday."

Andrew's announcement was met with silence, but he knew it wouldn't last. He counted the horse's hoofbeats. After thirty-six, he glanced at the older woman. He had expected an angry outburst, but when he saw that she was staring out the windshield with tears in her eyes, he pulled the horse to a stop.

"You could have told me before I came." She sniffed. "I need time to prepare myself."

Andrew leaned his elbows on his knees. "*Ja*, maybe I should have. But it was decided only three days ago."

Rose patted her eyes with a handkerchief. "This is very sudden. Do you even know this woman?"

"We've been friends since we were Mari's age. I know Bethany better than I know myself."

"But you married my daughter." Rose looked at him, her gaze drilling him with accusations. "Why did you marry Lily if you loved this Bethany?"

Andrew fingered the reins in his hand. Why did he marry Lily? Was it only because he knew Bethany didn't love him? The horse stamped, impatient to move on.

"I loved Lily with all my heart." Tears filled his own eyes and he blinked them away. "I'll never forget the time we had together."

"But how can you marry again so quickly? My Lemuel has been in the Blessed Land for ten years, and I still don't have any intention of marrying another man."

"Mari needed—"

Rose turned on him with a triumphant look. "A mother. Mari needs a mother who understands her. Who can love her. Who knows her. Can your Bethany say that? You know that I'm the best mother for Mari. I've known her since she was born."

Glancing at Rose, Andrew was ready to come to some

agreement with her, until he saw the gleam in her eye. Had her tears been real? This was why he had to bring Mari back to Indiana. Rose was too good at manipulating people. At manipulating him.

"I'm her father, Rose. Yes, Mari needs a mother and Bethany is going to be a good mother for her." He drew back his shoulders. "And Mari also needs her father. She needs me. I can't let you raise her." He lifted the reins, signaling the horse to go on down the road. "You're welcome to come to the wedding, but there will be a wedding."

Rose sniffed and dabbed at her eyes again. "I'm only thinking of Mari."

Andrew tamped down his ire. He had known Rose long enough to know that she was strong-willed, but her feelings could be hurt easily.

"As much as Mari needs a mother, she also needs a grandmother. She needs you, and she will be very happy to see you. She has missed you since we left Iowa."

"Is that right?"

"*Ja*, for sure."

Rose settled back in her seat, watching the farms as they drove by. It looked like Rose had accepted his announcement.

At least for now.

Cleaning Andrew's house was a chore that had taken nearly every hour of the past two days, but by midmorning on Saturday it was presentable. Bethany dribbled the bucket full of dirty water along the edge of the garden as Mari watched.

"Do the flowers like dirty water?" Mari was fasci-nated by the gray stream coming from the pail.

"*Ja*, for sure they do. Their feet are in the dirt, and they know how to take the water and leave the dirt behind."

Mari's eyes grew wide. She pulled one of the tall lily stems toward her and looked into the orange trumpet. "How do they know?"

"God told them."

"Why?"

"So they would grow to be strong, beautiful flowers. Just like He tells you to eat when you're hungry, so you grow to be strong, too."

"Why?"

"Because that's the way it is for children."

"Why?"

Bethany shook the last drips out of the bucket and straightened her back. "Because."

"Because why?"

Bethany touched the tip of Mari's nose with her fin-ger. "Because that's what God does for children."

"Why?"

"So they stop asking questions!" Bethany scooped up Mari with one arm and ran with her to the house. The little girl laughed all the way.

By the time Bethany had made up the beds in two of the three upstairs bedrooms and had prepared the down-stairs bedroom for Mari's grandmother, it was nearly noon and time to go home to fix dinner for *Daed* and her broth-ers. As she walked across the road with Mari, she went through her mental checklist. *Ja*, she had cleaned every speck of dust and dirt out of the neglected house, so that even the most diligent housekeeper would be satisfied.

She had moved Andrew's things to the front bedroom upstairs and had put Mari's clothes in the small room at the top of the stairs. After the wedding and after Rose went back to Iowa, Andrew would move into the downstairs bedroom and Bethany would sleep in the upstairs room next to Mari's. Meanwhile, there was a storeroom in the back of the house over the washing porch that Bethany would sleep in.

After the wedding. Bethany didn't want to think beyond Thursday. An unsettled feeling had been growing ever since she told Andrew she would marry him that day in Shipshewana. Was it only three days ago?

When they got home, Mari went into the front room to play with the toys John and James had brought down from the attic for her while Bethany finished preparing dinner. She had put a ham-and-potato casserole in the oven before going to Andrew's house, and now she started some green beans cooking on the stove and opened a jar of applesauce. After she set the table, she started slicing a loaf of bread. She had just set the casserole on the table when she heard the boys and *Daed* washing up before coming in for dinner.

With Mari settled on a stool and all the boys quiet, *Daed* bowed his head for the silent prayer. Bethany's mind fought against the quiet, settling calm of prayer. There was so much to do… And then *Daed* cleared his throat and prayer time was over.

"Well, Bethany, is Andrew's house ready for his

mother-in-law?" *Daed* asked as he helped himself to a scoop of ham and potatoes.

Bethany glanced at Mari, but she didn't seem to have noticed what *Daed* said.

"*Ja*, for sure. As clean as Martha kept it when she lived there." Andrew's mother had been the diligent housekeeper Bethany had in mind while she had been cleaning. "On Monday, I'll start cleaning our house for the wedding."

James and John giggled, while Nathaniel frowned. "When Bethany gets married, who is going to take care of us?"

Daed shrugged. "We'll have to do it ourselves."

John's giggles stopped. "*Daed, ne*, we can't. Won't Bethany come over to cook for us? She'll only be across the road."

"Bethany will have her own family to take care of. She won't have time to feed two families. But we'll be all right. I know how to cook."

As her brothers exchanged glances, Bethany looked at Aaron. They all knew what *Daed*'s cooking was like. They wouldn't go hungry, but the meals wouldn't be very satisfying, either.

"Perhaps I could cook some meals for you," Bethany said. "Rose will be staying for a week or two, so she'll be able to help out."

Mari's head snapped up. "*Mammi* Rose?"

Bethany stiffened. Andrew hadn't wanted Mari to know Rose was coming until she actually arrived, but her name had just slipped out. "*Ja*, Mari. *Mammi* Rose is coming."

"When?"

"Soon. I don't know if it will be today, though."

Mari grinned. "I love *Mammi* Rose."

"I know. Now eat your dinner."

Daed cleared his throat. "Does Rose know about the wedding?"

"Andrew was planning to tell her when he picked her up at the train station." Bethany's appetite fled. If Rose had been on today's train like she planned, Andrew might be breaking the news to her right now.

"Will she be happy about it?"

Bethany shook her head. "I don't know."

Aaron nudged her foot under the table. "Don't worry about it. You know you can't change anything by worrying."

"You can say that because you don't have anything to worry about."

Aaron shrugged, winking at her as he helped himself to another serving of casscrole. "I worry all the time."

"*Ja*, you worry about where your next meal is coming from."

Nathaniel took the serving spoon from Aaron and scooped more of the casserole onto his plate. "And he worries if Katie Miller will let him drive her home from the Singing tomorrow night."

Daed, his plate empty, sipped his coffee. He put his hand on nine-year-old James's shoulder. "You're being quiet. Are you feeling all right?"

Bethany hadn't noticed that James wasn't eating. She had been too involved in her own troubles and Aaron's teasing.

"I don't want Bethany to get married and move away. And I don't want Aaron to date Katie Miller."

"Why not?"

John scooted his chair closer to his younger brother. When James shrugged his answer, John said, "Things are changing too fast. Why can't everything stay the way it is? Bethany can live here and take care of us. And if Aaron marries Katie, he'll move away, too."

Daed sat back in his chair and looked around the table at all of them. His gaze fell on Mari last, and he smiled. "Families grow and change, son. Sometimes we don't like the changes. It was hard when *Mamm* passed away. But sometimes the changes are good, like when folks get married and the family grows. On Thursday, we're going to add a new big brother to our family, and you'll have a niece. Those are good changes, and before long it will seem like Andrew and Mari have always been part of our family."

As Nathaniel finished his last bite, Bethany rose to fetch the apple pie she had made for dessert. She set it on the table and cut it, the aroma of cinnamon and apples filling the air.

"But *Daed*," Nathaniel said, "you still haven't solved the problem of who is going to take care of us after Bethany gets married."

Daed held his piece of pie under his nose and took a deep breath, "Like Aaron said, you can't change anything by worrying. We'll just have to wait and see what happens." He took his first bite of pie. "We are certainly going to miss your cooking, Bethany. You'll have to make a pie for us once in a while after you're married."

"I'll take care of you, *Daed*." Bethany helped Mari cut her pie into bites. "You don't have to worry about that."

As they approached the farm, Andrew broke the silence that Rose had maintained since he had told her of his coming marriage.

"Did you want to get settled in the house first? Or do you want to see Mari?"

"Take me to see my granddaughter." Rose sat up, suddenly eager. "Are we almost there?"

"This is Bethany's home." Andrew turned the buggy horse into the Zook farm lane and pulled up at the hitching rail by the back door.

Jonah opened the door to greet them as Rose climbed out of the buggy. "Bethany said you would be along soon. Have you eaten yet? The boys have gone back to work, but there is still some dinner left if you'd like."

"*Ja*, for sure," Andrew answered, but Jonah wasn't looking at him. His gaze was directed at Rose, who had leaned over to brush a smudge of dust off her skirt.

Then Mari peered out of the door, past Jonah's knees.

"*Mammi* Rose!" She ran to Rose, who kneeled and gathered her in her arms.

After holding her for a long minute, Rose looked into Mari's face. "I've missed you since you went away."

"We didn't go away. We came home."

Rose gave Andrew a look that told him how she felt about that, but Andrew knew he was right in insisting that Mari saw Indiana as her home. Rose turned her attention back to her granddaughter.

"You have a new dress!" Rose smoothed the little skirt as Mari nodded.

"Bethany made it for me. She's going to be my new *mamm*."

Rose threw another look at Andrew. Could he do nothing right?

Jonah stepped forward. "Rose? I'm Jonah Zook, Bethany's father. Come in and sit down at the table. You haven't met Bethany yet."

Rose took Mari's hand and followed Jonah into the kitchen. When Bethany turned from the sink to greet them, Rose was cordial enough, but Andrew recognized her lifted chin and stiff smile. He had seen it many times. He mentally referred to it as her "top chicken in the henhouse" attitude.

"So, you're Bethany?" Her voice was as tight as the set of her mouth.

Andrew stepped around Rose and guided her to a chair at the table.

Jonah took the dish towel from Bethany. "We have some of the casserole left, don't we? And more applesauce?"

"For sure, we do. The applesauce is gone, but James picked some strawberries this morning." Bethany smiled, but Andrew could see how uncomfortable she was under Rose's stare. She moved too quickly to get clean plates from the cupboard, and her hands shook.

When Mari ran to the drawer to get forks to set beside the plates, Rose frowned. "Mari must spend a lot of her time here, rather than with you, Andrew."

"*Ja*, for sure," Jonah said as he took his seat at the

table with a cup of coffee. "Mari spends her days with Bethany, either here or at Andrew's place. I enjoy having a little one around the house again."

He smiled at Rose over the rim of his cup, then set it down as Bethany set a bowl of ham and potatoes on the table and a dish of fresh strawberries. Andrew bowed his head for a silent prayer.

As he helped himself to the casserole, Jonah continued. "I'm sure you have missed Mari while she and Andrew have been home."

Rose blushed. Andrew stared. He had never seen his mother-in-law blush. "You're right, I have missed her."

"We're glad you could come in time for the wedding."

Rose raised her eyebrows, her attention on Jonah. "You have agreed to this marriage?"

"Andrew and Bethany have known each other for years, and my wife and I always thought they would marry someday."

Rose pointed her fork toward Jonah. "But he married my Lily. Don't you think one happy marriage in a lifetime is enough for anyone?"

Jonah leaned back in his chair with a smile on his face. "A happy marriage is a wonderful blessing, but the Good Book says that widows should marry." He leaned forward again. "Not everyone who has lost a wife—or a husband—has to remain alone."

Andrew glanced at Bethany and she met his gaze. Jonah and Rose were talking as if they were the only people in the room.

Rose sniffed. "I've gotten along just fine since my Lemuel passed away, and I see no reason why Andrew needs to marry again. Especially so soon after—" A small hiccup escaped and they all waited for Rose to compose herself. "So soon after Lily's passing."

Jonah's smile faded. "There's the child."

"*Ja*, the child." Rose took Mari onto her lap, hugging her until Mari squirmed to get down. Rose looked after her as the little girl went into the next room, where her toys were waiting. "I know I can be the best mother for her. There is no need for Andrew to marry again so soon." She turned back to Jonah, her "top chicken" attitude back. "Perhaps if he wants to get married in a few years, then Mari can come back to Indiana and live with him again."

"A few years?" The words came out more forcefully than Andrew intended. He rose halfway out of his chair before Bethany's hand on his arm stopped him. He knew better than to let Rose rile him up. His mother-in-law went back to eating her dinner as if he hadn't said anything.

Andrew cleared his throat and began again. "I'm not going to let you take Mari away for a few years. Not even a few weeks. I'm her father, and I don't intend to be a stranger."

A glance from Jonah kept him from saying any more.

"Now, Rose," Jonah said in the voice he used when talking to a spooked horse. "Don't be unreasonable. Andrew is Mari's father, and she needs him. If you take her back to Iowa with you, then she will have lost both her mother and her father, and that is a terrible thing to put a child through." He turned his coffee cup in his hands, watching Rose from under his eyebrows. "I don't see why you couldn't stay here in Indiana, though. Stay for the wedding and as long as you need. You'll soon find that this new family that Andrew and Bethany are making is the perfect place for Mari to be."

"Well…" Rose drew out the word as she laid her fork on her empty plate. "I suppose I could do that. I'll live with Andrew and Bethany, at least until I'm sure that their home will be the right place for Mari."

Jonah cleared his throat. "Perhaps it would be better if you stayed somewhere else while the newlyweds are settling in. We have a *Dawdi Haus* that no one is using."

"I'll stay with Andrew and Bethany, or I'll take Mari home to Iowa on Monday. There are no other options."

Rose's voice held the no-nonsense tone Andrew knew too well. She had made up her mind and there was no arguing with her. He met Bethany's eyes. She shook her head slightly, and Andrew stood.

"Bethany, come outside with me." He took her hand and led her into the shady yard away from the kitchen window.

Once he stopped, she pulled her hand from his. "I don't think it's a good idea for Rose to live with us."

"You heard what she said." Andrew lowered his voice. "There isn't any arguing with her when she's like this. She has made up her mind. If she doesn't stay with us, then she'll take Mari back to Iowa on Monday."

"But Mari is your daughter. She can't do that if you don't want her to."

Andrew watched an ant crawl over his left shoe. For almost four years, Rose had said what he was going to do, and he did it. That was the way Lily had wanted it, and he had gone along with her to keep peace in the family. He didn't want to cause strife now, either, so the best thing would be to go along with what Rose wanted. The news of the wedding had been enough for her to take in for one day.

"You don't know Rose. Whenever I try to go against her plans, she always seems to get her own way in the end. I don't want her to take Mari away, so we'll just have to let her live with us." He shrugged. "What difference will it make?"

"Andrew, we're just starting out. I don't know what kind of marriage we'll have, but we need time with only us—you, me, and Mari. We need to become a family on our own, and we won't be able to do that if Rose is living with us."

His dinner churning in his stomach, Andrew faced Bethany. "It will be all right. I know Rose and how she thinks. Before long, she'll remember something important she needs to be involved in at home, and then she'll be gone."

She frowned, watching her feet. He lifted her chin, smiling at her until a corner of her mouth rose. "We have our whole lives to figure out what our family will be like, and Mari loves her grandmother. We can put up with her for a few weeks, can't we?"

Bethany sighed. "If you think so. But if anything goes wrong—"

He tapped her nose with his finger. "Nothing will go wrong. Trust me."

Chapter Four

"You're doing what?"

Bethany faced her friend Lovina Schrock, who was holding her one-year-old daughter, Rachel, on her hip. The Schrocks had come by to visit on this nonchurch Sunday afternoon, and Bethany was glad for an opportunity to confide in her friend as they stood in the shade of the house.

"You think I'm doing the wrong thing?"

"I don't think it's wrong for you to get married, I'm just wondering why it's so sudden. I know you and Andrew have known each other as long as we have, but aren't you jumping into this too quickly?"

"There's a good reason. Andrew's mother-in-law came yesterday, and she wants to take Andrew's daughter back to Iowa with her."

Lovina frowned. "Andrew has a daughter?"

Bethany told her friend the details of the story.

"Where are they today?"

"*Daed* invited them over, but Rose didn't seem very

interested. I would imagine she's tired from traveling so far."

"The biggest question is whether you and Andrew love each other or not."

Shaking her head, Bethany prepared herself for Lovina's reaction. "Not all marriages are based on love."

"Maybe not at first—"

"Andrew and I like each other. Neither of us have any plans to marry anyone else, so it is a convenient arrangement. A good arrangement."

Lovina swung her body slightly as Rachel laid her head on her shoulder. "Maybe you think it is now, but why settle for a good arrangement when you can have the best?"

"Let's go inside and you can lay Rachel down on my bed." Bethany led the way into the kitchen and poured two glasses of water while Lovina put her daughter down for her nap.

Sitting at the table, Lovina took a drink of the cold water, then set down her glass in front of her. "What aren't you telling me?"

Bethany ran her thumb through the condensation beading on her glass. "You know how we used to dream of getting married and having families."

"*Ja*, for sure I remember." Lovina smiled.

"This is my only chance. I'm twenty-four years old, and the only man who has even looked at me in the last year is Hiram Plank."

Lovina giggled. "I assume he isn't your first choice?"

Bethany laughed with her. "For sure, not. But there's more." She made another line through the beaded water with her thumb. "I long to be a mother, and Andrew is offering me that chance."

"You must like his daughter."

"I fell in love with her the first time I saw her. Already I feel like she's my responsibility, and my joy. Isn't that how mothers feel?"

Lovina nodded.

"Andrew and I…" Bethany chewed on her lower lip. "We won't have any more children. Mari is my only opportunity to be a mother."

Propping her chin with her hand, Lovina gave Bethany a thoughtful look. "Tell me about her."

"She's smart and funny, and full of energy. A lot like Andrew was when he was a boy. She isn't afraid of anything and keeps me running to keep up with her."

"How old is she?"

"Almost three, just about a year older than Rachel."

Lovina smiled. "Maybe they'll be good friends, just like we are."

Bethany smiled back. "That would be wonderful. I cherish your friendship, Lovina." She took her friend's hand. "Will you be able to come to the wedding on Thursday?"

"*Ach*, I can't. I'm so sorry, but I promised I would take Noah's aunt and uncle to visit some of their family on the other side of Middlebury."

"That's too bad, but I understand. You and Noah were my first choice of a couple to stand up with us, but Dave and Dorcas Zimmer are Andrew's first choice. I'm sure they'll be happy to do it."

Lovina turned her glass in her hands. "I hope this

is the right decision, but I can't help remembering how much Andrew hurt you."

Shifting in her seat, Bethany took a drink of water. "That was a long time ago."

"It was after Noah and I were married, and that was only five years ago."

"A lot has changed since then."

Lovina grasped her hand. "But has he changed? What if you find that you are falling in love with him?"

"I'm not about to make that mistake again." Bethany took her glass to the sink and refilled it.

"Love isn't always a choice. You said you loved him once, and you thought he loved you. It could happen again."

Bethany leaned against the counter. "But it won't. Andrew can't love me, because he still loves Lily. And he has Mari to remind him of her every day. I don't want to take Lily's place. I don't want to be his second choice."

Lovina's voice softened. "And you don't want to risk his rejection again." She patted the chair next to her and Bethany sat down again. "But just because he pushed you away then doesn't mean he would now."

The memory of her lips touching Andrew's smooth cheek rushed back. The scent of his shaving soap was strong as she had leaned close to him, waiting for his arm to clasp her close. Waiting for him to return the kiss. Her love for him had overflowed that day, but he had pushed her away, his face red. Then he had laughed at her dunking in the creek. She had been so embarrassed, even as she had run to Lovina for comfort. She would never risk her heart that way again.

"He won't get the chance." Bethany looked at Lovina. "I'll be his housekeeper and his daughter's mother. We'll have a good life together, and a good marriage. Mari will grow up, get married, and we'll love our grandchildren. But I will never make the mistake of trying to kiss him again."

"But marriage is more than just a friendship—"

"Aren't you and Noah friends?"

Lovina nodded. "He's my best friend. I don't know what I'd ever do without him."

"And that's the way Andrew and I will be. Best friends and partners."

"But there is so much more…"

Lovina's voice faded as Bethany shook her head. "Not in our marriage. But that's all right." She shrugged her shoulders. "We'll be happy, won't we?"

She ignored her friend's doubtful look as she finished her water.

Andrew felt like he was back in Iowa on his first Sunday home. It was a nonchurch Sunday for their community, and the other members would be visiting friends and relatives, taking advantage of the good weather to strengthen the bonds of fellowship.

But their Iowa church was different, maintaining that Sunday afternoons, whether a church day or not, should be spent at home. Activities were limited to resting, reading, or spending time in meditation of the previous week's sermons. Andrew had always thought that Rose's husband, Lemuel, had been the one to institute this practice in the Iowa community because Rose had always been most adamant in following it.

On this afternoon, Andrew was happy to rest from his normal work. The week had been tiring and eventful, and he hadn't slept well the night before. After a cold dinner of sliced ham and canned peaches, he was ready to nap, as was Mari. But as he carried the sleepy girl toward her bedroom on the second floor, Rose called to him.

"After you put Mari to bed, come into the sitting room. I want to talk to you about something."

By the time he came back downstairs, Rose was seated in *Mamm*'s rocking chair, tapping her fingers on the arm as she gazed out the front window. He sat in *Daed*'s armchair, placed near the rocking chair. *Mamm* and *Daed* had often sat here in the evening, especially in the winter. He never knew what they found to talk about, but they kept the chairs close enough together so that *Daed* could grasp *Mamm*'s hand if he wanted to. Andrew closed his eyes at the memory, suddenly feeling the empty coldness of the house he loved so much.

Rose shifted in her chair. "You know I want to take Mari back to Iowa with me. It's where she belongs."

"She doesn't belong in Iowa." Andrew rubbed his finger along the side of his nose. "She belongs with me."

"Then you should come back to Iowa. Forget about this broken-down farm and come home with me."

Andrew leaned on his knees and watched as he placed his fingertips together, matching his left hand to his right. "This farm can be productive with some work. We have a good well, and a spring, and there is plenty of water in the lakes and farm ponds around us. Iowa is still in the grips of the drought."

Rose crossed her arms. "The drought will be over soon. We've never had a drought last longer than two years. And once it starts raining again, then the Iowa farmland will be much more productive than this place. You just need to be patient."

"That dust storm last month took all our topsoil away with it, plus the seeds we had just planted. There is nothing there for me anymore."

Rose was silent for a long minute while the sound of voices from the Zook farm across the road filtered through the open windows.

"Lily is there."

Andrew almost missed her whisper, it was so quiet. "Rose, Lily isn't there."

"Memories of her are." A single tear found its way down Rose's cheek.

"I don't need to be in Iowa to remember Lily." Andrew laid his hand on Rose's where it rested on the arm of the rocking chair. "Mari and I are going to stay here."

Rose sighed. "All right, then. If you're going to stay here, I will, too. You don't need to marry that girl."

"I'm not going to change my mind. Mari needs a mother."

"You know how I would love to raise her…"

"She also needs a grandmother."

Rose's quivering chin stilled, and she turned a steel gaze on Andrew. Any signs of tears had disappeared. "You know I can be both. She needs me."

His stomach churning, Andrew caught himself before he nodded in agreement against his will. Lily had warned him of this. She had made him promise that if anything happened to her, he wouldn't let Rose raise Mari the way she had raised Lily. She had told him how Rose's love was genuine, but it was smothering. She didn't want her children growing up the same way she had, always afraid of the consequences of standing up for themselves. And now, Andrew was in the situation neither of them thought would ever be possible. He had to stand up to Rose for Mari's sake, no matter what the results might be.

"She needs a mother who is closer to Lily's age. Someone who can fill her shoes."

Rose's eyebrows lifted in disbelief. "That girl can never take my Lily's place, not in this family. She will never be your wife or Mari's mother. I forbid it."

"It isn't your choice. It's mine."

The older woman turned her gaze back to the window. "Be careful how you step, Andrew. You know how often your decisions turn out to be the wrong ones."

Andrew closed his fists, willing himself to control his feelings, to keep from lashing back at her with a biting comment. She is older, he reminded himself. She recently lost her daughter and is grieving. He waited to feel something for his mother-in-law. Forgiveness? He would have to work on that. Pity? *Ja*, for sure, he pitied her. But he wouldn't let his pity stand in the way of protecting his daughter.

"Is that Jonah Zook coming up the lane on a Sunday?"

Andrew stood, relieved that he had an excuse to leave

the room. "I'll talk to him outside so he doesn't disturb your rest."

"He should know better than to do something so frivolous on a Sunday. I didn't know this community was so easygoing with the *Ordnung...*"

Rose was still talking when Andrew went out the kitchen door, careful not to let the screen slam behind him.

"How are things going with Rose?" Jonah asked as he walked away from the house with Andrew, out of earshot.

Andrew sighed. "I don't want to be critical, but Rose can be difficult."

Jonah nodded as if Andrew's words were what he expected to hear. "I got that idea yesterday. Is she the reason we haven't seen you over at our place this afternoon? The Schrocks are there, and Noah was looking forward to visiting with you."

An easy excuse could be that Rose was tired from her trip, but that wasn't the true reason they had stayed home. "Rose believes that nonchurch Sundays should be spent at home."

Jonah crossed his arms and tapped pursed lips with his forefinger. "That's the way the church in Iowa does things?"

"I've missed the way we do things here. It doesn't seem right to neglect seeing other folks on nonchurch Sundays."

"Maybe I'll stop and visit with Rose. Meanwhile, why don't you go and join the others? Rose and I can take care of Mari."

Even though Rose would probably give him a stern lecture, Andrew couldn't keep from grinning. "I'll take you up on that offer. I'm afraid I'm sending you into a lion's den, though. Rose wasn't happy when she saw you coming up the lane."

Laughing, Jonah patted Andrew's shoulder. "Don't worry about me. I can hold my own when it comes to a woman like Rose."

Andrew left before Jonah could change his mind. As he turned from the lane onto the road, he glanced back at the window. Jonah had taken *Daed*'s chair and was gesturing as he and Rose talked. He wouldn't trade places with Jonah right now, but the older man had volunteered. Andrew couldn't help wondering if Jonah really knew what kind of scolding he was in for.

Chapter Five

Thursday morning was wet and dripping. A thunderstorm had moved in through during the night, and the rain following it had continued until dawn.

"It's a good rain, and we needed it," *Daed* said as he sat at the table while Bethany washed dishes after breakfast. "It looks like it will clear up in time for the wedding, though. The boys are clearing out the barn to make room for the extra horses just in case it doesn't."

Bethany's stomach lurched at the thought. Today was her wedding day. She glanced out the window as she put a stack of plates in the dishwater. "It's nothing but a gray, dreary morning. I wish it was sunny."

"Come sit down." *Daed* pulled a chair away from the table. "Let the dishes soak for a few minutes."

"But *Daed*, I have so much work to do."

"Then it's even more important that you sit down for a few minutes. Find some peace before you start the day. You barely sat down for breakfast."

Bethany slouched in the chair. "I wasn't hungry." Her

stomach lurched again. What if she was ill? Would they call off the wedding?

"Today is your wedding day." *Daed* smiled at her, as if it was the happiest day of his life.

"*Ja*, I know. That's why I have to get to work." Bethany started to stand, but *Daed* caught her hand and pulled her back to the chair.

"If I didn't know better, I'd think you didn't want to get married."

A sigh escaped and *Daed* got up to pour a cup of coffee for her. When he set it in front of her, she wrapped her hands around the white ironware cup, welcoming the warmth that seeped into her chilly fingers.

"It isn't that I don't want to get married, but this isn't the way I imagined it would be."

Daed took a sip of his coffee. "Things in life are rarely the way we think they will be. I remember your *mamm* on our wedding day, telling me we would have a dozen children." *Daed* smiled, a faraway look in his eyes as he remembered. "We were going to have a boy first, then a girl. She had it all planned out."

Bethany closed her eyes and remembered *Mamm*'s calm, gentle face. Her faith and her trust in the Lord had never wavered in all the years Bethany had known her. "Was she disappointed when I was born and wasn't a boy?"

Daed chuckled. "Not at all. You were the prettiest baby we had ever seen. Your *mamm* took one look at you and said, 'Well, Jonah, it looks like we'll have to have a boy the next time, because I'm not giving this one back.'"

Taking a sip of the hot coffee, Bethany smiled. "I miss her so much, but I love remembering what she was like."

"So do I." *Daed* turned his cup around. "You're not regretting your decision to marry Andrew, are you? It isn't too late to change your mind."

Bethany had wrestled with that very question through the long hours of the night as she listened to the thunder and the rain. "I don't regret it. But I think I wish the wedding was already over. I don't want to stand in front of all those people…"

"All those people are our friends and family. People you've known all your life."

"I know, but I'm still nervous."

"Andrew is a good man. He'll always take good care of you."

"I know that. I'm not worried about Andrew, or even being Mari's mother." Bethany turned her own cup around, then wrapped her cold fingers around it again. "I think I'm more worried about what other people will think. Andrew only returned home last week, and now we're getting married already. Folks will wonder about that."

"Let them wonder. After a few months or a few years, no one will remember the circumstances."

"And then there's Rose—" Bethany's voice broke. That was the center of what was bothering her. Andrew hadn't stood up to Rose, and it didn't look like he was going to. It looked like Rose might end up as the man of the house instead of Andrew.

"Don't worry about Rose. You'll learn to get along

with her. I wish she would move into the *Dawdi Haus*, but she is a determined woman."

Bethany couldn't look at *Daed*, but she had to know. "Now that you've met her, do you really think I'm like her?"

Daed studied his empty cup, turning it in his hands. "I don't think we've seen what Rose is really like. I think she's grieving the loss of her daughter and she is doing everything she can to make her life normal again. We need to be patient with her. Spending time with Mari will help, I think."

"I'm afraid that she's going to make our lives miserable."

"Not if you don't let her." *Daed* squeezed her shoulder as he got up and put his cup on the kitchen counter. "You can be just as stubborn as she is. Love her and show her that she's welcome in your home. You might be surprised at how well things might turn out." He peered out the window. "The sky is even clearing up. It looks like it will be a fine day."

After *Daed* went out to the barn, Bethany finished the dishes. She had put casseroles in the oven for the wedding dinner early in the morning, and others from the church had told her they would bring what they could. Her brothers had pushed back the walls of the downstairs to open the rooms for the church service and wedding ceremony, and everything was as clean as she could make it.

After she put potatoes on the stove to boil, she went into her bedroom to pack the rest of her things. The bed would go with her to Andrew's house, along with the rocking chair that had been her mother's and the chest full of quilts and other things she had made over the years. Bethany stripped the mattress, folding the quilt and sheets as she went.

When she lifted the pillow to add to the bundle, she fingered the flowers *Mamm* had embroidered on the edge of the pillowcase. They were purple lilacs, Bethany's favorite flower, and Bethany remembered when *Mamm* had given her the beautiful pillowcase for a Christmas present. Bethany had been twelve, and old enough to notice everything *Mamm* did in the days leading up to Christmas, but somehow *Mamm* had kept this present a secret until Christmas morning. When had she done the sewing? Late at night after Bethany and her brothers had gone to bed?

Bethany sank down on the bare mattress. This day would be much happier if *Mamm* was here to share it.

Andrew escaped from his house as quickly as he could. Breakfast had been another unbearable meal with Rose's barbed comments about today's wedding, comparing it to his wedding to Lily almost four years ago. He hoped that things would get better after the wedding was over and done with, but he could never anticipate what Rose would say or do. Once he and Bethany were married, nothing on earth could separate them. But he wasn't sure that Rose felt like she was bound to those rules.

He walked over to the Zook farm. Jonah had said he could use his spring wagon, and Bethany had promised to have her things ready to move to his house this morning. She wanted them out of the way before folks started arriving for the wedding.

The wedding.

He felt none of the anticipation and joy that had overwhelmed him when he and Lily had gotten married. That wedding, the beginning of their lives together, had also been his step into adulthood. He was no longer a boy or a youth. He had stopped shaving his beard, he had put his childish ways behind him and had joined the adult men of the church. He had responsibilities. A family. He had looked forward to a future with Lily.

Such a short time with Lily.

This wedding today felt like someone else's wedding, except he would be the one standing in front of the congregation with the bride. It didn't seem right that he would be a groom twice in such a short time.

He scratched his beard then smoothed the curly whiskers against his cheeks.

Was Rose right when she said he was making a mistake? Was it wrong to ask Bethany to enter into this marriage with him?

She was willing to do it, there was no mistake about that. And he would do everything he could to make her happy. He knew of marriages that had been built on a shakier foundation than the long friendship he and Bethany had shared, and those folks survived.

He batted away a deerfly and finished hitching the horse to the Jonah's wagon.

As persistent as the fly, the thought that had been in his mind for the last week came again. Was it enough to survive? Was it enough for Bethany to be Mari's mother, with nothing more promised in the marriage?

Bethany must have heard him coming and stepped out on the back porch as he drove the short distance from the barn.

"You're here for my things?"

Her face was pale, and her eyes looked as if she had been crying.

"*Ja*, for sure." Andrew jumped down from the wagon seat. "Are your brothers around? They can help load the wagon."

"They're out doing chores. I'm sure they'll be happy to help."

Andrew tied the horse to the hitching rail. "Do you have many things?"

"Only what we talked about. My bed, a dresser and my blanket chest."

Her voice sounded small. Flat. He should say something to make her feel better. Andrew glanced at her. She looked toward the barn, and he was struck again by how similar her profile was to Lily's. An uncomfortable thought drifted into his mind, that perhaps he had fallen in love with Lily because she had reminded him of Bethany. He shook his head to send that thought running. Lily and Bethany were two very different women. Bethany was his friend and nothing more.

"Today is a special day, isn't it?"

Bethany nodded, still looking toward the barn. "I was just thinking how I would like *Mamm* to be here today." She turned her gaze toward him. "But you don't have your mother here, either. Did you tell her about the wedding?"

"I wrote to her, but I haven't heard back. She wouldn't be able to come, anyway. She's needed in Iowa to take care of my grandmother."

"Oh."

"Bethany, I'm glad you said you would marry me." He let his mouth ease into a smile. "I know it isn't easy for you to step into Lily's shoes—"

"I'm not stepping into anyone's shoes, Andrew." Bethany frowned. "If you think I'm going to be just like Lily, then you need to think something else."

"I know you're not Lily." Andrew's face heated. That idea was preposterous. "I just meant that you'll be doing the things she did."

"But in my own way. I won't cook like she did, and I won't wash clothes like she did. I'll probably even sew your trousers in a different way."

"I know that." Andrew stepped back. At least he knew that now.

"I'll be your wife and Mari's mother, but I will never be Lily. That needs to be clear before we marry."

"I know." Andrew swallowed. He was repeating himself. "I won't expect you to be anyone but yourself." He sat on the top step of the porch and patted the spot beside him, inviting Bethany to sit with him. "Let's talk for a minute."

She hesitated, as if talking to him was going to interfere with her busy morning, but she sat. Then she leaned over and pulled a grass stem, sticking the pale green end in her mouth. The simple habit took him back to other summers, long ago, when they would both chew on the sweet ends of the grass stems while fishing on a hot afternoon. He pulled his own strand, tasting the sweet freshness. The fragile new growth of the grass.

Talking around the stem in his mouth, he said, "Are you sure about this wedding? You don't regret saying you'd marry me, do you?"

Bethany wove her grass stem between her fingers. "*Daed* asked me the same thing this morning. I told him I was sure that this is the right thing to do." She unwound the grass stem. "But I'm nervous, and I wish the day was over."

"*Ja*. Me, too."

"How is Mari?"

"She's fine." Andrew tried to forget the way Rose had talked incessantly of Lily during breakfast, as if to turn Mari's love for Bethany into a betrayal of Lily's memory. "She wanted to come see you this morning, but when I told her you were coming to live with us, she was happy."

"And Rose?"

Andrew rubbed his beard. "I won't lie to you. This is hard for her to accept."

"But she'll have to, right?"

Frustration vented itself in a sigh. "She'll have to." Aaron closed the gate of the pasture next to the barn, heading toward the house when he saw Andrew. "She won't have a choice."

Bethany's belongings were loaded quickly, and Aaron rode home with Andrew to help unload.

"The wedding is only a couple hours away." Aaron

grinned and gave Andrew a slap between his shoulder blades. "Are you nervous?"

Andrew shook his head as he pulled the horse to a halt by the kitchen door. "Not nervous, but I'd like it to be over so we can get back to normal."

Rose and Mari watched them carry the heavy blanket chest through the kitchen and up the stairs. Aaron started down the hall toward the front bedroom with his end of the chest, but Andrew stopped him. "This way," he whispered, heading down the hall to the opposite end of the house.

When they set the blanket chest down in the little room over the washing porch, Aaron closed the door. "Are you going to tell me why we're putting Bethany's things in here instead of the front bedroom? And why all the secrecy?"

"This is Bethany's room. It's the one she chose. Rose doesn't need to know we have separate rooms."

Aaron crossed his arms, leaning against the door. "So Nathaniel was right. You two won't really be husband and wife."

Andrew eyed Bethany's oldest brother. Aaron had always been a tease when they were younger, tagging along whether he and Bethany wanted him or not. But he had grown tall in the last few years and was acting like Bethany's watchdog.

"We will be husband and wife. We are getting married."

"But you won't be living together? Whose idea was this?"

"Both of ours." Andrew stepped closer to Aaron, and

lowered his voice. "If I don't get married and provide Mari with a mother, Rose will take her back to Iowa. I'll do anything to keep that from happening."

"So you will marry my sister, even if you don't love her? What kind of marriage will that be?"

Andrew ran his hand over his face. The room was hot and closing in. "Bethany and I are good friends. We like each other. We'll have a good marriage."

Aaron snorted and walked over to the window. He propped open the sash, letting in some fresh air. "It sounds awfully convenient, but not right. Have you really considered how this will affect everyone else?"

"It isn't convenient, Aaron. Not at all." Andrew sat on the blanket chest, his pounding head in his hands. "But will you keep this to yourself? Please?"

"*Daed* knows?"

Andrew nodded. "For sure he does."

"I'll keep quiet, then. Just make sure she doesn't ever regret marrying you."

"I won't." Andrew wiped the sweat from the back of his neck. "Don't worry."

Before the worship service was half-over, Bethany's lips were dry, and her heart was pounding. She couldn't faint. She wouldn't faint. Not while she was sitting here on the front bench of the women's side in front of everyone.

She and Andrew had had their final talk with Bishop before the service began, while the congregation had sung the familiar hymns. Sitting in *Daed*'s bedroom on the kitchen chairs one of the boys had brought up that morning, she and Andrew had answered Bishop's questions. But if anyone asked her now how she had answered, she wouldn't be able to tell them.

Finally, the last sermon was over, and Bishop signaled for her to come up front, along with Andrew. She stood next to him, the back of her dress damp where it touched her skin. As Bishop turned a page in his Bible, the slight breeze fanned her face.

Bethany barely heard Bishop's voice as he asked the first question, but when he reached the end of it, she nodded. *"Ja."*

Next to her, Andrew's firm voice echoed hers.

Bishop went on to the next question. "Do you solemnly promise—"

Bethany's mind raced. Could she promise? What promises was she making?

Then Bishop's voice broke through her thoughts. "—and not separate from each other until the dear God shall part you from each other through death?"

Death. Andrew and Lily had been parted through death. Would she have to survive Andrew's death, or would he be forced to bury a second wife? She shuddered, as if a chill wind had just blown through the house.

Andrew had stated his answer. His promise to stay with her until death. Bethany's stomach churned.

"Bethany?" Bishop waited for her answer. Everyone waited.

She felt the trickle of sweat reach the small of her back. *"Ja,* I do."

Then it was over. Other women served the food while

she and Andrew found their seats at the corner table. The couples table. Dave and Dorcas had stood up with them, and Dave sat at Andrew's side while Dorcas sat beside Bethany. Dorcas was preoccupied with watching her twins as they fussed in the arms of some younger girls, who had claimed their care for the afternoon, and Bethany was thankful for that small blessing. She didn't feel like talking to Dorcas, or anyone else. Her head pounded.

After the meal, folks visited while the children played in the shady yard. Out in the pasture, the men and boys were playing baseball. When Dorcas had left the table to feed the twins, Dave went to join the game, but Andrew fidgeted next to her.

She leaned close to him. "If you want to play ball, go ahead."

Andrew glanced at her, then out the door. "You don't mind? I don't want to leave you alone on your wedding day."

Bethany forced a smile. "I won't be alone. I'll sit out in the shade with the other married women and listen to them complain about their husbands."

Andrew's shocked look made her laugh. "Do they really complain about them?"

Bethany leaned against the wall behind their bench, finally relaxing. "Not in our church, they don't. Elisabeth Stoltzfus and the other ministers' wives won't allow it. So don't worry, and go ahead and enjoy yourself. It's your wedding day, too."

"I'll get you a glass of lemonade before I go, that way folks won't talk as much."

Andrew's hair was damp with sweat, his eyebrows puckered with…what? Worry? Concern for her? Bethany smiled at him, his face as familiar as her own brothers' faces. It wouldn't be a bad life, living with Andrew. The future was nothing to worry about.

"Lemonade sounds good, and I'm ready to go outside. It's too hot here in the house."

The kitchen was quiet. The dishes had all been washed and almost everyone had gone outside. Andrew poured a glass of lemonade and made a show of putting extra sugar in her glass and plenty of ice. He handed it to her, then was out the door, jogging toward the field and the crack of the baseball hitting a bat.

Bethany sipped her lemonade. The glass was too full to try to carry it outside yet, so she leaned against the shelf next to the sink and let the breeze that puffed through the open window cool her damp skin. She took another sip of the sweet drink, then held the cold glass against her cheek.

"I think the wedding happened quickly. Too quickly."

The voice came from outside the window, where some of the older women were sitting near the house.

"I thought so, too. As soon as Andrew told me he was marrying again I knew it was wrong. And less than a month since my Lily's passing."

Bethany set the glass on the shelf. She recognized Rose's voice. *Move away from the window,* she told herself. *Don't listen.*

"You don't think Bethany is in the family way, do you?" said another woman. Bethany didn't recognize her voice.

"How could she be?" That was Viola Schwartzendruber. Elisabeth Stoltzfus often needed to remind her not to gossip. "Andrew only came home a couple weeks ago."

"Andrew needn't be the father," Rose said. "It's a marriage of convenience. She needs a husband and he has the idea that she would make a better mother for Mari than I would."

"What are we talking about?" Elisabeth Stoltzfus's voice broke through the conversation, coming from the direction of the back porch. "For sure, there isn't any gossiping going on, is there?"

Bethany dared to peek out the window. Elisabeth was striding toward the group with a firm smile on her face. All the women in the circle below the window closed their mouths, unwilling to admit anything to Elisabeth, but Rose didn't know that she was a minister's wife.

"Join us, Elisabeth," said Viola. "Have you met Rose Bontrager? She is Andrew's mother-in-law."

"We were discussing the wedding," Rose said as Elisabeth sat with them. "My son-in-law didn't waste any time in taking a new wife, did he?"

"I think Andrew and Bethany know what they're doing," Elisabeth said in her quiet, steady way. "They have put the needs of your granddaughter before their own feelings, and with a beginning like that I'm sure God will bless their home."

"But I think that Mari will do much better if she returned to Iowa with me."

"Are you sure of that?" Elisabeth's question probed. "Isn't the best place for the child in a home with her father, and now a new mother?"

"But I love her." For the first time, Bethany heard a note of desperation in Rose's voice.

"For sure, you do. You want the best for her, I understand that. I have grandchildren, also. But sometimes it's difficult to let our children be their parents, isn't it?" Elisabeth paused and glanced toward the window. She smiled at Bethany, then patted Rose's hand. "I know Andrew and Bethany are happy you're here. I also know it is a blessing for you to have this time with Mari."

Bethany moved away from the window, thankful for Elisabeth's presence that stopped the gossiping women. Could they really think she was expecting a little one, and that's why she and Andrew had married so quickly? She shook her head. No one who knew her would believe that, and time would prove the rumor false.

Hearing a sound from upstairs, Bethany went to check on Mari. Rose had put her in Aaron and Nathaniel's room to take her nap, but that had been more than two hours ago. Bethany opened the door. Mari was sitting in the bed, her face flushed and eyes wide as she looked around the strange room. But when she saw Bethany, she held out her arms, her face crumpling in a cry.

"Shh, Mari, don't cry." Bethany sat on the bed and took the little girl onto her lap.

"I was alone." Mari sniffed.

"I was downstairs, and *Mammi* Rose is outside in the yard. We didn't leave you alone."

"Where is *Daed*?"

"He's out with the men. They're playing ball in the meadow."

Mari stuck her thumb in her mouth and leaned against Bethany.

"Are you thirsty? There is some lemonade in the kitchen."

"Too sour." Mari spoke around her thumb.

Andrew had said that Mari had quit sucking her thumb several months ago but started again when Lily passed away. Bethany would help her stop again, but not now. Not until their family was settled. She rocked Mari a little, wondering if she was going to go back to sleep.

"Are you my *mamm* now?"

Bethany stopped rocking and held Mari close. Of all the things that happened this day, this was the moment they were all leading to. The reason to put up with the gossip and Rose's disapproval. Elisabeth had been right. Nothing else mattered except for this little girl.

"*Ja*, Mari. I'm your *mamm* now."

Mari sat up, pushing out of Bethany arms, then put her hot palms on Bethany's cheeks, pulling her face closer. "Does that make you happy?"

Bethany smiled, even as tears filled her eyes. "Happier than anything."

"Will *Daed* be happy? And *Mammi* Rose?"

Kissing Mari's forehead, Bethany sighed as she drew the little girl close again. "I hope so. I do hope so."

Chapter Six

After being married for a week, Andrew and Bethany finally fell into a routine. They rose at the same time each morning, meeting in the hallway outside Mari's bedroom door. He would give her a nod, then head out to do chores, while Bethany started breakfast for them all.

Rose was often in the kitchen when they came down, drinking a cup of coffee. She would give them a curious look, as if she was estimating how long their marriage would last, and Andrew was always glad to escape to the barn.

Thursday morning was no different. Bethany followed him down the stairway. He gave Rose a nod as he headed out to do the chores. Behind him, he heard Bethany's greeting.

"It's another fine morning, isn't it?"

"If you think so," Rose answered in her tight, clipped voice.

Andrew went on to the barn, happy to get away from Rose's sour mood. It seemed the longer she stayed in

Indiana, the unhappier she became. She should make other plans soon, and then he and Bethany could start their lives together. With Rose in the house, he felt like he was plowing the same field over and over, but never making any progress.

But the question of where Rose would go and what she would do still remained. He couldn't send her back to Iowa, and she had no other friends or family that he knew of.

Thinking back to one of the sermons from Sunday, the one from Preacher John Stoltzfus, Andrew thought of the text of John's message. It was from Hebrews and spoke of following peace with everyone. As soon as John had read the text, Andrew had felt its weight. He was guilty of not following peace with Rose. He wanted to avoid her rather than mending the breach that Lily's death had caused. Mari's happiness and safety were more important, weren't they?

By the time he got back to the house, Mari was awake and dressed. She ran to meet him at the door as he kicked off his work boots.

"Does Dinah miss me? Can I see her?"

Andrew lifted Mari and kissed her cheek. "Dinah is happy and healthy, and she gave you some good milk this morning. I'll take you to see her after breakfast, unless your *mamm* has something else for you to do."

"I'd rather that she stays inside today," Rose said, not turning from her task at the stove. "I'm making her a new dress, and I want her to try it on."

Bethany shot a glance in his direction, but he

shrugged. "You can see Dinah another time. Maybe after dinner."

"That would be fine," Bethany said, but Rose interrupted her.

"You know that is Mari's nap time. If you take her to the barn, she'll be cranky and won't sleep when she comes back in." Rose set a dish of scrambled eggs on the table next to a plate of hotcakes. "Did you warm the syrup, Bethany?"

"I didn't think we needed to on such a pleasant morning." Bethany's voice was strained, as if she held back the words she would rather say.

Rose took the small ceramic pitcher from the table and set it on the back of the stove. "I always warm the syrup. It makes the hotcakes taste so much better."

Andrew helped Mari climb onto her stool, then took his seat as Bethany poured a cup of coffee for him. Rose joined them at the table and bent her head for the silent prayer. He gave Bethany a reassuring smile, then bowed his head. He was tempted to extend the prayer time past the usual couple of minutes, but he knew he couldn't avoid Rose's morning review of the day's events that way. She started as soon as he raised his head.

"I brought some fabric from home to make Mari's new dress," Rose began as Andrew reached for the hotcakes. "The one she has been wearing is looking a bit ragged."

Andrew glanced at Bethany. She stared at her plate, her bottom lip between her teeth. The dress Mari was wearing was the one Bethany had made for her when they had first arrived.

"Mari's dress is fine. I like it." Andrew spread butter on the hotcakes. "Bethany made it for her."

Rose sniffed. "I guess it will be all right for everyday. The new one can be her Sunday dress. I brought some pink fabric for her. Little girls always look best in pink." She smiled at Mari. "Eat your eggs, little one. They will make you strong."

Bethany wasn't eating. She fetched the syrup from the stove for Andrew, then poured a bit of cream in her coffee and stirred it.

"What are your plans today, Bethany?" Andrew smiled at her, trying to lighten the mood. He wouldn't let Rose spoil his breakfast.

"It's Thursday, so I'll clean the bedrooms upstairs and the hallway."

Rose fluttered her hand, as if to wave away Bethany's words. "Don't worry about that. I'll clean the upstairs for you."

Bethany gave Andrew a panicked look.

"I thought you were going to make the new dress for Mari." Sometimes all he could do was provide a fence between the two women. How did they manage when he wasn't in the house?

"That's right." Rose frowned slightly. "And there's churning to be done, isn't there?"

"With the cow giving so much milk right now, we need to make as much butter as we can. The store in Shipshewana will take the butter in trade." Bethany sipped at her coffee.

Rose sighed. "Those stairs are hard on my knees, anyway. I don't know why they made them so steep."

Andrew glanced at the stairway at the other end of the kitchen. It rose in a narrow enclosure and could be difficult for someone of Rose's girth. "My great-grandfather built that stairway. *Daed* always said the folks must have been smaller back then."

"So then, you can clean the upstairs, Bethany, and I'll stay down here with Mari."

As Andrew washed down his breakfast with his last swallow of coffee, Bethany nudged his leg with her foot. When he looked at her, she tilted her head toward the door. Rose was wiping Mari's face and hands with a cloth, not paying attention to them.

"Rose, Bethany is going to show me what she wants done in the henhouse."

"I'll be back in to clean up breakfast," Bethany said, starting toward the door. "I won't be long."

Andrew shoved his feet in his boots, grabbed his hat and hurried after Bethany.

"Wait a minute. Let me get my boots on."

She didn't stop until she reached the back of the empty henhouse, then she turned on him, eyes blazing. "I don't understand why you do that."

"Do what?"

"You let Rose have her own way every time."

Andrew picked at a piece of splintered wood on the henhouse wall. She was right. "Not every time."

"I'm surprised you didn't offer to rebuild the stairway to make it easier for her to get up there."

"Rose is difficult to deal with."

Bethany stepped closer to him. "Do you think I don't

know that? I have to work with her every day. We're trapped together in that house."

"I thought you liked our house. You always said how much you loved it when we were younger."

She shifted her gaze to the fallow fields needing to be plowed and the view of the prairie beyond. "I did. I still do. I love the kitchen with the Dutch door looking out on the barnyard. I would just rather not have to share it with Rose. I don't feel like it's our house, it's Rose's. While you're working, she is always telling me I do the housework wrong, or I talk to Mari the wrong way."

"She needs something to do outside the house."

"What do you suggest?"

"Is there a quilting soon? Don't the ladies meet every week?"

Bethany shook her head. "Only in the winter. There's too much work in the summer to spend time socializing."

"She can paint the henhouse. I'll mix up the white-wash this morning."

"Are you sure Rose won't think I can't do it because of my condition?" Bethany's voice held a tinge of sarcasm that Andrew had never heard her use before.

"What condition?"

She leaned against the henhouse wall, her arms crossed in front of her, and gave him a sideways look. "You haven't heard the rumors?"

"What are you talking about?"

"I heard some of the women talking the day of the wedding. Rose and some of the others seem to believe that we married so quickly because I'm expecting a little one."

"Where did that idea come from?" Then Andrew's knees grew weak. Dave had said there might be someone else. "You aren't, are you?"

She snorted her answer. "Of course not. You should know me better than that."

He shrugged. "Things happen. And I haven't seen you for four years."

"I know how things happen. People get married and have children, but not me."

She kicked at a tuft of grass, and a memory swept over Andrew of Bethany doing the same thing when Jonah had sold a colt she had wanted to keep when she was a girl. She must have been only twelve that day, but she had been hurt that her father hadn't understood her and her love for the young horse she had raised and trained. Instead, she had poured out her feelings to him, her best friend.

"Bethany." Andrew lifted a hand to caress her arm. To bring her close. To tell her he understood what she was going through. But he let it fall to his side. The barriers she put up warded him off. "Don't worry about it. We'll come up with a solution."

"When?" Her eyes blazed again, challenging him. "She acts like she's settling in very well. I'm not sure she plans to go back to Iowa. Not as long as Mari is here."

He met her challenge with his own glare. "Mari is staying here. There is no question about that."

"Then you need to ask Rose when she's going to leave. She is doing everything she can to make this situation unbearable, and you need to stop her."

Bethany didn't wait for his answer but stalked around the corner of the chicken coop toward the house.

Andrew pulled off his hat and wiped the sweat off his brow with his sleeve. She was right. He needed to confront Rose and tell her to stop interfering in their marriage. He had spent the last four years trying to avoid speaking to her so directly, but he had to do it soon. Otherwise there would be no living with Bethany.

When Bethany reached the house, she stopped outside the kitchen door. The top half of the Dutch door was open to let in the breeze, and she could hear Rose talking to Mari.

"No cream pie for you, dear. You just finished your breakfast."

Bethany put her hand on the latch, then another voice said, "Our Bethany is a wonderful cook, but this pie rivals even hers."

Daed?

Ja, for sure, *Daed* sat at the table, a slice of the sugar cream pie Rose had made for supper last night in front of him, along with a cup of coffee. His fork was poised to cut into the half-eaten wedge.

"What are you doing here, *Daed*?"

"I came to visit my daughter and her family." *Daed* took a bite of his treat, smiling. "And Rose offered me a piece of this delicious pie. I didn't realize she was such a good cook."

Bethany's anger, cooled by her walk from the henhouse, rose up again. How could Rose be so pleasant to *Daed*, and so infuriating to her?

"Jonah was just telling me about a nice picnic spot by a lake." Rose smiled at Bethany. "He thought our families could go there on Sunday."

"You must mean Emma Lake." Bethany hadn't been there for a picnic since before *Mamm* passed away.

"That's right," *Daed* said. "You and Rose can fix a lunch for us, and the boys and I will bring everything else we need."

Bethany laughed, in spite of her unsettled feelings. "What else is there to bring?"

"Our appetites." And then *Daed* winked at Rose and leaned over to tickle Mari. "And now I best be getting back to work. Is Andrew in the barn?"

"Either there or at the henhouse." Bethany gathered *Daed*'s plate and fork to add to the pile of breakfast dishes by the sink. "He wants to get the coop ready for new chickens this week."

"Good idea." *Daed* headed toward the door, but then turned back. "That was a good piece of pie, Rose. *Denki*."

"You're welcome, Jonah."

When Bethany went to the stove to get hot water for the dishes, she noticed that Rose's face was as red as if she had been in the sun. "Are you too warm, Rose? You might want to go in the other room to work if you are."

Rose fanned herself with her hand. "You're right. It will be cooler in the front room. I'll take Mari with me and she can play while I sew."

While Bethany washed the dishes, she considered the wink she had seen. *Daed* was only being friendly, wasn't he? Perhaps she had been mistaken, and *Daed*'s wink was for Mari rather than Rose. Of course, that was it. He had no reason to wink at Rose.

From the front room, she heard Mari say, "I like my blue dress."

"Pink is a better color for you. Your *mamm* always wore pink when she was a girl."

"She wears blue, now."

Bethany glanced down at her deep blue everyday dress. Was Mari talking about her, or Lily?

"I don't know what your *mamm* wears now. She's in the Blessed Land, and no one knows what they wear."

"Not that *mamm*. My new *mamm*. In the kitchen."

"Bethany isn't your real mother." Rose's voice dropped, but Bethany still heard as plain as day. "You need to remember that. She isn't your real mother."

Bethany grasped the pump handle and thrust it up and down until cold water gushed into the sink, the noise drowning out Rose's voice. How much longer could she take this? Andrew would have to talk to Rose soon.

When the noise of the running water faded, Bethany hummed a tune to block out Rose's voice as she dried the dishes and put them away. Still humming, she got the dust mop and cloth from their spot behind the door and ran up the stairs. Rose's words wouldn't follow her there.

She cleaned her own room first, dusting the furniture and under the bed. She put clean sheets on the bed and tucked in the blanket. Then she finished with the ceiling corners and the tops of the door and window frames. Before moving on to Mari's room, she glanced out the low window that overlooked the barnyard. The chicken coop was the closest building, then the barn beyond it, built into the slope of the hill. On the other side of the chicken coop was the garden, overgrown with lilies.

Halfway between the garden and the woodlot was the springhouse. It was built from round stones gleaned from the fields. Andrew had told her once that the first Yoder to settle this land almost a hundred years ago had built it for his wife, but Bethany was wary of going there now. Andrew hadn't cleaned it out since he'd moved home, and there were sure to be rats and other things living in the damp, cool darkness.

She liked to see it from her window, though, and think about the first Yoder bride who had lived in this house. Had her life been happy? It must have been. From what Andrew said, his great-grandparents had loved each other very much, and had married soon after their families arrived in Indiana from their homes in Pennsylvania.

Moving on to Mari's room, Bethany dusted and re-made the bed, adding the soiled sheets to the laundry basket in her room. She made sure Mari's special rag doll was on her pillow in the right spot. Mari's window looked toward the woodlot and birdsong drifted into the room. It was a pleasant room for a little girl to grow up in. Bethany leaned her head against the window frame with a sigh, thinking of Rose's comment. Mari liked her. She might even love her. But would she ever think of her as her real mother? Not with Rose filling her mind with the opposite thoughts.

Back in the hall, Bethany peeked into Andrew's room. His door was open, revealing his good shoes neatly placed below the clothes pegs that held his Sunday suit. She made quick work of dusting but didn't touch his bed. Rose was suspicious enough, and if she saw that sheets for three beds were in the laundry on Monday morning, then she would know something was amiss. Bethany would change Andrew's sheets next week instead of her own. After that? Perhaps after that Rose would be gone.

Next, Bethany dusted the walls and ceiling of the hallway, then the floor, before she moved to the staircase. As she went down the steps, dusting them one by one, she wondered about the secret she and Andrew were keeping from Rose. It was wrong to lie, but was keeping a secret the same as lying? It wasn't any of Rose's concern whether she and Andrew shared a room or not, and soon she would go back to Iowa, where she belonged. That thought was nearly as satisfying as getting rid of the dust and dirt that had collected on the narrow steps.

Bethany checked the clock as she finished the stairway. She still had some time before she needed to start dinner. Stepping into the front room, she found Rose in the rocking chair with her feet propped on the footstool. Pink fabric covered her lap and she took quick, neat stitches while Mari played with a set of blocks on the floor.

"Mari, do you want to come with me to visit Dinah?"

Rose stared at her. "In the barn?"

"For sure. I need to fetch the milk from this morning, and Mari can come with me."

Mari jumped to her feet, then shrank back when she saw Rose's frown. Bethany pressed her lips together at the sight. Mari shouldn't be afraid of her own grand-mother.

"Come, Mari." Bethany kneeled on the floor. "I'll help you put the blocks away, and then you can come with me."

Mari glanced at Rose again, but obeyed as Rose sewed silently, rocking the chair forward and back. Bethany took Mari's hand in hers and they went out into the yard. Bethany pushed away any thoughts of Rose as they walked through the grass, bright yellow and green with dandelion blossoms. Mari stopped to pick some, and Bethany helped her until Mari's fist was filled with dandelion stems.

"Pretty flowers." Mari buried her nose in the blossoms then grinned at Bethany, yellow pollen covering her chin.

"Very pretty. Do you want to take them to Dinah for a treat?"

Mari's eyes grew wide. "She eats flowers?"

"We can see if she likes them."

As Mari ran ahead to the fence at the edge of the pasture, Bethany's spirits rose. This was a good life, in spite of Rose, and in spite of Andrew's stubborn ways. She had her own home, even if she had to share it with Rose for now, and a sweet little girl to care for.

Mari climbed up the first two boards of the fence like a ladder and reached over the top. "Dinah, come get flowers."

She waved the flowers in the air as Dinah lifted her head from grazing and started walking toward her. By the time Bethany reached the fence, Mari was bouncing up and down with excitement. Bethany caught her and held her still as Dinah pulled the flowers out of Mari's hand with her long tongue and chewed, watching them.

"Her eyes are big," Mari said. "And her eye hairs are so long."

Bethany laughed. "Her eyelashes are long." She couldn't help correcting Mari, but from now on she would always think of eyelashes as eye hairs.

Everything that had happened over the last two weeks, the hasty marriage to Andrew and putting up with Rose's demanding ways, was nothing compared to the joy of being with this little girl.

Then Mari turned, looking into Bethany's eyes. "*Mammi* Rose said you aren't my real *mamm*."

Bethany's voice caught in her throat—she didn't know how to respond to Mari. The instructions she had overheard Rose give to Mari echoed in her mind, but Rose was wrong.

"I'm your new *mamm*." She caressed the little girl's soft cheek with her fingertip. "You had another *mamm*, and you will never forget her. But I am your *mamm* now."

Mari nodded, her curls bouncing. "I know. I feel it here." She patted her chest. "But *Mammi* Rose said you weren't."

"Sometimes, grown-ups are wrong. But that's all right. You and I know the truth, don't we?"

As Mari leaned toward her, Bethany gathered in her arms and held her tight.

"You are my *Mamma* Bethany," Mari said, clinging to her.

Bethany buried her face in the curly hair. "And you are my Mari."

* * *

"*Daed!* I fed Dinah the flowers!"

The sound of Mari's voice sent a ripple of panic through Andrew. He ran from the horse's stall to where Mari stood in the bright sunshine that fell through the open barn door, gazing into the high rafters. How soon would it be before she tried to climb up there?

"What are you doing out here?" He dropped to one knee and caught her in his arms. "Does Bethany know you're here?"

"I brought her with me to get the milk."

He hadn't noticed Bethany walk in behind Mari. She stood just inside the barn, hanging back as if she didn't want to speak to him unless it was necessary.

"The pail is in the dairy. I haven't skimmed the cream yet."

"I can do that. I'm sure Mari would like to spend some time with you."

She started toward the stairway leading to the dairy in the basement of the barn, but stopped when Andrew stood, picking up Mari. "We'll join you. How else will Mari learn to do that chore?"

"I'll do it. You can show Mari the horse. Have you decided on a name for him yet?" She took another step toward the stairway.

"Are you trying to avoid talking to me?"

"Our earlier conversation didn't turn out well."

Mari patted his cheek. "I want to see the horse."

"*Ja*, Mari, I'll show you the horse." He glanced toward the stairway, but Bethany had disappeared.

Mari's eyes grew wide as he brought her near the stall.

The gelding was tall and strong, but one horse wasn't enough to run the farm. He needed a team of Belgians like this one, and a driving horse, too. But that would happen in due time. Perhaps he'd find a teammate for this one at next week's auction.

The big horse stepped close and reached toward Mari with his nostrils wide, taking in the little girl's scent.

"He's smelling you." Andrew smiled at Mari to relieve her fears. "He only smells people he likes."

"Does he like you?"

"For sure, he does. I'm the one who feeds him."

Andrew took a carrot stub from his pocket and put it in Mari's open hand. She giggled as the horse lifted it from her palm. "His whiskers tickle."

"What should we name him?"

"Whiskers." Mari laid her hand on the gentle horse's soft nose. "His name is Whiskers."

"Don't you think that's a better name for a cat?"

Mari shook her head. "I like Whiskers."

"Whiskers it is, then."

"Does he have a *daed*?"

"For sure. But he's a big horse and doesn't live with his *daed*."

"His *mamm*?"

"He doesn't live with his mother, either."

Mari laid a hand on his beard and turned his face toward her. "I have my own *mamm*. Her name is *Mamma* Bethany."

Andrew froze. What should he say? Lily was Mari's real mother, but Bethany was…what?

"Bethany is your stepmother."

"That's what *Mammi* Rose said. But sometimes grown-ups are wrong."

That was true enough. "Who told you that?"

"*Mamma* Bethany."

"Do you know what that means?"

Mari shook her head. "*Mamma* Bethany is my new *mamm* and she loves me." She patted the horse's nose again. "Is she my real *mamm*?"

Andrew sighed. "Just because someone loves you doesn't mean they're your real mother."

"You're my real *daed*."

"For sure I am."

"You love me."

"For sure I do."

Mari nodded. "My real *mamm* loves me, too."

She was right about that. Lily had loved her daughter very much. But what did this have to do with Bethany?

"Your real *mamm* is in the Blessed Land, and you must always remember that she loved you."

Mari nodded. "*Mamm* loves me, and my new *mamm* loves me. And my *daed* loves me. And *Mammi* Rose loves me."

Andrew gave up. Perhaps when Mari was older she would understand.

"Let's go help Bethany with the milk."

"*Mamma* Bethany," Mari said as he set her on the floor. "Her name is *Mamma* Bethany."

"All right." Andrew followed her toward the stairway. "*Mamma* Bethany." Mari could be just as persistent as her grandmother.

Bethany had finished skimming the milk and was

covering the small cream pail with a cloth. Mari paused in the doorway of the room, taking in the sight of the bright metal buckets and the white walls.

"You're done already?" Andrew said.

"For sure. It doesn't take long to skim cream from one cow." She gave him a smile, then frowned, as if she just remembered that she was upset with him.

Andrew gestured at the walls. "We need a new coat of whitewash. I thought I'd do this room tomorrow, the same time we paint the chicken coop."

"That will brighten it up." Bethany shifted from one foot to the other. "I forgot to tell you that *Daed* came over this morning. He asked if we'd like to go on a picnic at Emma Lake on Sunday. It's an off-church week, and the weather should be good."

"That sounds like fun."

Mari tugged on his hand. "I like picnics."

"We don't have any chickens to fry," Bethany said, shifting the cream pail to the other hand, "but *Daed* has ham in the cellar at home, and we can make sandwiches."

"Will your brothers come, too?"

Bethany grinned. "Would they pass up a meal? Besides, it's Sunday. The family always does things together on Sundays."

A cool thread of memory ran through Andrew's mind. His family and Bethany's family picnicking at the lake on summer Sunday afternoons. Skipping rocks across the glassy water, watching the *Englischers* fish, relaxing in the soft grass. Even helping Bethany's little brothers catch frogs, and then watching their prizes swim away at the end of the afternoon. In Iowa it had been different, because of Rose's belief they should sit quietly in the house on a Sunday afternoon.

"Did Rose agree?"

Bethany handed the milk pail to him and started up the cellar steps. "She seemed to be happy about it when *Daed* invited her."

"What do you mean?" Andrew helped Mari up the steep steps.

"She was interested, and thought it was a good idea."

"That doesn't sound like Rose. She is very strict about how she spends Sunday afternoons, and they don't include picnics."

"Why not?"

Andrew shrugged as Bethany reached the top of the steps and turned toward him. "All of the church in Iowa believed that off-church Sundays should be spent reading and resting."

"That isn't the way we do it here. Resting, for sure. But also visiting with family and friends. Bishop says it's the way the church stays together, just like a family stays together."

"I remember that. But I'm still surprised Rose agreed to the picnic."

Bethany took Mari's hand before they reached the barn doors. "She didn't just agree. She looked delighted."

"Delighted?"

"She even gave *Daed* a piece of pie."

Andrew caught Bethany's elbow before she left the barn. "Wait. Rose gave Jonah a piece of pie?"

Bethany nodded.

"In the middle of the morning?"

"Earlier. Right after breakfast."

"Something is going on. That doesn't sound at all like Rose. Was she that nice to you, too?"

Bethany pointed to some dandelions in the barnyard. "Mari, would you like to pick more flowers for Dinah?"

As the little girl ran out to the grassy yard, Bethany watched her, chewing on her bottom lip.

"Rose isn't nice to me. Ever. I think she resents me and is trying to drive me away."

"Why? What does she say?"

"I heard her telling Mari that I'm not her real mother. She's trying to keep Mari from loving me."

"So that's why Mari told me she had two mothers. I think she's trying to please both you and Rose."

"That isn't fair, though, is it? A child shouldn't feel like she has to keep the peace between two grown-ups." Bethany faced him, one hand on her hip, the other dangling the small cream pail. "You need to talk to Rose, Andrew. Take control of her. This is your house and your family, not hers."

Andrew shifted the milk pail from one hand to the other, and then back, until Bethany finally took it out of his hand with an exasperated sigh.

"This reminds me of the time you broke the window in the front room. Do you remember that?"

He nodded, but he didn't want to revisit that day. He had been throwing a ball onto the roof and catching it as it rolled back to him, but then on one throw, the ball had gone through the window.

Bethany went on, her voice quiet. Accusing. "You knew you should tell your father, but you didn't."

Andrew scratched his beard. "I didn't want him to yell at me."

"You deserved it."

"I know."

"And you hid what you did."

Andrew nodded. He had pulled down the window shade, hoping *Daed* wouldn't notice the broken pane.

"Then it rained that night, and water blew in the front room, ruining your father's Bible and staining the furniture." Bethany stepped closer to him. "If you had only confessed to your father about the broken window, those things wouldn't have been ruined. You made the situation worse by trying to avoid facing him. You couldn't do the hard job."

Andrew watched Mari gathering dandelions, happy in the morning sunshine.

"This isn't the same as that."

"In a way it is. You don't want to do the hard job of telling Rose to either leave or accept that we're married."

"I told you, things will be fine. They'll sort themselves out."

"But Andrew, how long will Mari and I need to suffer under her poisonous words until that happens?"

Andrew had no answer but frowned at Bethany's back as she stalked toward the house with a pail in each hand. Mari followed her inside, her fist full of dandelions. He could do the hard things when he needed to. Facing Lily's death had been the hardest thing he had ever been through, and he had survived, for Mari's sake.

But facing Rose… Andrew scratched his beard. He wasn't sure what was holding him back, other than he had no idea what she should do. He couldn't send her back to Iowa, not as long as this drought held. And as long as she refused to move into the Zook's *Dawdi Haus*, he didn't have any other suggestions for her. And the whole idea of bringing up the subject of his marriage to Bethany with Lily's mother turned his stomach.

Maybe Bethany was right. Maybe he just didn't want to do it. Even if his delay only made things worse.

Chapter Seven

Emma Lake was beautiful on the warm June afternoon. The weather had cooled a little from the previous sweltering weeks, and Sunday brought many families to the lake, mostly *Englischers* with their fishing boats, but other Amish families were also there. Bethany spread an old quilt over the soft grass while Rose took Mari down to the edge of the water, holding her hand.

Mari was wearing her new pink dress over Bethany's objections that it would get soiled on the picnic, but Rose had her way. Somehow, Rose always got her way, no matter how hard Bethany protested. She had to admit, though, that Mari looked sweet in the new dress. Rose had even made her first *kapp*. She patiently put it back on every time Mari pulled it off, and now Mari seemed to be getting used to wearing it.

Rose wore a burgundy dress that reminded Bethany of ripe mulberries, and Mari's pink dress made a pretty contrast as she stood beside her grandmother. While Bethany got the dishes and food out of the picnic basket, *Daed* walked up to Rose and bent his head close to hers. Whatever he said, Rose responded with a good-natured laugh that carried all the way back to the picnic spot. The three of them strolled along the lakeshore until Bethany had to send James after them so they would be back in time for their picnic lunch.

"This is fun," James said after the prayer. He reached for a ham sandwich. "Can we go fishing after lunch?"

"Not on Sunday," *Daed* said. "You know that."

"What can we do, then?"

"I brought a ball," Nathaniel said. "We can play catch."

"I'm going to visit some of the other Amish families that are here." Aaron finished his first sandwich and reached for a second. "If that's all right with you, *Daed*."

"*Ja*, for sure. Didn't I see Katie's family down the way?"

Aaron blushed as his younger brothers laughed, but then he grinned. "Who knows? She might be family soon enough."

"You mean there might be another wedding in the works?" Rose said, and she smiled at *Daed*.

Bethany glanced at Andrew. *Ja*, for sure, he noticed it, too. Rose was being downright pleasant today.

By the time the lunch was cleared away, Mari was yawning.

"Why don't you and I sit on the quilt for a while?" Bethany said, moving the blanket close to a small tree to keep it in the shade. "We can watch the boats while you rest your head in my lap."

"No nap," Mari said as she rubbed her eyes.

"Only a bit of a rest."

Andrew sat with them as Aaron walked toward Katie's family and the other boys took their ball to an open space away from the water. Rose and *Daed* had disappeared. As Bethany waved flies away from Mari's face, the little girl's eyes closed.

"Where did Rose and Jonah go?" Andrew asked. He leaned back on his elbows as he watched the fishermen on the water.

"I don't know. They must have gone for a walk together, but I didn't see which way they went."

"Have you noticed how nice Rose has been today?"

Bethany waved a fly away from her own face. "Could it be that she's changing? Maybe being in Indiana is good for her."

"I think it's your father."

"You don't think she has set her sights on him, do you?"

"You mean marriage? Of course not. I don't know how many times she's talked about Lemuel and how she will never marry again. She's too old, anyway."

"No older than *Daed.*"

"That's just what I mean. People their age don't think about marriage. They have to be at least fifty years old."

"*Daed* is fifty-five." Rose leaned against the tree. "And he wouldn't marry again. He loved *Mamm* too much to ever think of replacing her."

Andrew laid back on the quilt, his hat over his face. "They probably just enjoy each other's company, since they're the same age."

Bethany nodded, but Andrew didn't see her. He didn't

talk anymore, either, and soon his breathing was as deep and even as Mari's.

The afternoon was warm and still, and Bethany must have nodded off, too. The next thing she knew, she heard voices behind her.

"Is there any cake left?" James said, his voice a whisper.

"*Ja*, I made plenty for you boys." Rose's whisper was slightly louder. "Go wash in the lake before you eat any, though. All of your hands are filthy."

Bethany heard pounding footsteps as the boys ran toward the lake, and she was just dozing off again when *Daed* lowered himself to sit on the opposite side of the tree she leaned against.

"They love your cake, Rose. And you spoil them."

Wide awake now, Bethany didn't move for fear of waking Mari. Rose spoiled her brothers?

"It's only cake," Rose said. "And I've heard that growing boys need a lot of food."

"You and Lemuel only had one daughter?"

Rose sighed. "Only Lily. Lemuel always said he loved her, but I knew he was disappointed that we never had a son."

"It sounds like he was a fine man."

"He was a good man and loved the church. There aren't many like him in this world."

The boys came back then, noisy as ever, and both Mari and Andrew woke up. By the time Bethany and Mari returned from the outhouse next to the boat launch, the rest of the family was sitting on the quilt, eating cake as if they had never had dinner.

"I have cake, too?" Mari asked.

"For sure you can." Bethany helped her find a place to sit next to John as Rose handed her a piece of cake.

"Bethany, look." John showed her a tear in his trouser knee. "Nathaniel threw the ball out of my reach, and when I went to get it, I slipped. You'll need to mend it."

"Bring it over tomorrow, and I'll wash it, too."

Daed cleared his throat. "I hoped I could bring all of our laundry to you. There is quite a pile, and none of us can take time off our work to wash it."

Inwardly, Bethany groaned. A pile of her brother's dirty work clothes on top of Andrew's? For sure, she would do it, but it would be a job and a half.

But before she could agree, Rose jumped in. "I'll come over in the morning and take care of it, Jonah. Bethany has enough to do with her own laundry. And there's no reason to cart it back and forth across the road."

Bethany blinked. "Are you sure, Rose? You don't know how dirty my brothers' clothes can be."

"It's been ten years since I've washed a man's laundry, but I remember how. It will be a pleasure to help out a neighbor."

Andrew froze, his last bite of cake halfway to his mouth. He looked at Bethany and she shrugged. It seemed that he was just as confused by this change as she was. But at least Rose was finding a way to make herself busy away from the house. Tomorrow could be a peaceful, productive day.

Rose left the house before Andrew went downstairs on Monday morning, leaving the kitchen feeling empty and quiet. Mari was still sleeping, but Bethany was already on the washing porch, sorting the laundry into piles of dark clothes and light.

Andrew paused before heading to the barn. "It's a fine morning, isn't it?"

Bethany straightened, looking up at the deep blue sky with pink and orange streaks on the eastern horizon. "For sure, it is. I've been so busy that I haven't noticed."

"The chicken coop is ready for new chicks. Have you found any for us, yet?"

"Lovina Schrock said she would have some this week."

"Do you want to take the spring wagon over there later?"

"You're sure you don't need the horse?" Bethany stopped sorting clothes, a hopeful expression on her face.

"I need to have a team to get the plowing done. I'll go to the auction on Wednesday to look for one, but until then, you might as well take him." Andrew took a step closer to her, watching the way the early morning light gave her face a golden glow. "He's gentle and well-broken, so you don't have to worry about him."

"That would be *wonderful-gut*, Andrew. *Denki*. I'll take Mari with me after I hang the clothes on the line."

As Andrew turned toward the barn, Bethany stopped him.

"When do you think you'll be able to plow the garden? It's past time to get the seeds planted."

Andrew glanced at the wild profusion of day lilies filling the old garden spot, their orange blossoms opening to the early morning light. If dandelions had been growing there, or clover, or anything else, he wouldn't hesitate to plow them under and let the nutrients fertilize the garden bed. But lilies? He took a step toward the barn.

"I don't know when I can get to it. Perhaps you should share Jonah's garden this year. You're taking care of it, anyway, aren't you?"

Her puzzled frown made him take another step away. "I suppose I could share *Daed*'s, but it would take less than half the morning to plow it, and you don't need two horses. You could do it after breakfast."

"I'm busy after breakfast. Too much to do. I really don't think I'll be able to plow it this spring." Andrew turned and walked the rest of the way to the barn.

Taking out those lilies just didn't feel right. They were beautiful, even in their wild profusion, and Mari loved them. Andrew let his mind drift to the lilies that had grown along the roadside at their Iowa farm. Before the drought started and the dust started to blow, the flowers had been Lily's delight. She would gather the blossoms and bring them into the house, keeping a fresh bouquet on the kitchen table all through the summer.

Andrew went down the steps to the cellar. Dinah was waiting for him, nosing her feed box. He poured in her feed, then started mixing a bucket of soapy water to wash her before milking.

He thought back to that day in April when the neighbor's cattle had broken out of their bare, dusty pasture and had eaten every green thing in sight, including the day lily shoots along the road. Lily had cried over them and said, "I know they're only flowers, but now they're gone, like everything else."

And he had laughed at her.

He gazed out the cellar door to the patch of day lilies by the garden. She would have loved to see the flowers here. Why hadn't he come home sooner? If he had, then maybe she would still be alive.

By the time chores were done and he was back at the house, Mari was up and dressed. She was helping Bethany set the table, but as soon as she saw him, she ran to the door.

"*Daed*, I'm helping *Mamma* Bethany." She threw her arms around his legs.

"That's good. Give me a kiss, and then keep working until the job is done." He leaned down to receive a moist smack on his cheek. "And now back to your chore."

She ran back to the table and finished putting a spoon at each place. Andrew watched Bethany's back as he hung his hat next on the hook next to the door. She stood at the stove flipping hotcakes on the griddle. He thought she might ignore him, but once she turned over the last cake, she gave him a nod.

"How is Dinah this morning?"

"She's settling in well. She was waiting for me when I got there."

"She knew it was breakfast time."

"Or she wanted to be milked." Andrew sat at the table just as Mari laid a fork next to his plate. "I'm glad she's such a gentle cow and an easy milker. Mari will be able to take over that chore in a couple years."

"I thought we'd start her on the chickens, first. That's a better job for a little girl." Bethany put the hotcakes on a plate and set them on the table. She poured coffee for the two of them and put a glass of milk at Mari's place. "Mari, it's time to sit in your chair."

After placing a platter of eggs and bacon in the center of the table, Bethany sat and bowed her head for the silent prayer. Andrew gazed at the top of her *kapp* before bowing his head. He recited the prayer he had learned as a child in his head, but his thoughts were on Bethany's comment. Things had gone well between them during the past week, if he didn't count the friction between Bethany and Rose, but should he stand his ground on this? Or should he let Bethany have her way? By the time he lifted his head, he knew. Mari was his daughter, and he would have the last word in how she would be raised.

"I think it's better for Mari to learn how to milk, first. Especially since Dinah is such a gentle cow. You know chickens can be hard to handle sometimes." He helped himself to three eggs and six strips of bacon.

Bethany put an egg on Mari's plate. "Chickens are easy to take care of. I started when I was four."

"And you never got pecked?"

"For sure I got pecked. It taught me to be careful."

"I don't want Mari to learn that way. She should be older than four before she starts gathering eggs by herself."

Mari tapped on her plate with her fork. "What chickens?"

Bethany smiled at her. "We're getting baby chickens this afternoon. When they grow up, they'll give us eggs."

"Are they mean?"

"Only if we're mean to them." Bethany leveled her gaze at him. "We'll be gentle with our chickens."

Andrew finished his eggs and poured syrup on his hotcakes. "We'll start her out on milking."

"Chickens. Her hands aren't strong enough to milk."

"Milking." Andrew cut his hotcakes with the edge of his fork.

"Chickens, and that's final."

Mari's round eyes looked from Bethany to him, and back to Bethany. Andrew suddenly realized that he and Bethany were arguing as if they were still children.

"We'll finish this discussion later." He held Bethany's gaze until she nodded her agreement. "Meanwhile, I had a thought about the garden. The spot where it is now is overgrown and too shady in the afternoon. I thought we could put it closer to the road and away from the trees."

"In the front yard?"

"Between the house and the road. There's plenty of room there, and it's in the sun all day."

Bethany nodded as she sipped her coffee. "Won't it be more work for you, though?"

"I don't think so. I'll have to take out that young maple tree, but that won't be difficult."

"It seems like it would be easier to take out the day lilies or move them."

Andrew laid down his fork and took a deep breath. Was she going to argue with him about every little thing?

"I like the day lilies, and they're going to stay where they are."

Mari grinned at him. "I like the lilies. *Mamm* likes them, too."

Bethany set down her cup. "I like the lilies, Mari. But

there are so many of them. We can cut them back and they'll still be pretty."

Mari shook her head. "*Mamm* wouldn't like that. She cries when the cows eat the flowers."

"Oh." Bethany stood, her chair shoving back. "You mean Lily." When she faced Andrew, her chin was quivering. "You want to move the garden because Lily liked the flowers."

He stared at his plate. He didn't have an answer for her. Didn't know what to say.

Without a word to either of them, she left the table and ran upstairs. As Andrew met his daughter's questioning gaze, the bedroom door slammed.

Bethany stalked to the window, to the view she had enjoyed until now. Below her was the garden with its profusion of orange lilies. Mocking her.

Andrew wanted to keep the lilies because they reminded him of his first wife. She could understand that. She had kept several things to remind her of *Mamm*. So why did it bother her so much? She wasn't jealous, was she?

Slumping on her bed, Bethany fingered the edge of the quilt as all the memories of Andrew's rejection of her came rushing back. She had almost forgotten it. Almost. Until Lovina brought it up on the Sunday before the wedding. He had rejected her, then moved away, then married someone else. Mari's mother. The much-beloved Lily. While she had waited at home, willing to forgive him and forget the whole thing, if only he had written to apologize.

But there had been no letter. Only silence. And now she knew why.

One hot tear rolled down her cheek and she pushed it away.

Andrew had fallen in love, and he was still in love. Every decision he made about his marriage to her was made in the shadow of Lily's memory.

Bethany wiped at another tear. She had been so foolish to enter into this arrangement with Andrew. If she hadn't been so... Bethany sighed. If she hadn't been so desperate. She thought this was her chance to be a mother, to have a family of her own. But she hadn't taken the time to consider what role Lily would take in their lives.

Rose was bad enough, with her constant comments about her daughter and undermining Bethany's relationship with Mari. But eventually Rose would leave, and Bethany had once thought that they could be a happy family then. But that wasn't going to happen. Not with Lily's constant presence in every moment of Andrew's life.

But then there was Mari. The little girl was confused enough, and when her parents bickered at the table, it only made her life worse.

This wasn't the family life Bethany had dreamed of. This wasn't the marriage she had hoped for.

One thing she could do to make their lives better would be to give in to Andrew's desire to move the garden. She couldn't expect Mari to forget her first mother, and she didn't want to. If letting the lilies grow would help Mari, then she would let the patch keep growing in the backyard for her sake.

Bethany stood and gazed at the lilies again. She might

have made a mistake when she married Andrew, but it was done. She had to make the best of it, and she would, even if she was only the second best. The second mother. The second wife. And she would do it for Mari's sake.

Straightening her shoulders, Bethany lifted her chin. *Mamm* always said that life was what you made of it, and it was time to go back downstairs and start making this life of hers one that would please God. She gave one last tear an impatient swipe and went back to the kitchen.

Andrew had cleared the table and was helping Mari wash her hands when Bethany walked in. He gave her a crooked smile.

"Are you all right?"

Bethany forced her own smile as she nodded. "For sure. I just needed to be alone for a few minutes." She cleared her throat. "I'll plan on driving over to Lovina's house later this morning. I'll leave a casserole in the oven for your dinner in case we aren't back in time."

Andrew dried Mari's hands. "Don't bother. I'll make a sandwich for myself. I know you're busy enough with the laundry this morning."

"Denki." Bethany leaned against the kitchen shelf as he stopped by the door to put on his hat. "And I think your idea about the garden is a good one. The front of the house is a good, sunny spot."

"I was thinking about that, too." Andrew paused, framed by the doorway. "The front yard isn't level and taking that tree out won't be easy. I'll cut the day lilies back a little bit and extend the garden on the other end."

Bethany nodded, accepting his compromise. "I'm glad we could work it out."

"We can work out anything as long as we do it together." Andrew gave her one last smile, then went back to the barn.

Mari tugged at Bethany's skirt. "Are you sad?"

Bethany kneeled so she was level with Mari. "I'm not sad. I only needed to think about some things."

"*Daed* said you were sad."

"I was for a little while."

"Why?"

How could she say what she felt so that Mari would understand? "You and your father loved your mother very much."

Mari nodded.

"You miss her and that makes you sad sometimes." She drew Mari close and looked into her eyes. "I never met your mother, but I need to help you remember her. I don't want you to forget her."

"That's what *Mammi* Rose said."

"We'll keep the day lilies growing to help you and your father remember her. Would you like that?"

Mari grinned. "And we won't let Dinah eat them."

Bethany laughed. "We'll keep Dinah far away from them." She stood up. "Now, it's time to wash the dishes and then we need to get started on the washing. We have a lot to do today."

That afternoon, when Bethany and Mari drove back into the yard with a box of chicks in the wagon, James was waiting for her on the back step. When he saw them, he ran over.

"Do you need help with anything?"

"*Ja*, for sure," Bethany said, pulling the wagon to a

halt. "You can unhitch the horse while Mari and put the chicks in their new home."

James took Whiskers' bridle. "I'd rather help you with the chicks."

"Then we'll take care of the horse together, and then the chicks."

As James led the horse into the barn with Mari beside him, Bethany asked, "What brings you over today?"

Her youngest brother made a face. "Rose is at our house."

"What's wrong with that?"

"John says she's got her eye on *Daed*, and I don't like it."

"You've heard her say she isn't interested in marrying again, didn't you? I think she only wants to talk to someone her own age."

James shrugged. "Maybe." He unfastened the harness on one side while Bethany did the other with Mari's help. "She sure makes a good dinner, though."

"What did she fix?"

"Fried chicken, potatoes, green beans and biscuits. And she made a pie for dessert."

Bethany peered under the horse to catch James's eye. "She made all that on a laundry day?"

"She sure did. And she was on the laundry porch even before *Daed* got up, working away. She had the clothesline full by the time I went out to do chores."

They hung up the harness and Bethany took Whiskers into his stall while James pushed the spring wagon into its place. Rose must have gotten up long before dawn if she had finished the laundry that early.

Bethany picked up the box of chicks and the three of them walked out to the chicken coop. "What makes John say she has her eye on *Daed*?"

"They are always smiling at each other." James looked up at her. "I haven't seen *Daed* smile this much for a long time."

Mari ran ahead to the pen Andrew had built for the chickens and waited until Bethany opened the gate. "Can I hold one?"

"We'll close the gate first, and then I'll help you hold one."

When she set the box on the ground, the peeping intensified as Bethany lifted the lid. The chicks stretched up their necks, trying to climb over the edge of the shallow box. As James lifted them over the side of the box and set them on the dusty ground, Bethany picked up one fuzzy yellow ball and put it in Mari's hands, keeping her own hands cradled underneath.

Mari's eyes widened as she held the chick. "It's a baby."

"For sure, it is. It will grow up right quick, though."

"Its feet tickle." She giggled. "Can I hug it?"

"Little chicks are too fragile to hug. Let's put it down so it can get a drink."

Andrew had filled the water can for the chicks while she had been gone and a bucket of cracked corn sat next to it. While the chicks crowded around the waterer, James showed Mari how to scatter the corn.

Once the chicks were settled, it was time for Mari's nap. James followed them into the house. By the time Bethany had made sure Mari was on her way to sleep, she came back into the kitchen to find James sitting at the table with a glass of milk and a plate of cookies.

"I thought you said you had a big dinner." Bethany covered her mouth, trying not to laugh at her little brother.

"That was at least an hour ago," James said, taking another cookie. "Where is Andrew?"

"I'm not sure. I thought he might be at your house, since we didn't see him in the barn."

James swallowed his cookie, then drank the milk in big gulps. Bethany broke a cookie in half, and took a bite, waiting for James to tell her why he came over. It had to be more than to spend time with her. James never did anything without a purpose behind it.

"These are good cookies," he said, taking another one. "You make the best cookies."

"Better than *Daed*?" Bethany couldn't help teasing him.

"For sure. Better than Aaron, too."

"Aaron made cookies?" Bethany couldn't imagine Aaron working in the kitchen.

James wrinkled his nose. "He tried. They were all flat, and they burned. He gave them to the pigs."

"You can take the rest of these home with you, if you want to."

James shook his head. "I'm not going home."

"Why not?"

"It isn't the same without you there. I want to live here."

"But what would *Daed* do without you?"

"He has John, and Nathaniel, and Aaron. He doesn't need me. But you do. I could do your chores for you and help Andrew."

His eyebrows went up as he looked at her, his expression as hopeful as a puppy begging for scraps.

"You know that Rose lives here, and I thought you didn't like her."

James took another bite of his cookie before he answered. "I like her all right, and I like her cooking. I just want things to go back to the way they were."

"Then you don't really want to live here?"

He stared at the half-eaten cookie in his hand. "I guess not. It just isn't right without you at home."

Since it was only the two of them in the kitchen, Bethany opened her arms and he climbed into her lap, the way he had when he was little, in the months after *Mamm* passed on.

"I know you don't like things to change, but everything will work out."

James tried to lay his head on her shoulder, but he was too tall. He sighed. "I wish *Mamm* was still here."

Bethany thought of the bright profusion of orange lilies. "Do you remember much about her?"

"I remember what her apron smelled like when I hugged her. And I remember when she tucked me in bed at night." He still held his half-eaten cookie. "I wish she hadn't died."

Holding him close, Bethany leaned her cheek on his shoulder. He smelled of hay and little-boy sweat. "So do I."

Chapter Eight

Andrew was eating his lunch of a bread-and-butter sandwich when he heard a wagon drive into the yard. He shoved the last bite into his mouth, brushed the crumbs off his lap and grabbed his hat on the way out the door.

Dave met him at the edge of his drive as he tied his team to the hitching rail by the back porch.

"I was hoping you would be home. I heard about a farmer selling out south of here and thought you might like to come with me to see what he has."

Andrew glanced at the noon sun. "Isn't it a little late in the day for a sale?"

"Not this one. I heard the man is selling whatever he has to whoever comes along. Daniel Miller bought a set of plow shares from him, and said the man has some livestock and more tools. I'm looking for some parts for my combine, and I know you need another horse."

"For sure. I'll be right with you."

As they drove west, and then south at the next crossroad, Dave said, "I haven't seen you since the wedding. How are things going?"

Andrew shifted in his seat. "Well enough."

Ja, well enough, but nothing like the first couple weeks of his marriage to Lily.

"What's wrong?" Dave kept his eyes on the horses' ears.

"Bethany can be prickly." Andrew scratched his beard. "We haven't become comfortable together yet."

Dave laughed. "From what I remember, the first few months of wedded life aren't supposed to be comfortable."

"It's different than what I thought it would be."

His friend glanced at him, then back at the horses. "You aren't regretting this marriage, are you?"

"Regret? I don't think so. I appreciate Bethany's care of the house and Mari. Of course, Rose is still living with us."

Dave drove to the next corner and turned the team west again before he spoke. "That could cause some difficulties. We certainly appreciated Dorcas's mother when she came to help with the babies, but it was a relief when she went back home last week." He flicked a deerfly away from the near horse's ears. "Is Rose going back to Iowa anytime soon?"

"The drought out there hasn't let up. When I left to come back here, none of the farmers had crops going. The wind had buried all the seeds too deep in the dust, and then the next windstorm blew everything away. There hasn't been any rain in months, even after the hard winter. I don't know what she'd do if she went back."

"She lives alone?"

Andrew nodded. "She supported herself with her garden and her chickens, and she rented out the farm fields. But the chickens didn't survive the winter, and there's no use trying to plant a garden this year. I don't want her to go back to dust and more dust."

"What does Bethany think about that?"

"That's the problem. Rose and Bethany are like sandpaper and wool. One of them is always complaining about the other, and Bethany constantly asks me when I'm going to send Rose home. She doesn't understand what it's like in Iowa. The biggest problem is that I don't think Rose understands it, either. She still thinks she can take Mari back there to live with her and everything will be the same as it's always been." Andrew sighed. "She keeps saying that this drought has to be over soon. That they never last more than two years." He brushed at some caked dirt on his trouser leg. "I can't ask Rose to leave, knowing what she would be going back to."

"Maybe we could build her a *Dawdi Haus*."

"Jonah offered the one on his farm, but she refused." Andrew shifted in his seat again. "I don't want to burden you with my problems. We can talk about something else."

Dave shrugged. "What else are friends for?"

"How are those twins doing?"

As Dave talked about the babies, Andrew listened with one ear, but his thoughts were on Bethany. She wasn't happy. He wasn't happy. Rose and Mari seemed content, but they were the only ones. He didn't want

Bethany to regret marrying him, but what could he do to fix the problem?

When they reached the farm, Dave pulled his team to a halt at the end of the lane. The barn had been neglected and half the roof had fallen in. Overgrown bushes hid the house, and the lane itself disappeared into a patch of weeds. The only sign of life was a crooked For Sale sign tacked to a fence post.

"Is this the right place?"

Dave turned the horses into the lane. "If it isn't, then maybe someone here can direct us to the farm we're looking for."

As they approached the house, a man stepped out from behind the bushes with a shotgun cradled in his arms.

"Y'all from the bank?"

"No, sir. We heard you might have some stock or equipment for sale," answered Dave.

The man laid the shotgun on the porch and walked toward them. "Now that I look at you, I can see you ain't bankers. Come on in the barn and we'll see if I have anything you want."

Leaving the wagon by the house, Andrew and Dave followed the man to the half of the barn that was still standing.

"You boys from around here?"

"Up toward Emma," Andrew said, blinking as they passed from the bright sunshine into the shadowed barn. "I see you're selling your farm, too."

"Yep." The man gave a satisfied grunt. "Told my woman it wasn't worth coming up here to farm, but she wanted to be near her folks. That was twenty years ago. Wife finally up and died, so I'm heading back to Tennessee. I'd rather hardscrabble in the hills than here in this swampland."

Andrew kept his thoughts to himself, but in twenty years, the man could have built this place into a fine farm. Swampland was very fertile once it was drained.

"Here's the stock I have left." Opening a gate in the back of the barn, the man gestured toward a draft horse. "You can put this rope on him and lead him out in the yard, if you want."

As Andrew slid the frayed rope over the horse's head, the beast looked at him sideways. "Is he gentle?"

"As a lamb. Well broke, too."

"How old is he?" Andrew watched the horse's gait as he led him toward the barn door.

"The man I got him from said he was seven years old when I bought him a while back. I'd say he's probably a little over ten."

In the sunlight, Andrew ran his hand along the horse's side, feeling the ribs. The hooves needed trimming, and the coat was dull, but the horse was curious about him and pricked his ears forward as Andrew came around to his front again. At least the man was right about him being gentle. The horse let Andrew examine his teeth and run his hands down each leg. Andrew guessed he was over fifteen years, but the legs felt sound.

"How much do you want for him?"

The old man grinned and started haggling. By the time Dave returned with a handful of machine parts, they had reached a price that Andrew thought was fair.

He handed the man the last of the cash he had gotten from selling his stock back in Iowa.

After loading Dave's purchase into the wagon and tying the horse to the back, they set off for home. Whatever breeze there had been in the morning had stilled and the sun beat down on them in shimmering waves. Grasshoppers buzzed among the dusty weeds along the road. It was so dry that the back of Andrew's shirt was stiff from dried sweat.

"It looks like we're in for a hot, dry summer. It reminds me of the last couple years in Iowa."

Dave glanced his way. "You don't think we could be in for the same kind of dust storms here, do you? The one that came through in May was pretty bad, and I wouldn't want to repeat it."

Andrew leaned on his knees. That big storm in May had started somewhere west of his farm in Iowa, chasing dry clouds and crackling lightning ahead of it, and had gone all the way to the east coast, carrying the dirt of the plains with it. It had been the day Lily died.

"We can't." He shook his head, clearing his throat of the dust he still felt sometimes. "It can't get as bad here."

A stray gust of wind kicked up a dust whirl in the road in front of them that disappeared as quickly as it had formed. Andrew closed his eyes and forced himself to remember Emma Lake, shimmering in the Sunday afternoon sun. The drought couldn't get as bad here as it was in Iowa and farther west.

Bethany submerged the breakfast plates in the dishwater as she stared out the window. Thursday morning, two weeks to the day after her wedding, and she didn't feel any more married than she had then. Or maybe she did. Maybe all married people were as miserable as she and Andrew seemed to be.

"*Mamma* Bethany, can I help?"

Turning to smile at Mari, Bethany helped her scoot her stool over to the sink. "For sure you can. You can be my little dishwasher."

Bethany mentally shook herself. She wasn't miserable. Not really. It was only that Andrew seemed to be distant, keeping himself away from the house as much as possible.

"Where is *Mammi* Rose?"

"She went to my *daed*'s house to cook dinner for the boys."

Mari swirled the dishrag through the soapy water and across the plates the way Bethany had shown her. "They don't have a *mamm*?"

"I used to take care of them, but now I'm here with you."

"Will *Mammi* Rose be their *mamm*?"

Bethany almost laughed at that. "I don't think so. That means she would marry my *daed*, and that isn't going to happen." She rinsed the plate Mari had washed, then picked up a towel to dry it. "But while she's gone, you can help me with today's work. We're going to clean the upstairs bedrooms. You can use the dust mop and clean under the beds."

Mari grinned at her. "I like the dust mop." She rubbed the rag across the last plate. "Can Dinah help?"

"Cows don't help with housework. They're too big to

come in the house." She dried Mari's hands and helped her down from the stool. "Dinah has her own job."

"What is it?"

Bethany took the dishpan out to the garden and Mari followed her. "Dinah's job is to eat grass and make milk for us. She works hard at her job every day."

"I like Dinah."

Mari stood back as Bethany flung the dishwater over the garden in an arc. She had planted the first seeds two days ago, but still looked for green shoots.

"It's too early for the seeds to be sprouting."

Bethany jumped at Andrew's words. She hadn't heard him coming up behind her.

"Daed!" Mari ran to him and he lifted her into his arms.

"What are you up to this morning?"

Bethany opened her mouth to answer, but then saw that Andrew was addressing Mari. He wasn't interested in what she was doing.

"I'm going to use the dust mop."

"Are you going to dust the garden?"

Andrew's smile when he teased Mari reminded Bethany of the old days, when they had been young. She had borne the brunt of his teasing then. Mari laughed as Andrew tossed her into the air and caught her again. Bethany turned to walk back into the house so she wouldn't intrude on Andrew's time with Mari.

"Can I see the new horse?"

Bethany didn't hear Andrew's answer to his daughter's question but hurried into the house. She had been wrong. Andrew wasn't miserable when he was around

Mari, but he was when he was in the house with her. Sighing, Bethany grabbed the cleaning supplies and headed for the stairs. She would tackle the dirt and hope that made her feel better.

Dropping onto the step halfway up, Bethany leaned against the wall. Work wouldn't help. Talking to Andrew was impossible, and she couldn't confide in *Daed*. She needed a woman to talk to. Someone who would understand, and definitely not Rose.

Elisabeth Stoltzfus. Bethany smiled at the thought of the minister's wife, who had been *Mamm*'s good friend. Elisabeth would be the perfect one to talk to. She would use Andrew's spring wagon or borrow *Daed*'s buggy and drive over as soon as she finished cleaning.

As she continued up the steps, Mari came running to join her.

"Don't forget," she said, taking the steep steps one at a time, "I get to use the dust mop."

"I haven't forgotten. Which room do you want to do first?"

"My room. It's dirty under my bed."

As Bethany hurried through the Thursday morning chore, she told herself she could make up for it next week. She wanted to get to Elisabeth's and return before dinnertime. It wasn't long before she had hitched Whiskers to the spring wagon and was on her way, with Mari sitting on the seat beside her.

"Where are we going?"

"To visit my friend Elisabeth."

"Does she have girls?"

"She has big girls. Rebecca and Mandy. Do you remember them? They played with you at church on our last meeting day." Lovina's seven- and nine-year-old sisters were always happy to play with the little ones and keep them occupied during the fellowship meal.

Mari nodded and stuck her thumb in her mouth as Whiskers walked along. A buggy horse would trot briskly, but Whiskers was too heavy for more than his normal plod. She hoped Andrew would be able to buy a buggy horse soon.

When they reached the Stoltzfus farm, Mandy and Rebecca came running from the backyard to greet them.

"Can Mari play? We have baby rabbits."

Bethany smiled at the girls. "For sure, she can. Just help her be careful so she doesn't squeeze the bunnies."

She followed the girls to the backyard, where Elisabeth sat in a shady spot, paring off the tops of strawberries into a pan.

"If you have another knife, I'll help." Bethany sat on the bench next to Elisabeth.

"Mandy was helping for a little while. You can use her knife." Elisabeth gave her a warm smile. "I'm glad you came over. What brings you by?"

Bethany used the point of the knife to take off the top of the first strawberry, sliced it and let it drop onto the bowl Elisabeth had already filled more than halfway. "I just want to visit, I guess."

"How are things for the newlyweds?"

Picking up the next strawberry, Bethany shrugged. "I thought things would be different."

Elisabeth took off the tops of two strawberries before she answered. "You and Andrew have difficulties to overcome."

"I can't seem to make him happy."

"Why do you say that?"

"I know he has to work hard, but it seems like he avoids coming into the house unless he has to." Bethany sliced her strawberry and reached for the next one. "And every time we talk, we seem to end up in an argument."

"It sounds like you aren't very happy, either."

"I don't want to complain."

"You don't have to say you're unhappy for me to tell."

Mari came running over to Bethany, a young rabbit in her arms. "*Mamma* Bethany, look. It's a bunny."

The rabbit struggled in Mari's arms. Bethany repositioned the little girl's hands so that she was holding the rabbit's hind feet. "If you support his feet, then he feels safe and he won't wiggle."

Mari smiled, then walked back to the rabbit pen on the other side of the backyard.

"It's easy for a man to feel like he's failed. And when he doesn't feel like he has support, he struggles, just like that rabbit." Elisabeth's voice was quiet. "Andrew has lost his first wife and left his farm in Iowa. He's come home and has had to start over again."

Bethany nodded. "He works hard."

"But?"

"He never smiles at me."

"He has a lot of responsibilities. You, Mari, Rose, the farm…"

Bethany dropped more strawberry slices in the bowl.

"That's part of the problem. Rose is still here. She refuses to go home."

"I overheard Andrew tell John that Rose didn't have much to go back to in Iowa. The last letter from Martha said that no one can raise crops or even a garden this year because it is too dry and dusty."

She stared at Elisabeth. Andrew had gotten a letter from his mother?

"He never told me that."

"Maybe he didn't want to burden you." The older woman cut off the top the last berry in her pan. "Would it make a difference if you had known Rose's situation?"

"I'm not sure."

"You and Andrew need to learn how to work as a team. In a good marriage, the husband and wife work together toward the same goals, and each one is equally important."

"Like a team of horses?"

Elisabeth laughed. "I'm not sure I want to compare myself to a horse, but they have to learn to work together, just like we do."

Bethany thought of the new horse Andrew had brought home to be a teammate for Whiskers. It had been three days, but the horses still weren't getting along well.

"How do I do learn to work with Andrew?"

Elisabeth picked up the bowl of berries. "I need to take these into the house before the flies bother them too much. Come in with me while I start on dinner."

Bethany followed her into the kitchen, carrying the

knives and empty pans. The pan of strawberry tops would go to the chickens.

"The first thing you and Andrew need to do," Elisabeth said as she set the bowl of berries next to the sink, "is to realize that you are partners. You'll be together for the rest of your lives, so the sooner you do that, the better."

"So I just need to tell him?"

Elisabeth shook her head. "Words don't mean anything unless they're accompanied by action. Show him you're ready to work with him. Don't ask for more than he can provide, and don't pester him about chores he hasn't been able to do yet."

Bethany thought of the garden she had reminded him to plow several times before he got the job done.

Elisabeth went on. "And show him that you love him. That you're thinking of him, even when he's out working. Make his favorite dishes for dinner and keep your conversations peaceful. No one likes to bicker all the time."

"What if I'm not the one doing it?"

"It doesn't matter. Your attitude can make all the difference."

Bethany ran her finger along the edge of the kitchen shelf. It all sounded so easy when Elisabeth said it, but what would she do about Rose? Would the same plan work for her, too?

Elisabeth reached into the cupboard for an empty jar and spooned some strawberry slices into it.

"Take these with you and make a strawberry shortcake to have with your dinner. I guarantee that it will show Andrew how you feel about him."

Bethany took the strawberries with thanks and rounded up Mari to head home.

For sure, Andrew would enjoy the strawberry short-cake, but Elisabeth was wrong when she thought they loved each other. They only needed to get along, not fall in love.

Something woke Andrew from a sound sleep. He waited, then heard it again. A noise outside the open window. A bush rustled, then a branch cracked. Some-one was out there.

It could be an animal, but he had heard the rumors of tramps in the area. Men out of work and homeless, living on whatever they could find as they made their way west or south. Looking for work or a handout, ei-ther one. Some of the farmers had reported thievery. Chickens disappearing. Even clothes off the clothesline. Andrew kept still and waited.

The noises faded. Whoever, or whatever, it was had gone around the end of the house.

Next came a crackle. The noise of pebbles bouncing off a window.

Andrew sat up. There was a time when he had been the one tossing pebbles at a window, back in Iowa when he was courting Lily.

Waiting, keeping his breathing shallow and quiet, he heard low voices, but couldn't make out any words. After several minutes, he heard the footsteps going to-ward the road and peered out the window. A furtive figure followed the edge of the front yard, then disappeared through the shrubs that lined the ditch by the road.

He punched his pillow and lay back down on the bed, but he only stared at the ceiling, wide-awake. Bethany was his wife, even if she didn't think so. How could she consider a friendship with another man? Especially one who came calling during the night. And when he had asked her there was anyone else before they entered into this marriage, she had denied it.

She had lied. How could she do this to him?

To Mari?

He had trusted her.

Was this why she had been so kind after she returned from visiting Elisabeth this morning? She had even made strawberry shortcake, his favorite dessert.

A cold, bitter thought washed over him. Had she really gone to visit Elisabeth? Or had that been the excuse she used to meet the other man?

But she had taken Mari, who couldn't stop talking about the rabbits at the Stoltzfus farm, even at bedtime.

He frowned. Maybe only Mari had spent the hour with Mandy and Rebecca while Bethany had taken the opportunity to meet someone.

Flopping over on the bed, he punched his pillow again.

If he hadn't seen the man sneaking away, he wouldn't believe it. Bethany wouldn't act so treacherously. Not the Bethany he knew.

But people changed.

As the long hours passed into gray morning light, Andrew thought of a plan. He wouldn't confront Bethany.

That would only give her an excuse to lie to him again. But a dog on the place would chase away any intruders, and the rumors of tramps would be the only excuse he would need for getting one.

He couldn't look at Bethany during breakfast, but he didn't need to. Rose kept the conversation going.

"Do you think this is the right time to plant the corn and tomatoes?" she asked.

Andrew's fork stopped partway to his mouth. Rose was asking his opinion?

"It's the third week of June. We're almost too late."

"Jonah gave me some seeds when I was there yesterday, so I thought I'd plant them today. Mari can help me. Would you like to work in the garden today, too, Bethany?"

Bethany choked on her coffee and shot a glance his way, but Andrew ignored her.

"I'd like that."

"Good." Rose smiled at all three of them. "We'll be able to get the whole garden planted this morning. Won't that be *wonderful-gut*?"

Andrew dared to exchange glances with Bethany. He wasn't sure how to respond to this new Rose.

"I'm going to start plowing the cornfield this morning." He ate the last bite of his toast and stood up.

"Will Whiskers and the new horse be able to work together?" Bethany stood also and started clearing the table.

"They'll have to learn," Andrew said. Bethany didn't look like she had lost any sleep last night. "But before I start, I'm going over to Jonah's to see if he knows where I can find a good dog."

"Why do we need a dog?"

Andrew watched Bethany's face closely as he said, "I thought I heard a prowler last night."

Rose gave a nervous laugh. "A prowler?" she asked.

"You don't have to worry. A dog will scare anyone off who doesn't belong here."

Bethany's face hadn't changed. It was as if she didn't feel any guilt at all.

Jonah was washing the breakfast dishes with John and James when he arrived. His father-in-law waved him in.

"Would you like some coffee?"

"I just finished breakfast." Andrew sat with Jonah at the table while the boys finished their chore. "I was wondering if you knew of anyone who has a dog they want to give away."

"My cousin Levi's dog had a litter of puppies a couple months ago. You could see if he's still looking for homes for them."

"I was hoping to find an adult dog."

"Are you having problems over there? Is there a fox after your chickens?"

Andrew nodded. It was a fox, for sure. "I just want to keep any varmints away, human or animal."

"So you've heard the rumors, too." Jonah combed his beard with his fingers.

"The Smiths have a dog they want to give away," John said. "Joe told me that they have two, but they only want one."

"Where do they live?" Andrew asked.

"Their farm is east a mile," said Jonah. "It's an *Englisch* farm with a big red barn. You can't miss the place."

"Thanks for the help. I'll head over there right away."

"I'll go with you," Jonah said. "I borrowed a fence-post puller from Eugene last week and this is a good time to return it and introduce you to him."

Jonah hitched up his buggy and they were soon approaching the Smith farm. The *Englisch* family hadn't lived here when Andrew had moved to Iowa. As they turned into the farm lane, two large brown dogs came rushing from the barn, barking.

Jonah chuckled. "They do this every time. But as soon as they see who it is, they'll stop."

Jonah was right. The dogs soon stopped their barking and followed the buggy to the hitching rail by the barn, their tails wagging. Jonah jumped down from the buggy and rubbed both dogs behind the ears, but they didn't approach Andrew. They sat near Jonah, watching the stranger with distrustful eyes.

"What do you think?" asked Jonah.

"They're suspicious of me, and that's exactly what I'm looking for. One of these will keep the place safe at night."

He held out a hand to the nearest dog, who sniffed it, but didn't step closer. This was the dog for him.

Chapter Nine

On Tuesday morning when *Daed* stopped by for a cup of coffee, Bethany was no longer surprised.

"You're making this a habit," she said as she poured a second cup for him.

Daed leaned back in his chair. "I hope you don't mind. I didn't think I'd miss you so much when you got married."

Bethany sat down across from him with her own cup. "Do you miss me? Or do you miss someone taking care of the cooking and cleaning?"

"*Ja*, for sure, that might be it." *Daed* smiled at her.

"Aaron should marry soon, and then his wife can take over."

Daed blew across the steaming surface of his coffee. "Or maybe I should marry again."

Bethany laughed until she realized he wasn't joking. "You're serious?"

"Why not? Men my age remarry. And you know your younger brothers could use the guidance of a loving mother."

"I suppose you're right." Bethany tried to imagine someone else working in *Mamm*'s kitchen. "Do you have anyone in mind?"

Shrugging, *Daed* set his cup on the table. "Where are Rose and Mari this morning?"

"They went out to the garden to see how the early vegetables are doing. I hope they find some radishes that are ready."

"I saw Andrew out plowing. The new horse seems to have settled in."

"It took a few days. Andrew had to work with them for hours before they would let themselves be harnessed next to each other. Yesterday evening he said they finally started pulling together."

"It takes some time to get used to someone new."

Bethany took a sip of her coffee. Was *Daed* talking about the horses, or marriage?

"What do the boys think of the idea of you marrying again?"

"It depends. On the days when Rose comes over to cook for us, they're all for it. But when evening comes I think they'd rather not face another change in their lives." *Daed* watched his coffee. "There's something to be said for being a group of bachelors."

"No one to tell you to clean up after yourselves?"

Chuckling, *Daed* nodded. "Or complaining about animals in the house."

"Did John adopt one of the lambs? He tries that every year."

"He has a bum lamb that he's bottle-feeding, and somehow that thing ends up in his bed every night."

"Why don't you hire someone to cook and clean for you instead of getting married?"

Daed ran his fingers through his beard, his gaze set on something past Bethany's shoulder, somewhere out the kitchen door. "Now that you're married, you know how a husband and wife form a bond that's different than any other. Your *mamm*'s been gone for a few years now, and sometimes..." He looked at Bethany. "Sometimes I just get lonely. I start wondering if there is anyone else I might love like I loved her."

Bethany couldn't meet *Daed*'s eyes. She and Andrew didn't have this bond he spoke of, and she doubted if they ever would. But she remembered the way *Mamm* would rest one hand on *Daed*'s shoulder while she leaned over him to put food on the table, or the way *Daed* would take her hand while they talked in the evenings. Their affection for each other showed every day. Affection didn't have to be based on love, though. She liked Andrew, most of the time. Perhaps a small show of affection was what Elisabeth meant when she said to show Andrew that she was willing to be by his side as a team.

Just then, Mari and Rose came in.

"*Mamma* Bethany," Mari said, "we found pink potatoes."

"She means radishes." Rose laid a basket on the table with a few radishes and some fresh lettuce leaves. "We'll be able to pick some spinach tomorrow, and the tomato plants are doing well." She glanced at Jonah. "I didn't know you were here."

Daed's expression changed to one of mock hurt. "It is Tuesday, isn't it? I thought you would be expecting me."

"I never know what to expect from you." Rose took a bowl from the cupboard and started putting the radishes in it, tearing off the tops as she went. "I suppose you want me to cook dinner for you again today."

"If you don't have anything else to keep you busy."

Bethany glanced at *Daed*. In spite of Rose's harsh tone, he kept a smile on his face as he watched her.

"I used the last of your ham on Saturday. Do you want me to fix a chicken?"

"I'll have one of the boys get it ready for you." *Daed* leaned forward. "I do love chicken pot pie."

"As long as I'm making pie crust, perhaps I'll bake a rhubarb-custard pie for you to have with your supper tonight."

"Now that hits the spot."

Bethany dared to peek at Rose. The frown was gone, and she had replaced it with a look of pleasant satisfaction. Rose certainly enjoyed compliments on her cooking.

"Mari, do you want to come with me to fetch the milk, or do you want to stay in the house?"

Mari slid off of Bethany's lap. "Fetch the milk. I want to see Dinah."

"Don't spoil my brothers too much, Rose," Bethany said as she started toward the door with Mari. "When you're not cooking for them, they have to make do with *Daed*'s meals."

Laughter followed her out the door, from both *Daed* and Rose. It was good that they enjoyed each other's company, but when Rose went back to Iowa, *Daed* would be even more lonely. Perhaps that was why he was considering marriage again.

The new dog met them at the door, tail wagging. Mari had named her Jenny, and Bethany supposed she was a good dog. At first, she had been afraid the dog might be too active to be around the little girl, but Jenny seemed to know that Mari was young and was always gentle with her.

"Jenny," Mari said, slapping her thigh the way Andrew did. "Jenny, come here."

The dog came close to her, sniffing Mari's fingers.

"I don't have food for you."

Jenny wagged her tail and let her tongue hang out, looking as if she was smiling. She stepped closer to Mari and thrust her head under the little girl's hand.

"She wants you to pet her," Bethany said, reaching down to scratch the dog's head.

When Mari patted her softly, Jenny's tail wagged in circles. "Good dog," Mari said. She rested her hand on Jenny's back as the three of them walked the rest of the way to the barn.

Bethany was surprised to find Andrew standing at the workbench when they walked in. Mari ran over to him and wrapped her arms around his leg.

"We came to get the milk," she said. "Is Dinah down cellar?"

Andrew kneeled so he could be on her level. "Dinah is in the pasture, but the milk is in the springhouse waiting for you."

"The springhouse?"

"I cleaned it out yesterday afternoon. We need to use it to keep the food fresh in this hot weather."

"The milk will cool faster there."

Andrew met Bethany's gaze. "I haven't skimmed it yet."

She smiled, hoping that would ease his worried look. "It isn't a problem for me to do it. I know you're busy with the plowing and all the other work you do."

Andrew gestured toward the workbench with a sigh. "I should be plowing now, except that the harness broke. I'll be able to mend it, but I've lost an hour already."

"You could ask *Daed* if he or Aaron could help you get the plowing done."

"They have their own work to do, but if I have any more delays, I'll be sure to ask. I need to get the seeds in the ground soon if we're going to have a crop this year."

Bethany stepped closer to him. They should be a team, Elisabeth had said.

"Is there anything I can do to make things easier for you?"

Andrew stood, picking up Mari. "You're already doing it." He gave Mari a hug, not meeting Bethany's eyes. "You're caring for Mari and making sure I have my meals on time and clean clothes to wear. What more could I ask you to do?"

"With four brothers around, I've never done much field work," Bethany said. "But I know how to harness the horses and drive a plow."

He glanced at her. "Wouldn't you rather visit your friends?"

She laughed. "My friends are as busy as I am this time

of year. We can catch up with each other on Sundays. When there is work to be done, I'd rather be at home."

Andrew's eyes narrowed. "There isn't a special friend that you'd rather see than help me?"

"What do you mean?"

He shook his head. "Forget about it. I don't want to keep you from your work."

Bethany went on to the springhouse with Mari. Andrew had been acting strangely for a few days now, but she couldn't figure out what was bothering him. Perhaps he'd tell her eventually, but if there was something about the farm or anything else that he was concerned about, he should share it with her. She had to show him that they could work together as a team.

After the house was quiet on Wednesday night, Andrew opened his bedroom door, listening. Light from the full moon streamed through his window and illuminated the upstairs hall. No sounds came from Mari's room or from Bethany's room at the other end of the house. He crept down the narrow stairs, stepping over the one that creaked—the third one down. His bare feet made no sound in the dark stairway or as he walked through the kitchen. Even Rose's room off the kitchen was silent, without her usual soft snoring.

Nearly a week had passed since Andrew had heard the nighttime prowler, and even though Jenny had alerted him to strangers on the road during the day, she hadn't barked once in the nights since he had gotten her from the Smiths. Tonight he intended to keep watch. It could be that she spent her nights wandering back to her old home rather than staying put like she was supposed to. He had no delusions that their nighttime visitor wouldn't return.

Jenny came running to greet him as he let himself out the kitchen door. He patted her, then looked for a place to keep watch. The doghouse was next to the oak tree and sat in heavy shadow on this moonlit night. Andrew pulled on his boots and walked over to it, his footsteps crunching faintly on the driveway. Jenny followed him, thrusting her nose into his hand. He sat in the dark next to the doghouse and Jenny lay alongside him as he scratched her side.

The moon showed the time to be an hour or so after sunset. Andrew yawned and leaned against the doghouse wall. If a prowler came around, he and Jenny would take care of him.

He yawned again, watching the shadows move slowly across the yard as the moon climbed in the sky. Andrew blinked. The shadows had jumped ahead and were beginning to stretch toward the east. Stretching his stiff muscles, he stood. He hadn't meant to sleep, but he must have. Jenny was nowhere around. He might as well go to bed.

Halfway across the drive, he saw a figure moving toward the road and froze. There was Jenny, walking beside the man as if she intended to follow him home. Andrew ran to the house and peered around the corner. The figure had stopped at the edge of the road and motioned back toward the house. Jenny turned around and trotted toward her doghouse as the figure disappeared into the shadowed road. Andrew couldn't tell which direction he went.

Some watchdog. The prowler had made friends with her. Maybe Bethany had warned her friend of the dog and he had brought a treat of some kind to ingratiate himself to her. But how could Bethany have warned anyone? She hadn't talked to any man but Jonah at church on Sunday. Unless Lovina or one of her other friends was in on the secret.

Andrew shook his head. It was the middle of the night and he wasn't thinking straight. He'd figure this out in the morning. He let himself into the house and went up to bed.

Dawn came too quickly. Andrew sat up in bed, scrubbing his face with his hands. He had to get to the bottom of this soon because he couldn't afford to lose any more sleep.

He had just finished milking Dinah when Bethany came to find him.

"You're up early," he said, spreading a clean piece of cheesecloth over the pail of milk. He took it out to the springhouse to cool and Bethany followed him.

"So are you. You left the house before I got up. I wanted to talk to you about something." She drew closer to him and lowered her voice. "I think there was someone outside the house last night."

He tried to keep the surprise off his face. If the prowler was visiting Bethany, then why was she bringing it up?

"Why do you say that?"

"I heard someone tossing pebbles at a window."

Andrew scratched his beard. "I thought I heard that same sound a while ago, too. That's why I thought we needed a dog."

"I couldn't figure out why she didn't bark if there was really a person out there."

"Did you see anyone?"

Bethany shook her head, clearly as puzzled as he was. "Who do you think it could have been? And what was he doing out there?"

"And why didn't Jenny bark? She barks if a stranger drives past the farm during the day."

"If I didn't know better, I would think that someone is courting Rose. The noise sounded like it came from her window." Bethany waited outside the springhouse as he put the pail of warm milk in the shallow trough. The water ran through the trough before leaving the springhouse, keeping anything they placed there cool, even on the hottest days.

"Rose?" Andrew laughed. "You know she wouldn't put up with that, and we'd certainly hear about it if anyone came snooping around her window at night." He followed her out of the dairy and picked up the manure fork. "You could ask her about it during breakfast."

Bethany shook her head. "I'm not going to bring it up. You can if you want to." She started up the steps. "Breakfast will be ready in a while."

"All right." Andrew started cleaning the milking parlor.

If Bethany did have someone visiting her at night, it would be very clever of her to make him think the man was visiting Rose. Was she that clever? Did she know he had been keeping watch last night?

But the biggest question was, why didn't Jenny bark?

By the time he finished the barn chores, it was time for breakfast. When he walked in the kitchen, Rose was standing by the table helping Mari onto her stool, and she was humming.

"You must have slept well last night, Rose," he said as he sat in his chair.

"Wasn't the moon bright?" Rose said, smiling at him. "I could have worked in the garden by moonlight, like I did when I was a girl."

"Did it keep you awake?"

"Not for long. And then I had a beautiful dream."

Andrew exchanged glances with Bethany. This didn't sound like Rose at all.

After their silent prayer, Rose went on. "I don't think I'll be going back to Iowa after all. I like it here too much, and Mari is so happy."

Bethany pressed her lips together in a tight line as she caught Andrew's eye and shook her head slightly.

Andrew cleared his throat. "I never did want you to try to go back to Iowa. I hear the drought is worse this year than it's ever been."

He felt Bethany's foot push his leg under the table.

"What are your plans, then?" Andrew poured syrup over his hotcakes. The logical place for Rose to live was here with them, but Bethany wouldn't be happy with that. "Jonah still has the empty *Dawdi Haus* on his farm."

Rose blushed. "I might look at it. Jonah was right when he said that I shouldn't impose on the two of you, being newly married. And Jonah's place is right across the road, so I would be able to see Mari almost as much as I do now." She cut Mari's hotcakes into bite-sized pieces.

Bethany smiled at that. "I'm certain that would work out well for you. No one has lived in the *Dawdi Haus* since my grandfather passed away, so it will need to be cleaned."

Andrew folded a piece of his hotcake on his fork and shoved it in his mouth as the turning in his stomach settled down. For the first time since Rose's arrival, he felt like things were going his way.

Now, if he could solve the mystery of the night prowler, life could start being normal again.

Buoyed by Rose's talk of moving out of the house, Bethany felt the burden she had been carrying since the wedding lift. Even though her relationship with Rose had been better since the older woman had taken on caring for Bethany's brothers a few days a week, she knew that once Rose moved out, then she and Andrew could make their marriage work better.

Mari helped Bethany clean the upstairs after breakfast on Thursday morning. Rose had closed herself in her room, saying she wanted to write some letters, so Bethany felt like she had the house to herself. This was the way her marriage was supposed to be, she thought as she and Mari climbed up the stairs. She and Mari working together through the day, taking care of their own home without Rose's unwelcome interference.

"I use the dust mop," Mari said as they reached the top step.

Bethany handed it to her. "For sure, you can. And you

can take the sheets off your bed. We'll start with my bed and I'll show you how to do it, then you can do yours."

Bethany took extra time dusting, since she had done the chore so quickly last week. Mari pushed the dust mop around, banging it into the corners, while Bethany thought about her conversation with Elisabeth last week. So far, she didn't feel like she had made any progress with Andrew. In fact, their friendship might have even cooled a little bit. During the past week, their conversations had been shallow, dwelling only on the weather or Mari. And when she had told him about the noises she had heard last night, his face had grown tight and closed, as if he knew something he didn't want to share with her.

Mari helped her strip the sheets off the beds, and then Bethany made the beds with clean sheets while Mari dusted the hallway. For sure, Mari missed the corners, but she improved every week. When they got to Andrew's room, Bethany remade his bed with clean sheets, too. Since Rose had been doing laundry for *Daed* and the boys on Mondays, there was no reason to try to hide the fact that she and Andrew weren't sharing a bedroom. By the time Rose returned home after dinner on Mondays, the sheets were washed, dried, ironed and put away in the cupboard.

The upstairs rooms were getting hot when they had finished their cleaning. Bethany made sure the windows sashes were raised and the doors propped open so the air could circulate through the house. Years ago, *Mamm* had shown her how the air blowing across the upper floor of the house would act like a chimney, pulling fresh air into the rooms downstairs and up the stairway. That, and lowering the window shades to keep out the strongest rays of the sun, kept the house cooler on these hot summer days.

When Bethany and Mari came downstairs, Rose's bedroom door was still closed, and it was too early to start preparing dinner. Elisabeth had told Bethany to work with Andrew, to show him she was willing to be his partner, but how?

Mari tugged at her skirt. "I'm thirsty."

As Bethany got her a drink of water, she thought of a way she could help Andrew.

"Should we take some water out to your *daed*?"

Mari nodded. "We can take water for Whiskers and Dandy, too."

"*Daed* will take care of the horses' water."

Bethany got an empty jug out of the cupboard and washed it out. She put some ginger and vinegar into the jar, then filled it with fresh, cold water. Stopping up the opening with a clean rag, she and Mari went out to the field, with Jenny running ahead of them.

Andrew saw them coming and stopped the horses in the shade of a tree at the edge of the field. "What brings you out here? Is anything wrong?"

Mari ran to him. "We brought you water."

Bethany handed him the jug. He nodded his thanks and took a drink while Mari searched for worms in the newly turned earth.

When he lowered the jug, he grinned at her. "You made ginger water."

"Your *mamm* was the one who taught me how to do it."

He took another drink. "I'm glad you remembered."

He wiped the sweat from his face. "It's going to be a hot one today."

"How much more do you need to plow?"

Andrew waved his arm over the field. "Another few acres, and then I'll be ready to plant this field." He gestured toward another field. "I've already planted the corn there, and if we get rain, it should be sprouting soon."

Bethany looked at the blue sky. "There's no sign of rain?"

Andrew shook his head, then took another drink. "I'm not sure what we'll do if it doesn't rain soon."

"Is it that bad?"

"I spent every dime I had bringing this farm back, but I don't want to worry you with my problems."

"We're married, Andrew." He looked at her. "Your problems are my problems, too. We're partners, aren't we?"

Andrew sighed. "Are we?"

"For sure we are."

He pushed the cloth back into the mouth of the jug. "I need to get back to work. The water was good."

Elisabeth had said that Bethany needed to show Andrew that they were partners, not just tell him. But how?

"I'll take the jug back and refill it so you can have fresh water after dinner."

As she took the heavy stoneware jug from him, their hands touched, and she looked into his face. Worry lines framed his eyes. Where was the happy, energetic boy she had grown up with?

"You're worried about more than just the rain, aren't you?"

"*Ja*, for sure I am."

"Is it anything I can help you with?"

She couldn't read the expression on his face after her question. It was as if it had surprised him.

He nodded. "I need you to stick by me, Bethany. I know you want things for the house. A buggy horse, and material to make new clothes for us..."

"Those things don't matter."

"Don't tell me you don't want a new dress."

"Not if a new dress means the farm doesn't do as well." Bethany set down the jug at her feet. "You and Mari come first, and the farm. A new dress isn't important, but other things are."

Andrew rubbed his right shoulder, frowning as if he was bothered by something he couldn't quite identify. This was her Andrew. Lily may have his heart, but the rest of him was Bethany's. His life, his work and his family. They were partners, whether he admitted it or not.

On an impulse, she laid her hand over his, bracing herself on his shoulder as she rose on her toes to place a kiss on his cheek.

She was sorry immediately. His face turned dark red as he turned away from her, just as he had when she had been foolish enough to kiss him so many years ago. How could she had been so stupid? So naive to think that he would welcome her kiss, even as one friend to another?

Her eyes blinded with tears, she dusted off Mari's skirt and started the long walk back to the house.

Chapter Ten

The horses had rested while he talked with Bethany, so Andrew lined them up for another pass across the field. The ground had been well-worked four years ago, and it was still easier to plow than the clay soil on his farm in Iowa. Still, the horses could only plow about an acre each day. By Saturday night, this field would be done.

As he walked behind the plow, he thought back to Bethany's kiss. She didn't mean anything by it, he was sure. She had done the same thing a year or so before he moved to Iowa. Just a kiss on the cheek, like girls did. He had laughed it off then, thinking that she had turned girlish and was trying to start something romantic. But after she got over being mad, they went back to being friends.

At least he thought they had.

But now, after being married before and understanding women a little better than he had then, he was sure this kiss from Bethany had only been to thank him. Romance took two people, a give-and-take. If she was going to be romantic with anyone, it would be her mysterious visitor. Maybe she had only been happy because she didn't think he knew.

Andrew swiped at a deerfly, only to have it come back at him again. He had to stop thinking this way. Bethany was his wife and took her commitment to their marriage as seriously as he did. Her worry about their nighttime prowler should be enough to prove to him that whoever it was wasn't coming around to visit her. He had to trust her, and that was final.

Where was this jealousy coming from, anyway? It couldn't be because he was in love with her.

It was only because they were married, and she was his responsibility. That was all. She didn't mean anything by that kiss.

Maybe if he kept telling himself that, he would forget how her scent had wrapped around him as she had leaned in to brush her lips against his cheek.

The plow got caught in a tangle of dead weeds and stopped.

"Whoa, horses. Back up some."

Whiskers flicked his ears around and took a step back. Dandy shook his head but moved back to match his teammate.

"Ready?" The horses leaned into their collars. "Pull!"

They strained together, and the plow pulled through the web of roots and stems. In a few more steps they were at the edge of the field. Andrew measured the sun's position and judged it was nearly noon and time for dinner. He left the plow at the edge of the field and drove the horses to the barn, following behind on foot. After he removed the harness, he made sure there was fresh water in their trough and hay in the basket on the pasture fence. He'd let them rest for an hour, then feed them a bit of grain before going back to work.

Andrew pulled off his hat and fanned his face. The sky was brassy yellow in the noonday sun, and the temperature was rising. He should take more than an hour to rest. No reason to wear out the horses and risk heatstroke. He could finish the acre this evening, after an early supper. It would be cooler then and better for the horses and him.

When he reached the house, Bethany had a full dinner waiting for him, in spite of the heat. When she took the chicken casserole out of the oven, she stirred the embers to separate them and closed the dampers.

"We'll have a cold supper tonight, if that's all right," she said as she put the casserole on the table. Her face was bright red from the heat. "It's just too hot to keep a fire going."

"If the heat doesn't let up, you should plan on cold meals tomorrow, too." Andrew had washed up at the pump in the barnyard, and his hair dripped water into his eyes. He wiped his face on his shirt. "I'm going to wait until this evening to finish plowing. It's going to be too hot to work the horses this afternoon."

Rose's bedroom door opened. She was fanning herself as she came out.

"Did you get the letters written that you wanted to?" asked Bethany.

The older woman nodded. "I fell asleep, too. I can't understand that, but I was so tired."

"This heat will do that to you." Bethany helped Mari onto her stool. The little girl's face was flushed, and she yawned. "It looks like someone else will be ready for a nap soon, too."

After dinner, Bethany took Mari upstairs to bed while Andrew strolled out to the front porch. On the north side of the house, the porch was shaded until evening, when the setting sun would peek under the low-hanging eaves. The afternoon was quiet, with insects buzzing in the long grass. He was nearly asleep in his chair when Bethany came out to the porch.

"You should go upstairs if you're going to sleep." She sat on the porch swing.

"I can't do that. I always get cranky if I try to sleep during the day."

"What do you call what you were doing just now?"

"Resting my eyes. That's all."

"I'm still worried about that prowler I heard last night." She pushed against the porch floor with her toes, setting the swing in motion. The familiar creak sounded like home as much as the spring on the screen door. "Is there anything missing from the barn or outbuildings? Could he be trying to get into the house?"

"We don't have anything a thief would want to steal." Andrew had considered that possibility. "And why would he come back? He's been here at least twice, maybe more times."

"And then there's Jenny."

Andrew thought about Jenny's reaction to the man last night. She had acted like she knew him. "It couldn't be one of the Smiths, could it?"

"Eugene Smith is a good neighbor, and a friend of *Daed*'s."

"How many are in the family?"

"Joe is the youngest. He's good friends with John. Then there are three older boys, I think. Sam is married, but Will and Trey still live at home."

Andrew tapped his foot. If one of the Smiths was the prowler, that would explain why Jenny didn't think they were a threat. "How well do you know them?"

"As well as any other *Englischers*. *Daed* knows them better than I do. I see Mrs. Smith at the store in Shipshewana sometimes." Bethany leaned toward him. "You can't think the prowler is one of the Smiths."

"Why not?"

"They're good people. They wouldn't think of bothering us."

"Maybe you're right." Andrew pushed his suspicions away as he yawned. "But we need to find out who it is and what he wants. I'd keep watch again tonight, but I'll be plowing as long as the moonlight holds."

"When will you sleep?"

"I'll catch a few hours before dawn, and maybe I'll rest my eyes a bit now."

"Then I'll leave you to it. I'm going to work on my sewing. And since you'll be working late tonight, I'll do the chores for you in the morning. I know Dinah needs to be milked at four o'clock no matter what time you go to bed."

As Bethany passed by him to go into the house, she patted his shoulder. Andrew felt a smile form. It was a nice gesture, and just like Bethany to do it.

He laid his head against the back of the chair and closed his eyes. After their prickly start, it seemed that this marriage might be pleasant after all. Even if they didn't share love, they could be friends, just like they always had. Bethany had been a big part of his life as long as he could remember, and it felt good to think she would remain next to him into the future. He still missed Lily, but having Bethany around eased the pain a little bit.

He tried to remember Lily's face, her smile, the way she greeted him in the morning, but as he drifted into sleep, he couldn't tell if the face he saw was Lily's or Bethany's.

As far as Bethany could tell, the prowler didn't show up during the night. She milked Dinah and fed the horses and the chicks. The little things were covered with an ugly combination of feathers and down, but they would become pretty with time, and start laying in a few months, too. Until then, they still relied on *Daed*'s hens for their eggs.

"What are your plans for today?" Rose asked while they ate their breakfast.

"I'm going to borrow *Daed*'s buggy and go visit Lovina. On Sunday she told me someone gave her clothes for her little girl, but they're too big for Rachel and she thought we could use them for Mari."

"Will you take Mari?"

"For sure. I'd love the company, and she can play with Rachel."

Rose sipped her coffee. "I thought I'd make dinner

for Jonah and the boys, and work in their garden. The weeds are taking over."

"I'm glad you cook for them so often," Bethany said. "I think they might starve if you didn't."

Rose chuckled. "Your brothers are terrible cooks, that's for sure. But Jonah has a few recipes he does well."

"Like scrambled eggs."

"And hotcakes," Rose said.

"If it was up to him, they'd have hotcakes every morning for breakfast."

Rose laughed at that and Bethany joined in.

Mari looked at both of them. "I like hotcakes. Are they funny?"

Rose wiped her eyes as Bethany said, "Only when *Datti* Jonah makes them."

Later in the morning, as Bethany drove to Lovina's house, she realized that she and Rose had gotten along very well that morning. Had Rose changed? Or had *she* changed? Maybe both.

"Where are we going?" Mari asked. She stood on the floor in front of the seat, watching Melba, *Daed*'s buggy horse, trot along the road.

"We're going to my friend's house. She has a little girl a little younger than you."

Mari climbed on the seat next to Bethany. "Will she be my friend?"

"For sure, she will. You will remember her when you see her. She's a nice little girl."

"Does she like cows?"

Bethany laughed. "I don't know. You'll have to ask her."

As they turned in the farm lane, Lovina was in the garden while Rachel played in the nearby yard.

"*Hallo*, Bethany." Lovina put down her hoe and came toward her. "I'm glad you stopped by. The clothes are in the house, but can you stay for a bit? Or do you have to get home?"

Before Lovina finished her sentence, Mari had climbed out of the buggy and was staring at Rachel.

"I don't have to hurry home, and I'd love to visit."

"Ellie and her children were here earlier, and Johnny helped me hoe for a few minutes," Lovina said as she pointed to a hoe that had been dropped at the edge of the garden. "You can pick up where he left off."

Bethany bent beside her friend as they worked their way along the rows of sweet corn. "Your garden looks good. Ours got a late start."

"How are things going?" Lovina asked.

"We're doing fine." Bethany's reply was automatic and too quick.

For sure, Lovina noticed. "Fine? Are you certain?"

"All newly married couples have trouble adjusting at first, don't they?"

Lovina chopped at a weed in the dirt between the rows of corn. "What's wrong?"

"Andrew is acting strangely and won't tell me what's bothering him." Bethany cleared away a couple of dandelion plants and moved on to a sprig of grass. "Have you noticed any prowlers around your place?"

"Prowlers? Like tramps?"

"Maybe. Or possibly thieves."

"Has anything been stolen?"

Bethany shook her head. "That's what is strange about it. Andrew has even seen someone, and we've both heard something."

Lovina leaned on her hoe. "What did you hear?"

"I thought I heard pebbles being thrown against a window."

Her eyes grew wide. "Like someone trying to get your attention?"

"But it wasn't my window, and it wasn't Andrew's. And I don't want to ask Rose if she heard it."

"Why not?"

"I don't want to worry her. If she can sleep through the prowler's visits, then that is best."

"You need to get a dog."

"Andrew got one, but she doesn't bark at night."

"Then you need to get a dog that doesn't like strangers."

"She barks at everyone else who drives by. The only person she doesn't bark at is *Daed*."

"That is a puzzle." Lovina went back to her hoeing, then stopped again. "What does Andrew say?"

Bethany faced her friend. "Not much, but sometimes I get the feeling he thinks I have something to do with it. What should I do?"

"If it was Noah and I, I would just ask him if he thought I was involved." Lovina went back to her hoeing. "You know, a marriage is a partnership. You have to work together."

"That's what your mother said."

Lovina grinned. "And she's usually right." She stopped to chop through a dandelion root. "But you have to work at it. Most men don't like to talk much, and they don't like to worry their wives with things they think they can handle on their own. Sometimes we need to bring up the subjects they won't."

"So I should ask him if he thinks I know the prowler?"

"It would be better than him being suspicious and doubting you." Lovina laughed. "Listen to me talk. We know Andrew doesn't have any reason to doubt you. And I know you two will fall in love before too long, right?"

Bethany's face grew hot. "I don't think so. He still loves his first wife. I don't think he'll ever love me."

"Why?"

"I kissed him again."

"What did he do?"

"Nothing. He just turned away from me. He hasn't mentioned it since."

Lovina kept working until she reached the end of her row, then waited for Bethany to catch up. "You and Andrew need to be patient with each other for Mari's sake and for your own happiness. He'll come around."

Bethany watched Mari and Rachel chase each other around a bush. "I'll try, for Mari's sake."

Lovina started on the last row while Bethany walked next to her. "How are things going with Rose? Is she still making life difficult for you?"

"That's the strangest thing," Bethany said. "We had a pleasant conversation this morning. It has happened gradually, but when I think of how her comments were so hurtful a couple weeks ago, I'm surprised at the difference."

"Maybe she is learning to like you now that she knows you better."

"That could be it. Or maybe it's because she's found a way to make herself useful." Bethany stopped to let a garter snake slither by in front of her as it fled from Lovina's hoe. "She has taken my place at *Daed*'s house, in a way. She spends at least three days a week there, doing laundry, cooking for them, doing their mending, cleaning the house. Whatever needs to be done."

Lovina paused, letting her hoe rest on the ground. "Anyone is more pleasant to be around when they're busy and feeling appreciated."

"*Ja*, but I miss seeing my brothers. *Daed* comes over a couple mornings a week. He says he misses me, and James came over one time, but I thought the others might need me, too."

"Do you know what I think?"

"What?"

"I think you might be a little jealous of Rose."

Bethany crushed a dirt clod with her toe. "I thought she was jealous of me because Mari and I get along so well."

"I'm sure that's true, too."

"I know what you're going to say next."

"What?" Lovina picked up her hoe and they started walking toward the garden shed.

"You're going to tell me to be nice to Rose and Andrew so we have a happy and peaceful household."

Lovina laughed. "That's what my mother would tell you."

Bethany smiled and linked her arm in Lovina's. "And

that's why we're such good friends. You let me talk and talk, and then you give me the best advice."

Andrew slept later than he had for years and woke to a quiet house. He intended to let the horses rest today after working all night, so he got to work doing some odd jobs that had been piling up.

The first one was to satisfy his curiosity. What did the prowler do when he was here? Andrew had only heard noises, and then he had seen that figure walking toward the road from the far side of the house. Wild conjectures had gone through his head while he had been plowing the field last night, including the thought that they might not be alone on the farm. The place had sat empty for four years, and the woods to the east of the house might be a good place for bootleggers to use for a hideout. Or perhaps tramps had a camp there, far enough away from the house that they hadn't noticed them.

Andrew walked around the house, going slowly and looking for any sign of an intruder. Jenny bounded ahead of him, stopping every few steps to snuffle at the ground. Andrew finally found a spot where it looked like someone had been standing. The lily-of-the-valley plants under Rose's bedroom window were broken down in places, and some of the flowers had been ground into the dirt. Had someone been looking at Rose through the window? Or had they thought they might gain entrance into the house that way?

But if he stood where the prowler would have stood, the window was too high. The house was set on a hill, and on this side of the house, the foundation rose up three feet before the first floor of the house started. The bottom of the window was at least seven feet from the ground. Andrew couldn't see any damage to the window frame, and the foundation of stones was covered with moss. If anyone had tried to get in by climbing up to the window or digging through the stone wall, there was no sign of it.

He continued to the front of the house but didn't see any other evidence that anyone had been around. There were no tracks leading from the woods to the house, and even though he listened closely, the only sounds he heard came from Jonah's farm across the road.

Later, he was replacing the rungs of the windmill ladder when Jenny started barking, alerting him to Dave driving up the lane in his spring wagon. Andrew climbed down, happy to take a break, and Jenny stopped barking. Instead, she circled the two men, tail wagging.

"Taking the day off today, Dave?"

Dave jumped down from the wagon seat. "Dorcas had a list of things she needed from town, so I thought I'd stop by to see if you or Bethany needed anything."

"I can't think of anything, but if you have a minute, I want to show you something." Andrew led the way around the house. "We've had a nighttime prowler around the house, and I'd like to know what you think it might be."

He stopped by Rose's window and Dave leaned down to look at the footprints. "It's a man, and he's wearing boots. I can see the tread in this footprint." Dave looked up at the window above them. "He couldn't climb in there unless he had a ladder, and there's no sign of anything like that. What room is that window in?"

"Rose's bedroom."

"Has she said anything about hearing something outside her window? She probably keeps it open at night."

"Nothing, even though Bethany and I have both heard noises. And I saw the man the other night."

"What about your dog? She barked loud enough to wake anybody when I drove up."

"That's the strangest thing. Jenny is a good watchdog, but she doesn't bark at this prowler. When I saw him walking across the front yard, she walked right along with him. I think she would have followed him if he hadn't told her to go back."

"Where did you get the dog?"

"From the Smiths, Jonah's neighbors to the east."

Dave nodded. "I know the family. Their oldest son, Trey, is a little wild at times, but nothing more than drinking too much and making noise. I've never heard of him bothering anyone's property."

"Jenny wouldn't bark at him, but anyone wanting to rob the place or something like that wouldn't come around more than once." Andrew stared at the footprints as if they could reveal their secrets.

"Do you have any other ideas who it might be?"

"At first, I thought it might be a friend of Bethany's."

Dave frowned. "What kind of friend would come in the middle of the night?"

"You said you thought there was someone Bethany was fond of, and that's why she turned down your marriage proposal."

"That was just a feeling I had. I've never seen her with anyone." Dave looked up at Rose's window again. "If it had been someone visiting Bethany, then why was he outside Rose's window?" They started walking back to Dave's wagon. "Besides, Bethany is married to you now. You know you can trust her to stay true to her promise."

Andrew nodded. He had come to the same conclusion.

"There's one possibility you haven't mentioned. Maybe someone is courting Rose is secret."

"Rose? Being courted like a teenager?" Andrew laughed. "If there's one thing I know about Rose, she isn't going to get married again. She holds her husband up on a pedestal, even though it's been ten years since he passed on."

"You don't think anyone else might turn her head?"

"Maybe if she was younger. But she's too old for romance now, and too set in her ways."

Dave paused before he climbed onto the wagon seat. "How are you and Bethany doing, other than dealing with this prowler?"

"Things are going well. In fact, it seems to be going better every week."

"But?"

Andrew rubbed a bit of dried mud off the front wagon wheel. "I can't remember what Lily looked like. I used to be able to close my eyes and see her in my memory, but now it's Bethany's face that I see. I don't want to lose my memories."

"Does Mari look like her?"

"For sure, she does. But Bethany does, too. I hadn't realized how much Lily looked like Bethany until I came home and saw her again."

"Then Lily must have been lovely, inside and out."

Andrew nodded. "She was."

"Did you ever think that you might have been attracted to Lily because she reminded you of Bethany?"

"Are you saying that it was a mistake to marry Lily? That I should have stayed here and married Bethany in the first place?"

Dave shook his head. "I can't tell you that. Maybe it was God's will that you married Lily, and that you had Mari."

"Then it was a mistake to marry Bethany." Andrew felt like he had been kicked by a cow at that thought.

"Do you think it was?"

"Ne," Andrew said. Then he said it again, more certain this time. *"Ne*, it was no mistake."

Dave laid a hand on Andrew's shoulder. "You married Bethany because you thought it was the right thing to do, *ja*?" When Andrew nodded, he went on. "Then don't try to rethink the decision again, like a cow chewing its cud. You made the decision, you're married and there's no going back to do anything different. You and Bethany make a good couple, and you'll have a good marriage. You believe that, don't you?"

"For sure I do. At least, I hope so."

"Then trust her and trust yourself." Dave swung up onto the wagon seat. "And don't be surprised if you end up falling in love with her." He slapped the reins on the team's back and set off down the lane, Jenny running behind the wagon, barking all the way to the road.

Andrew sighed, then picked up his hammer again. Trust Bethany? He could try to do that. Trust himself? Only a fool would trust himself. He gazed up at Bethany's window, above the back porch.

The thing he couldn't trust was love. He had learned that love could disappear with the speed of a lightning bolt. Dave was wrong. Dead wrong. He would never put his trust in love again.

Chapter Eleven

The first Sunday in July was a nonchurch day, so breakfast was relaxed. Andrew read from the *Christenflicht*, the book of prayers, for a time of prayer and meditation after breakfast was over. Even Mari listened to the old German words as Andrew read. When he reached the end of the prayer, one that had praised God for His mercies during the Exodus of the Israelites from Egypt, he sat silently, thinking of his own journey that had brought him to this place.

Was Dave right, that neither his marriage to Lily nor his marriage to Bethany had been the wrong choice? Could it be that both marriages were part of God's plan? But Andrew didn't want to try to guess the intricacies of God's ways.

With a sigh, he closed the little book, then looked at Rose and Bethany.

"Did I hear Jonah say we should stop by over there today?"

Bethany stood, gathering the breakfast dishes from

the table. "Folks end up at *Daed*'s house most nonchurch Sundays during the summer, unless we go to the lake for a picnic like we did a couple weeks ago."

"I like the lake," said Mari. "Can we go there?"

"Another day." Andrew got up to return the *Christenflicht* to its shelf. "We need to plan ahead of time for a picnic like that."

"When would Jonah expect us to come by?" Rose asked as Bethany got ready to wash the dishes.

"Not until afternoon. We can spend the morning resting, or reading," Bethany said.

"Can I play with Jenny?" Mari slid off her stool and stood by Andrew's knee.

"Today is a rest day for dogs, too. But we can take a walk outside and visit her."

"Dinah, too?"

"For sure. We can visit all the animals."

Mari wrapped her hand around Andrew's finger and they went outside together. Jenny came running up to them, tail wagging.

"We didn't bring her any food," Mari said, looking up at him.

"She's already had her breakfast. I fed her when I fed the rest of the animals."

"Does she eat grass?" Mari petted the dog's back.

"She eats scraps from our table." Andrew didn't tell her that part of Jenny's job was to hunt the rats that lived in the barn.

When they reached the barn, the horses heard them and came inside from their pasture. Andrew got a carrot from the box by the grain bin and broke it in pieces.

"Here's one for Whiskers," he said, handing it to Mari. "And I'll give the other one to Dandy."

Both horses crunched their treat while Mari giggled.

A soft *woof* from Jenny made him look up at the hay-mow, in the direction her nose was pointed. He hadn't been up there yet, since he had no hay to store. He would need to clean out the big hay-storage area before late summer. But when he looked up there from the barn floor, he couldn't see beyond the edge of the mow. No sign of anything that might be disturbing the dog.

Jenny woofed again, the hackles on her shoulders rising. Something, or someone, was up there.

"Let's go see Dinah," Andrew said, taking Mari's hand and leading her toward the barn door.

Once they reached the pasture fence, Mari picked dandelions and fed them to the cow while Andrew watched for Jenny. She didn't come out of the barn, and he could imagine that she was still looking at the hay-mow.

Looking at the barn, Andrew realized that the hole he had patched in the barn roof when he first arrived home was over the same part of the haymow that Jenny had been watching. He nearly laughed at his own nervousness. The raccoons that had caused the hole in the first place had probably come back, and that's what had alerted the dog. He would have to take the ladder in there and get rid of the raccoons once and for all. He didn't mind the curious animals, but he didn't want them living in his barn, either.

By the time he and Mari returned to the house, he was ready for a rest. Mari played with her doll while he and Bethany sat in the front room. Rose had gone to her room. Andrew sighed. It felt good to have nothing to do.

"Have you thought any more about our night visitor?" Bethany asked.

Andrew opened his eyes. Bethany looked nervous.

"Why?"

She twisted her fingers in her lap. "I just have a feeling that, well, you think I might know more about it than I do."

Andrew sat up. Was she going to confess? Had he been wrong about her?

"Why do you say that?"

"The way you look at me when we talk about it." She glanced at Mari, but his daughter was playing and not paying attention to the adult conversation. "It's like you think I'm lying."

"I admit that the thought crossed my mind that our prowler might be visiting you."

"Who would visit me in the middle of the night?"

Andrew shrugged. "That's the conclusion I came to. And then I found footprints under a different window." He didn't want to mention Rose's name while Mari was in the room.

Bethany didn't take her eyes from him but frowned as she watched him.

"You thought someone was courting me?"

He rubbed his hand over his face, embarrassed to think he had mistrusted her.

"Not really. I mean, I thought it was possible that someone might…but not you." He licked his lips. "I trust you."

She continued frowning.

"When I thought about it, I knew you couldn't know the—" He glanced at Mari. "The visitor. You were as surprised as I was."

"But you trust me."

Andrew nodded. "I do. That other, it was just a fleeting thought. I don't know what I was thinking."

Bethany released him from her gaze. "Lovina said I should mention it and bring it out in the open. She said that would be better than doubts and suspicions."

"I don't doubt you, Bethany. I know you're as committed to our marriage as I am."

She sighed. "It's harder than we thought it would be, isn't it?"

She glanced at him without the challenge her gaze had held earlier. It was a look that offered a truce, an invitation to work together.

"I have a feeling marriage is never easy, even in the best circumstances. We both need to work hard to stay friends."

Bethany smiled. "I'm willing to work if you are."

Andrew grinned at her. "We always make a good team, don't we?"

On Sunday night, Bethany was glad to climb into bed, ready to fall asleep as soon as she closed her eyes, but it didn't happen. She stared at the ceiling, remembering the afternoon.

Andrew had been true to his word, and they had worked together as a team as they had visited with their family and other friends who had stopped by *Daed*'s.

She and Andrew had even taken turns watching Mari, so they both had an opportunity to spend time with their friends. It had been a good time.

She was just drifting off to sleep when Jenny barked. Bethany sat up in bed. She had heard Jenny bark many times, but this sounded different. She grabbed her blanket from her bed and wrapped up in it as she went out into the hall. Andrew met her at the top of the stairs.

"You stay here," he said, starting down the steps.

"What is it?"

"I don't know, but I don't want you outside."

Bethany followed him down the steps, resolved to stay in the kitchen, but she had to know what had made Jenny so upset. Andrew lit a lantern in the kitchen, then went outside.

Through the window, she saw the lantern bobbing toward the barn.

"What is it?" Rose stood behind her, trying to see.

Bethany moved over so Rose could see out the window as well as she could, and they both watched. The moon wasn't up yet, and light clouds obscured the stars. The lantern was a pinpoint of light against the dark barn, and Jenny continued her barking.

"Something has that dog upset," Rose said.

Bethany watched the lantern. It seemed to stop, then rise. She heard Andrew's voice shouting, then a dog's yelp. Rose clutched Bethany's arm.

The lantern swung in the air, then went out. Shadowy forms ran down the lane toward the road, and Jenny started barking again, running after them.

"I'm going out there."

"You can't." Rose's voice was a squeak.

"I have to see what happened to Andrew. You saw those men running away, and Jenny has followed them to the road. She'll warn me if they try to come back."

Gathering her blanket tightly around her, Bethany stepped out into the night. Jenny barked in the distance, then she heard the sound of an automobile on the road. She hoped that meant the prowlers were driving away and wouldn't be back. She stayed on the grass as she walked toward the barn, listening as she went. As she got closer, she heard someone moan.

"Andrew?"

"Bethany? I told you to stay in the house."

"They're gone. I heard them drive away in an automobile. What happened?"

"They knocked the lantern out of my hand and pushed me down. I got the wind knocked out of me."

Bethany groped in the space where his voice came from, and her hand found his head. He grabbed it and stood up, breathing hard.

"Let's go back to the house. Where's Jenny?"

"She followed them to the road."

Rose had lit the lantern in the kitchen, and the light gave them a path to follow in the dark. Andrew pushed Bethany in the door, then looked back out into the yard. He whistled once, then came in with the dog. He got a crust of bread from the slop bucket and tossed it to her.

"You did a good job tonight, girl. Go get some rest."

Jenny wagged her tail then went back outside while Andrew sat down on a chair at the table.

"Who were those men?" Rose asked.

Andrew shook his head. "I have no idea. But this morning, Jenny barked at something in the barn. Maybe they were tramps."

"Tramps wouldn't have an automobile," Bethany said.

"Bootleggers," Rose said. "That haymow hasn't been used in years. I wouldn't be surprised if a gang of bootleggers used it to stash their stuff."

Bethany thought of the men running away.

"When they left, they weren't carrying anything with them. It must still be in the barn."

She met Rose's gaze, then looked at Andrew. He was staring at the table, drumming his fingers.

"I'm going to bring Jenny inside the house, and we'll keep watch. If they come back, we won't interfere with them. If we don't get in their way, they probably won't bother us."

"Do you think they'll come back tonight?" Bethany asked.

"If whatever they had in the barn is valuable, they can't risk leaving it there until morning." Andrew stood. "You two go back to bed. Jenny and I will stay up and make sure they don't bother the house."

Rose shook her head. "I won't be able to sleep. I may as well stay out here with you."

"The same for me." Bethany crossed her arms. "I won't be able to close my eyes if I try to go to bed."

Andrew called in Jenny, and she lay down by the door. Then the three of them sat at the table, waiting.

When Bethany woke up, it was light in the kitchen. She was stiff from sleeping with her head pillowed on her arms at the table. She blew out the lantern and looked at Rose and Andrew, their heads still pillowed on the table. Jenny whined from her spot by the door and Bethany let her out.

The dog ran to the barn, her nose to the ground. She cast back and forth, then trotted back to her doghouse. Bethany trusted the dog enough to know that if their visitors had returned in the night, they had left again.

After finishing the morning chores, Andrew wandered around the barnyard before going into the house for breakfast. He found his lantern outside the barn door, where the prowlers had knocked it from his hand, and he found the ladder propped against the edge of the haymow. He climbed it but saw nothing in the empty loft. If there had been anything there, the men must have come back during the night and taken it away.

He went in to breakfast. When Mari ran to him for her morning hug, he held her close until she struggled to get free. The thought of violent strangers on his farm made him want to cling to his daughter and never let her go.

"*Daed, Daed*, we have hotcakes for breakfast." Mari patted his beard.

"Is that your favorite breakfast?"

She nodded. "And it's your favorite, too."

After the prayer, Bethany looked at him, her tired face looking worried.

"Did you find anything?"

He shook his head. "If it hadn't been for Jenny, we might not have known anyone had been around."

Mari looked up, a bite of hotcake speared on her fork. "Did Jenny bark?"

"For sure, she did. She was a good dog."

"Did you give her a treat?"

"I gave her some bread."

Mari nodded. "I'll give her a hotcake. She will like a hotcake."

"Do you think this will be the end of it?" Bethany asked.

"The end of what?" Rose looked at both of them. "Have they been here before?"

Andrew cut his hotcakes into squares and thrust his fork into a stack. "We've seen a prowler around the house at night."

Rose concentrated on her coffee.

"I don't think these were the same men, though."

"Why not?" Bethany asked.

"We can talk about it later," he said. He didn't want to frighten Mari or Rose.

After breakfast, Andrew shoveled manure into the spreader. He planned to spread it on the hay field, but before he could hitch up the team, an automobile drove into the yard and Jenny started barking. He stepped out of the barn to see what the *Englischers* wanted. He called Jenny to him and told her to be quiet.

The men all wore suits and felt hats. The first one showed him a badge.

"Hank Phillips, FBI." He looked around the farm. "Have you seen any suspicious activity around here?"

"What kind of suspicious activity?"

"Automobiles driving fast along the road, that sort of thing."

"Or men in my barn in the middle of the night?"

That got the *Englischer*'s attention.

"You saw them?"

"Not really. It was dark, and they knocked my lantern out of my hand." Andrew gestured for the men to follow him into the barn and showed them the ladder. "This wasn't in here yesterday."

Two of the men brought a leather case and opened it. It was filled with glass jars, brushes and other items Andrew couldn't name. They started spreading the powder on the rungs of the ladder.

"Had you ever seen these men before?"

Andrew shook his head. "I couldn't tell you. Like I said, it was dark. But I don't think they've been around my farm since I moved in."

Hank Phillips, FBI pulled a notebook from his jacket pocket. "When was that?"

"The end of May."

"You didn't think to call the police when they were here last night?"

"They didn't harm anything, and they left in a hurry. We don't involve the police in something like this."

"Did anyone else see these men?"

Andrew didn't want to mention Bethany, but she had seen them running. "My wife, but it was dark. She didn't see their faces."

Hank Phillips looked at Jenny. "Did your dog bark at them?"

Andrew scratched Jenny's ears. "She woke us up."

"That looks like one of Eugene Smith's dogs."

"He's the one who gave her to me."

"And you say she barked at the men the whole time?"

Andrew rubbed the back of his neck. "Just before the men knocked me down, I heard her yelp, then she stopped barking."

Hank Phillips wrote in his notebook.

"Is that important?"

"It could be. It might just be the evidence we need to arrest a suspect." He put his notebook back in his pocket. "Would you be willing to testify in court and tell what you know, just as you told me?"

"I would rather not, but I will if you insist."

"Good enough." Hank Phillips nodded toward the barn. "We're going to be busy in there for a while, gathering evidence. I hope that won't disturb you. You and your family can go about your usual day."

Andrew walked back to the house to tell Bethany what was going on. She met him at the door.

"I'm glad Rose is over at *Daed*'s this morning. She would hate to see all these *Englischers* around. What are they doing?"

"They were asking about our visitors."

"Did you tell them about the other times we've had prowlers?"

"I don't think these men had anything to do with our other prowler."

"Because Jenny barked at them?"

Andrew nodded. "And because they didn't come near the house. Our other prowler stays by the house and doesn't go near the barn." He didn't tell her about Dave's idea that the prowler might be courting Rose.

Bethany watched the men go in and out of the barn. "How long will they be here?"

"He said it would be a while."

"Since I'm not going to get any laundry done today, I'll make some cookies for them. They look like they don't get home-baked cookies very often."

"I'll stick around the house while they're here. I don't want to be out in the fields in case they need me for something."

"I thought you were going to stay for my cookies."

Andrew grinned at her. "I'll be playing with Mari. Let me know when the cookies are ready."

Chapter Twelve

As July wore on, the heat grew without the relief of any rain to cool the air. Every afternoon, Bethany would look out the kitchen window, watching white thunderheads gather in the sky like wool from a sheared sheep, until she thought they couldn't climb any higher. Sometimes the clouds would rumble with thunder, but no rain would come, and they would disappear when the sun went down.

They hadn't seen any sign of the men in the barn since last Sunday night, and she hadn't heard the other prowler, either. Bethany was glad about the absence of both of them.

On Sunday, the church was to meet at Dave and Dorcas Zimmer's house for services, so on Saturday morning Bethany met the other women of the church there to help Dorcas clean, leaving Mari at home with Rose.

"It certainly is hot today, isn't it?" Dorcas said as she met Bethany at the door. "Both twins are fussy with a heat rash."

Lovina, coming into the house behind Bethany, said, "I'm sure that means you haven't slept, either."

"You're right." Dorcas led the way to the kitchen. "Either Betsy or Matthew was crying all night long."

"Then you rest and let us do the work," said Elisabeth Stoltzfus. "There are six of us here now, and we can get the job done before noon if we keep at it."

The women worked together, Elisabeth taking charge, and started in the front room. Bethany washed the windows while Lovina scrubbed the white-painted window frames. Others moved the furniture out of the room or swept the walls and ceiling.

"Did you hear that the youngest Smith boy has the measles?" asked Lovina.

"I heard there were three children in Shipshewana who have the disease," said Viola Schwartzendruber. "Have any of our children contracted it?"

"Not that I've heard of." Elisabeth was sweeping the floor with dust mop. "But once an illness like that starts in an area, there is no telling where it will land."

The conversation went on to the weather, then droughts of the past, then how everyone's garden was doing and how often they watered the plants, and before Bethany knew it, the work was done. She had ridden to the workday with Lovina, and as they drove home, the subject of measles came up again.

"I wonder if we should keep our children home from church tomorrow," Lovina said.

"I have to admit, I know nothing about measles, except that the child comes down with a rash. I don't remember when my little brothers had them."

"They can be dangerous if the child isn't cared for properly. The rash is what you see, but the fever is the worst part of it."

"Will you keep Rachel home tomorrow?"

Lovina turned into Andrew's farm lane. "It depends on what Noah says. If none of the children in the church has them, then there shouldn't be a danger."

Rose was setting food on the table for dinner when Bethany came in. "We're having a cold dinner today."

"That's a good idea." Bethany carried a plate of to-mato slices to the table. "Is this the first tomato from our garden?"

"It's from Jonah's garden. Ours were planted late, but we should get tomatoes before too long. I picked the last of the radishes this morning, though. I'm afraid they're quite spicy."

Mari frowned as she climbed onto her stool. "Pink potatoes."

"Don't contradict," Rose said. "They are radishes."

Mari kicked the table leg. "They're pink potatoes."

"Radishes." Rose turned to look at her red-faced grand-daughter. "What is wrong with you today?"

"Let me get her something to drink. Perhaps she's just tired." Bethany picked up Mari and took her to the sink.

Mari pointed to the dish of cottage cheese waiting on the counter. "I don't like that."

"Cottage cheese is good for you. We make it from the milk Dinah gives us." Bethany looked at Rose. "Has she been this way all morning?"

"She worked in the garden with me, and she was fine.

The heat might be getting to her, though. I know it has made me tired, even before I do any work."

By the time Andrew came in for dinner, Mari was almost asleep on her stool. Bethany carried her into the living room and laid her on the couch.

"Go to sleep, Mari. You'll feel better after a nap."

"I'm hot." Mari pulled at her dress.

Bethany brought her light cotton nightgown from her bedroom and dressed her in the loose garment, leaving the top buttons open.

"Is that better?" She smoothed the sweaty curls away from Mari's face.

Mari nodded and closed her eyes while Bethany went back to the kitchen.

"Is she all right?" Andrew asked as Bethany sat down.

"I think so. I know she didn't sleep well last night in this heat."

Andrew cut a slice of tomato with the side of his fork. "Every day when those thunderheads start building, I wonder if this is the day that we'll get rain. It reminds me of last summer in Iowa."

"All things come to an end," Rose said. "The drought will end, and the heat will, too. Do you remember how cold it was last winter? We get one or the other, and it's no use complaining about either one."

Andrew laughed. "Somewhere in between the two would be best, wouldn't it? And with some rain thrown in for good measure?" He took another bite of his tomato. "Those *Englishchers* stopped by again today."

"The ones from the FBI?"

Andrew nodded. "They said they caught the men who

were in our barn Sunday night. You were right, Rose. They were bootleggers. Trey Smith was one of them."

"We don't have to worry about them coming around again then, do we?" Rose settled back in her chair with a sigh. "I'm sorry for those men, though. They will go to jail, won't they?"

"For sure, they will," Andrew said. "And I agree with you, Rose. I'll be glad to sleep without wondering if we'll be pulled out of our beds again."

The rest of the day passed slowly, but at last night came with a slight breeze that cooled the upstairs rooms enough to try to sleep. Leaving the doors open helped the air move, and Bethany lay on her bed with her night-clothes on, waiting for sleep to come. The evening bird-songs had faded as the darkness grew, and in the woods two owls hooted to one another. The house was quiet.

Bethany was nearly asleep when she heard the soft sound of a pebble hitting glass. Sitting up in bed, she strained to hear more. *Ja*, for sure. Another pebble. Following the direction of the sound, she made her way to Mari's room and looked out the window. When she saw a dark shadow standing between the house and the edge of the woods, she caught her breath, covering her mouth so no sound escaped. As quietly as she could, she ran to Andrew's doorway.

"Andrew!" she whispered, but he didn't stir. She peeked in the open door and saw him in the faint light, lying on his back with his arms spread wide.

"Andrew!" she whispered louder, but he didn't move. She took one step into the room and grasped the toe hanging off the edge of his bed.

He turned over, then sat up, rubbing his eyes. "What is it?"

"The prowler is back. I saw him standing below Mari's window."

Andrew got up and went to the middle bedroom while Bethany followed. Side by side, they gazed out the window, trying to see into the darkness through the cheese-cloth screen. They could see nothing.

"Are you sure you saw him?" Andrew asked.

"Shh! I hear something."

A quiet sound drifted up to them. A voice. But Bethany couldn't distinguish any words. Then the sound of footsteps in the grass reached them and Andrew stood.

"Where are you going?"

"I'm going to try to catch him. I need to know what he's doing here."

Bethany grabbed Andrew's hand. "What if he's dangerous? What if it's one of the bootleggers?"

"It isn't a bootlegger. I have to know what's going on."

Andrew went down the steps and Bethany followed as closely as she dared. As they went out the front door and onto the porch, Bethany saw the shadowy figure slip through the shrubs by the road and disappear. Jenny had followed the man, but when she saw Andrew and Bethany on the porch, she came trotting toward them, woofing a welcome.

"So you'll bark at us, but not at a stranger?" Andrew ruffled the fur around the dog's neck and then straightened up. "I guess I'll just have to try another time."

Suddenly, Bethany remembered that they were both wearing their nightclothes as they stood on the porch.

Andrew's eyes, dark in the shadows, found hers and she stood, motionless. He took a step toward her, then ran his fingers through his hair.

What would this moment turn into if they were truly married? Would they kiss each other here on the front porch, and then laugh and go back to bed? Would he take her hand in a sweet, loving gesture?

But as Andrew turned away from her and into the house, her what-ifs disappeared like a popped bubble. They didn't love each other, and they wouldn't. She was his second choice, and no matter how well they got along, their marriage was a lie.

Monday morning brought no relief from the heat. Andrew hurried through his chores so he could get as much field work done as possible before noon. The horses would need to rest in the shade of the barn during the afternoon.

As the team pulled the harrow between the rows of corn, breaking up the soil and exposing the weeds to the hot sun, he thought about the sermons from church the day before. While Preacher Stoltzfus and Bishop Yoder had spoken on the verses in Luke chapter twelve that talked of not being anxious, the visiting preacher from Millersburg had spoken on some verses further on in the same chapter.

"Pay attention to the signs of the times," he had said. He had talked of knowing that the heat will come when the south wind blows and knowing that a rain shower would come when a cloud rises in the west. Then he urged the congregation to look at the events of the world around them, and to be prepared for the judgment to come.

It had been an unusual sermon for an Amish service, and the preachers had questioned the man's wisdom of his prideful assurance of being able to discern the details of God's will. But Andrew wondered if the preacher was right. The world was going through hard times, for sure. And he had heard snatches of conversations among the *Englisch* of a new, dangerous leader in Germany. But were those signs pointing toward the end of the world, as the preacher seemed to think?

After he turned the horses for the next pass across the length of the field, his thoughts went to Bethany. Even though she and Rose seemed to be getting along better every day, she still looked unhappy at times. The only time he saw a true smile on her face was when she was with Mari. She loved his daughter, and Mari returned that love. Sometimes he felt a twinge of regret that the most important woman in Mari's life was someone other than Lily. He couldn't let go of the thought that Lily should be the one who was raising Mari and the other children they had hoped to have.

Saturday night, as he and Bethany had stood on the front porch, he had almost kissed her. But had that thought come to him because she looked so much like Lily? Or was it because Bethany had been so beautiful in the dark, and there had been no one around to see if he had stolen a sweet kiss? But if he had kissed her, he would have regretted it, just as he regretted considering it. In his heart, he was still married to Lily, and he couldn't betray her memory.

As the sun climbed to the top of the sky, Andrew unhitched the harrow and walked the horses back to the barn. He unharnessed them, then walked them around to the shady yard in front of the barn. He took his time, walking them slowly back and forth until their breathing was soft and even. Then he washed the sweat from their coats with the lukewarm water from the trough, gave them a good brushing and put them out in their pasture for the rest of the afternoon.

Bethany hadn't rung the dinner bell yet, so he gave himself a splashing bath by the pump, knowing his wet clothes and hair would dry by the time he got to the house. As he shook drops of water from his hands, he looked out toward the west. Thunderheads were beginning to form, just as they had every afternoon for the past week. Signs of things to come? Not this year. The clouds were only empty promises of rain that never fell.

"I'm sorry we're having a cold dinner again," Bethany said as he came into the kitchen. "I hope egg salad is all right."

"I like it on sandwiches," Andrew answered as he took his seat.

Bethany shook her head. "We're out of bread. I plan to bake tonight, while it's cooler in the kitchen. If I tried to use the oven now, it would heat up the entire house."

Rose came from the front room with Mari. "We had a fine time on the swing, didn't we, Mari?"

Mari came over to him and climbed in his lap. "I like the swing." She coughed, then stuck her finger in her mouth. On such a hot day, Mari's little body felt like a furnace on his lap.

"Sit on your stool, and we'll have our dinner."

Andrew's silent prayer was longer than normal, as he prayed for rain and cooler weather. Finally, he raised his head and gave the nod to signal that it was time to eat.

"How are the crops doing?" Rose asked.

"Drying up in the fields. If we get rain soon, they'll make it." He didn't continue. He didn't have to tell Rose what would happen if the rain stayed away.

"I'm glad we have a good well and the spring. At least we can water the garden." Bethany scooped some egg salad onto her plate next to her lettuce with vinegar dressing. "It's too bad we can't do the same for the crops."

Andrew let that thought filter through his brain as he ate. Could he hope to water enough of the corn plants with a pail to save the crop? Or perhaps he only needed to save enough to provide feed for the animals over the winter and have some to use for seed next spring.

After dinner, he went out to the front porch and sat in the old rocking chair. The heat was building, but a fitful breeze brought an occasional puff of air to cool him. After a few minutes, Bethany opened the screen door.

"I think Mari might be ill," she said.

Andrew turned to her, the sight of her worried face and the way one hand clung to the door frame hitting him with the certainty that he would remember this moment for the rest of his life.

"What do you mean?" He stood, facing her.

"She has a fever and a cough." Bethany chewed on her bottom lip. "It could be nothing."

"What can we do?"

"All I know to do is to try to keep her fever down and let her rest. But could you go get Elisabeth? She would know what to do."

"Have you asked Rose?"

Bethany looked over her shoulder into the house. "I never even thought to."

Once Rose learned that Mari was ill, she climbed the narrow stairway without hesitation. Bethany went ahead of her to Mari's room as Andrew followed, dreading what they might find.

"You're right. She has a fever," Rose said, feeling Mari's forehead and cheeks. "And you said she had a cough?"

Bethany nodded. Andrew stood in the doorway of the small room, anxious to help, but not knowing what to do.

"She was fine at breakfast this morning, but I remember her coughing once or twice." Rose's voice sounded strained, as if she was worried. "We'll watch her closely for the rest of the day. If her fever goes up any higher, we'll use cool, wet cloths to try to bring it down. Meanwhile, all we can do is wait."

"I'll stay here with her," Bethany said. Her face took on the determined look he knew so well.

"I'll sit with her first." When Bethany started to protest, Rose took her hand. "I had a long nap this morning and I'm rested. I'll sit with her this afternoon while you try to get some sleep. Then you'll be ready to watch her through the night."

Andrew stepped close to the bed. Mari's face was flushed and tense, not relaxed in sleep. He laid the back of his fingers on her hot cheek. "What can I do?"

"Be ready to go for the doctor. You should ask Jonah if you can use his buggy horse."

Bethany met his gaze over Rose's head and he tried to give her a reassuring smile. "Mari will get better soon. You know how fevers are in children—they come and go so quickly."

He glanced at his daughter's face again. She had to get better soon. He tried not to think about how dangerous a child's fever could be, and how quickly she could be taken from them.

Bethany didn't think she would sleep at all when she lay on her bed. The room was warm, but a breeze had come up and blown through the house.

Mari was sick, but how sick? Rose was clearly worried, and that made Bethany worry. Would they know when it was time to call the doctor?

She woke when her door slammed shut in the rapidly rising wind. She closed her windows against the black sky just as a lightning bolt flashed against the rolling clouds. When she opened her door, Andrew was coming up the stairway.

"I closed all the windows downstairs, but this is a bad storm. I think we had better go to the cellar."

"What about Mari?"

Andrew ushered her into Mari's room, where Rose was closing her windows, too. "You two get anything Mari needs and go down to the cellar. I'll carry her downstairs." He flinched as a crack of thunder sounded almost overhead.

Rose gathered blankets and started down the stairway while Bethany found Mari's favorite doll.

"Mamma—" Interrupted by a cough, Mari's voice was hoarse. "I don't like the storm."

Bethany took a deep breath. She needed to help Mari stay calm. Sitting on the edge of Mari's bed, she pushed the little girl's damp hair off her forehead. "I know you don't. But it won't last long, and then you'll be up and playing again."

Another crack of thunder sounded just as Andrew came in the room. Mari grabbed Bethany's hand as she moved to let Andrew pick up his daughter. "Don't leave me alone."

"We won't, little one." Bethany smiled as lightning flashed outside the window once more. "We'll never leave you. We're just going downstairs."

Mari closed her eyes as Andrew lifted her into his arms. Bethany took Mari's pillow and the doll and led the way down the staircase. By the time they reached the kitchen, hailstones pelted the windows. The noise was deafening as Bethany went out on the washing porch to the trapdoor leading to the cellar. Rose had left it propped open, and a light shone from the darkness below. Andrew carried Mari down the steep stairs, then Bethany followed, closing the door on the chaos outside as she went. The noise muted suddenly.

Andrew sat on a box with Mari on his lap. She was crying as he rocked back and forth, trying to comfort her. In her cries, Bethany heard her call *"Mamma, Mamma"* in a weak voice.

Bethany kneeled on the dirt floor and stroked Mari's cheek. "I'm here, Mari."

Mari shook her head and clung to Andrew, still sobbing.

Bethany looked at Andrew. The lamplight shone on his stricken face. He stared into the blackness of the far corner as if he was living in a nightmare and flinched with every crack of thunder.

Laying her hand on his knee, Bethany felt his leg quivering. She spoke softly. "Andrew, what is it?"

He turned toward her as if he had forgotten she was there. "This storm... Lily was killed in a storm like this. It came up suddenly, with lightning everywhere and thunder splitting the air..." He closed his eyes. "Lightning followed by the wall of dust." He held Mari close as she cried, her voice hoarse. "She ran out to take care of the hens, to shut them in before the storm hit, but a bolt of lightning came out of nowhere, and she was gone."

Sinking back, Bethany was helpless. As the storm forced Andrew to relive Lily's death, he comforted Mari. What memories did the little girl have of that day? Did she understand that the thunder and lightning had caused her loss? Bethany wanted to comfort Andrew, but she felt like an intruder. An outsider witnessing something that was private, shared only by the man she was married to and his daughter.

The muffled sound of the storm outside lessened, so she went up the steps and lifted the trapdoor. A gentle rain was falling, following the first violent outburst that had passed on to the east. To the west, the clouds were darker, as if this rain was only a calm peace as the storm gathered itself for another blast. She propped open the door to let fresh air into the cellar and went back down the steps.

"It looks like another storm is coming, but it doesn't look as severe as the last one."

Andrew still held Mari, but her crying had stopped. "She's so hot. Is her fever going up?"

Rose felt Mari's arm, then her cheeks. "For sure, it has gone up."

"We need to get her out of this damp cellar," Andrew said. "But I don't want to take her all the way to her room in case we need to come down here again."

"We'll make a bed for her on the kitchen table," Rose said. She handed Bethany the pile of blankets she had brought from Mari's room and from the closet at the top of the stairs. "She'll be comfortable there, and it's close to the cellar."

Bethany followed Rose's instructions, making a soft bed for the little girl. Andrew laid her down and Rose covered her with a sheet. Bethany tucked Mari's doll in next to the sleeping girl. She was lying too still. Sleeping too deeply.

Rose felt Mari's forehead. "We need to bring the fever down, but not too quickly. Look here." She ran her finger along Mari's brow. "She's getting a rash. It looks like it might be measles."

"Do I need to go for the doctor?" Andrew pumped cold water into a basin and put it near Mari's head.

Rose wrung out a cloth in the water, then laid it on Mari's forehead. "You can't go if there's another storm coming."

"I can if Mari is sick."

Rose dipped the cloth in the water again. "If it's measles, then we're already doing as much as we can."

"But what if you're wrong? What if it's something even worse? I'd rather have the doctor look at her."

Rose pressed her lips together. "Then go now, before the next storm comes."

Andrew hesitated, his hand on Mari's small body as if he was afraid to leave her. "If the storm gets bad again, will you be able to carry her down?"

Bethany nodded. "Don't worry about us. We'll head down to the cellar again if we need to."

Andrew backed away from the table with reluctant steps, his eyes on Mari's flushed face.

He glanced at Bethany. "You be careful, and don't risk your safety or hers."

"I could say the same to you. Be careful. You'll borrow *Daed*'s buggy?"

Nodding, Andrew grabbed his hat and started toward the door. "I'll be back as soon as I can."

After the door slammed shut, Bethany put her hand where Andrew's had been, holding on to Mari's fragile life. What if he didn't come home? What if the storm swallowed him up and he never came home again?

As Rose started bathing Mari's forehead and cheeks again, Bethany glanced out the window. Rain still fell lightly, but in the west, dark clouds flashed with lightning. To her surprise, it was still afternoon. She felt like it was the middle of the night.

"You're worried," Rose said as she pumped fresh water into the basin.

"Aren't you?" Bethany took a damp cloth from Rose and laid it on Mari's hot chest. Her skin was covered with a red rash.

"For sure, I'm worried about Mari. And about Andrew." Rose sighed. "But I also know that the outcome of this is in the Good Lord's hands."

"Andrew said that Mari's illness could be worse than measles, but I can't imagine anything worse."

"Scarlet fever is much worse. But either one could be deadly." Rose wrung out another cloth and laid in on Mari's forehead. "If we can bring the fever down, then we have hope."

"And if we don't?"

Rose didn't answer, and she didn't meet Bethany's eyes.

Chapter Thirteen

Jonah's horse trotted patiently through the downpour, not even flicking his ears at the rumbles of thunder.

"That was some storm that passed through earlier, wasn't it?" Jonah asked.

Andrew stared at the horse, willing him to trot faster. "For sure it was."

"Did you get any damage at your place?"

"I didn't take the time to look. Once Rose said that Mari needed the doctor, I went straight to your house."

"And we'll get to Shipshewana as quickly as we can. The doctor has an automobile, so the trip home will be much faster."

Andrew rubbed his cold arms. The temperature had dropped when the storm came through, and now it was chilly. "I'm just worried about Mari. You didn't see how still she was. She's very sick."

"Children get sick. You know that. If Rose had been too worried, she would have had us take Mari to the doctor to save time." Jonah pulled the horse to a halt at the intersection with the state highway and looked both ways before turning onto the paved road. "Mari is in good hands. Rose knows what she's doing."

"I wish I could be as certain as you are. I can't bear the thought of losing her."

Jonah grunted. "One of the benefits of growing older is that you have more experience trusting the Good Lord to take care of the things that are beyond your reach. You do your best but leave the outcome to the Lord."

Andrew whooshed out a breath. "Do you think He knows how much Mari means to me?"

"Not only that, but that little girl means even more to Him. You need to trust that no matter what the outcome of this illness is, God cares."

The rain let up a little as the thunder faded in the distance.

"Do you think He cared when my Lily passed away?"

Jonah studied his face. "Is that what you're worried about?"

Andrew nodded. "I just can't believe that God cares when he let Lily die. Why should I trust Him to keep Mari from dying, too?"

The horse's hooves beat against the pavement in a steady rhythm while Jonah stared ahead.

"When my wife passed away, I had similar thoughts. I was afraid for my children, thinking that they might be taken from me, too." Jonah's voice broke and he cleared his throat before going on. "But then I met a man from Millersburg whose wife is dying of cancer. She was bedridden and in much pain. Horrible pain. This man cared for her every need, but it was so hard for him to watch her suffer. He asked me why the Good Lord saw fit to prolong her agony. Why she didn't die so she could be free of the pain that is part of every single hour of her day."

"What did you tell him?"

"God's ways are not ours. Sometimes death comes quickly, almost easily. A sudden accident, or an illness that strikes quickly. Sometimes death is drawn out and painful. We can't choose, and we can't know why God chooses the way He does." Jonah pulled the horse to a stop at the intersection in the middle of town. They were in Shipshewana. He turned to the right and drove past the grain elevator. "But we can trust that God's ways are right."

"So it isn't any use to pray for God to spare Mari?"

Jonah turned onto a side street and stopped in front of the doctor's house and office. He turned to Andrew before they went in. "God tells us to pray, and the Lord Jesus showed us how to pray. So we must pray always. I don't know how God uses our prayers, but He does."

Andrew climbed out of the buggy, almost afraid to ask the next question. "What if God's answer to our prayer is 'no'?"

"Then we trust that it is the right answer. The best answer," Jonah said as they walked up the gravel walk to the front door. "And when we face hard times and hard decisions, He is right beside us, facing them with us."

Jonah knocked on the door.

Once Dr. Hoover heard why they had come, he grabbed his hat and bag.

On the way out the door, he turned to Andrew. "You'll

ride with me, won't you? We'll be there in about ten minutes."

Leaving Jonah to drive the buggy home, Andrew got into the car. He had never ridden in an automobile before, but he found that it wasn't much different than riding on a train. Even so, it was the longest ten minutes he had ever experienced.

When they reached the farm, the doctor strode ahead of Andrew into the house, ignoring Jenny's barking. Mari was still on her makeshift bed on the kitchen table and Rose and Bethany were sponging her with wet cloths.

The doctor took Mari's temperature and looked at the thermometer with a grunt. He used a tiny light to look into Mari's eyes, ears and down her throat. He listened to her chest with a stethoscope. Then he examined the rash that had spread across her face and body while Andrew had been away.

He looked at Bethany. "It is definitely measles. How long has she been ill?"

"We noticed the fever today, but she has been out of sorts since yesterday or the day before. I thought she might be coming down with something, but I hoped it was only the heat."

The doctor nodded. "That sounds about right. It takes about three days for the rash to show, so she was probably already ill on Friday." He felt Mari's shoulders and elbows, then uncovered her and did the same to her knees and feet. "How long has she been asleep like this?"

"All afternoon," Rose said. "Her fever rose, and we

couldn't get her to wake up. That's why we sent Andrew to get you."

"You did the right thing." The doctor put his equipment back in his bag but handed the thermometer to Bethany. "Now, Mother, you must take her temperature every hour, just like you saw me do. If it goes much above one hundred four degrees, send someone for me right away. It is right at that temperature now. Continue what you've been doing to reduce her fever and keep her comfortable. When she wakes up, give her some cool beef or chicken broth and let her drink as much water as she desires. You should begin to see some improvement in a day or two but keep her inside until the spots are gone." He zipped up his bag. "And keep her from coming into contact with anyone who has never had the measles until then. We don't want this to spread any further."

Andrew met Bethany's eyes and nodded. She had insisted that she keep Mari home from church yesterday, and he was glad he had listened to her.

As he walked with the doctor out to his car, the clouds were clearing away and the sun was setting in a wash of orange and pink.

"Thank you for coming. I know I need to pay you, but…"

The doctor grasped Andrew's shoulder. "I know. No one has any money. You recently moved here from Iowa, didn't you?"

"How did you know?"

Dr. Hoover chuckled. "I hear things. I was called to the Smith house a few days ago to look at their boy. He has measles, too. Mr. Smith was telling me how he gave you one of his dogs."

"Do you really think Mari is going to be all right?"

"Don't worry, son. As long as the fever stays down, she'll be fine."

"How can I pay you?"

The doctor rubbed his chin. "Folks have been paying me in food, since no one has cash, but our larder is about full. I need new posts on my porch, though. The old ones are about rotted through. Can you do that kind of carpentry work?"

"For sure I can. Will that be a fair trade, though?"

"I'm satisfied if you are." The doctor shook Andrew's hand. "Whenever you can get to it, but I'd like it done before the end of the summer."

Andrew nodded. "It will be done before the end of the summer."

He waved as the doctor drove away, and then leaned down to scratch Jenny's ears. "Why didn't you bark at him that time? Because you knew he was leaving?"

Jenny grinned at him, her tail wagging.

In spite of the doctor's encouraging words, Mari's fever remained high. Andrew had carried his daughter back to her own bedroom, and Bethany prepared to spend the night watching over her. She brought her rocking chair from her room and set the doctor's thermometer on the small table beside the bed, along with a glass of water. The ever-present basin and towels were at her feet, ready for the constant bathing to keep Mari's temperature from going too high.

Andrew came into Mari's room with Bethany's supper of cottage cheese and canned peaches in a bowl.

"Rose went to bed right after she finished her supper," he said, sitting on the edge of Mari's bed across from her. "She said to call her if you can't stay awake."

Bethany shook her head. "Rose will take her turn tomorrow while I sleep. She needs to get as much rest as she can." Andrew's face was sculpted with lines of worry. "You need to get some rest, too. Morning will be here before you know it."

"I can't sleep. Not until she wakes up. I don't like to see her like this."

"The doctor didn't seem too worried."

"He was worried enough." He rubbed the back of his neck. "Have you taken her temperature? Is she all right?"

"I was going to take it at ten o'clock." Bethany pointed to the clock she had set on the table next to the water glass. "She doesn't feel any warmer to me, but I thought I'd check it every hour."

Andrew sighed. "Hand me one of those towels. I can help you as long as I'm here."

Bethany wrung out a fresh towel and handed it to him, then folded a second one and laid it across Mari's forehead. She ate her supper, then sponged Mari's chest and arms. The towels dried quickly in the heat from Mari's body. She and Andrew worked together without talking. After the long and exhausting day, Bethany didn't have the energy to do more than refresh the towels, one after another.

When the little alarm clock said ten, Bethany took the thermometer and shook the mercury down the way the doctor had shown her. Then she slipped the glass tube under Mari's tongue and waited while the clock ticked. Andrew watched the mercury in the thermometer, as if it could tell him if Mari was well or not.

"You have to wait for three minutes. If you look before then, the reading won't be accurate."

"I know." Andrew ran his hand through his hair. "I heard the doctor, too. How long has it been?"

Bethany glanced at the clock. "One minute."

The seconds ticked by.

"I don't know what I would do if she doesn't pull through this." Andrew's voice was almost a whisper.

"She will. You have to believe that. Everything will be all right."

"It doesn't always turn out that way." Andrew got up and walked over to the window, leaning against the frame as he took a deep breath. "You know that as well as I do. People die."

"But that doesn't mean we give up."

He turned toward her, his face shadowed. "I'll never give up." He sat down again. "How long has it been?"

"Almost three minutes." Bethany waited while the seconds passed, then held the thermometer to the light. "It has gone down a little bit. It's just above one hundred three degrees."

"That's good?"

Bethany couldn't keep from smiling. "That's wonderful." She put a fresh towel on Mari's forehead. "Now you should get some sleep. I'll wake you if anything changes."

"Whether the news is good or bad?"

She nodded. "Either way."

"All right. But don't forget."

"I won't forget."

She listened to his quiet footsteps as he went into his room and closed the door. Now that she was alone with Mari, she could let the tears fall that she had held in all afternoon. They trickled down her cheeks as she sponged the little girl's stomach, which was bright red with spots. The tears dripped off her chin as she laid a damp towel on Mari's forearm to cool her hot, dry skin. She blew her nose, then replaced the damp cloth on Mari's chest.

Over and over, she freshened the towels. Once she had to take the basin down to the kitchen to refill it, and she hurried back up the steps, not wanting to leave Mari alone for longer than she needed to. When she took Mari's temperature at eleven o'clock, the thermometer read one hundred four degrees again.

Bethany freshened the wet towels on Mari's forehead and chest, then walked to the window, trying to stay awake. Would Mari survive? Measles could be deadly, and she was so young. Her small body was burning up with the fever, no matter how often Bethany bathed her.

What would happen if they lost Mari?

Bethany shook her head, not wanting to consider the possibility. She loved the little girl so much that the strength of her feelings surprised her. Every day was a joy only because Mari was part of it. She couldn't imagine never seeing Mari's bright smile again, never looking into her deep blue eyes. The pain of losing her would be unbearable.

But an additional worry thudded against her consciousness like a loose shutter swinging in the wind. Andrew had only married her to provide a mother for his daughter. It was a convenient arrangement made only for Mari's sake. If she was no longer here, what would happen to their marriage? Andrew could quickly resent being tied to Bethany for the rest of his life. What if he fell in love with someone else? It didn't matter. They were married, and nothing could change that, short of abandoning their faith and the church.

Bethany closed the window blinds. Lack of sleep and fear for Mari had turned her thoughts in directions she didn't want to follow. Mari would recover. She had to recover.

At midnight, Bethany took Mari's temperature once more. It was slightly above 104 degrees, continuing to climb. She freshened the damp towels once more. The air in the room was oppressive and Mari grew restless, pushing the covers away in her sleep, and her face shone with perspiration.

A little later, Mari opened her eyes. *"Mamma?"*

"I'm here."

"I don't feel good."

"I know. Do you want me to hold you?"

Mari shook her head. "I'm too hot." She pushed at the covers.

"Do you want a drink?"

When Mari nodded, Bethany helped her sit up, holding the glass of water as Mari took a sip and swallowed. "It hurts."

As Bethany helped her settle back down on the bed

again, she felt Mari's cheek with the back of her hand. It felt cooler. Or perhaps she was only imagining it. It was nearly one o'clock, so she took Mari's temperature. The thermometer read just under 102 degrees. Could she dare hope that her fever had broken?

Andrew came in the room as Mari's eyes closed again. "I heard voices. Is she all right?"

"She woke up for a few minutes, and her temperature is going down. Do you think we might be over the worst of it?"

As Andrew felt Mari's forehead, she opened her eyes again. When she saw her *daed*, she smiled.

"Are you feeling better, little one?"

"It hurts when I drink."

"I know. But you still need to drink some water." Andrew helped her take another sip.

When he laid her back on the bed, Mari pushed her damp hair out of her face. "I'm hot."

Andrew looked at Bethany. "Do we dare open a window? It's very hot and stuffy in here, even with the door open."

When she nodded her agreement, he lifted one of the blinds and opened the window a few inches. The air that came in was cool and refreshing. Mari's eyes closed once more, and Bethany covered her with a sheet, but the little girl stirred and reached for her.

Taking her in her arms, Bethany sat on the rocking chair. As Mari relaxed, Bethany put her feet up on the bed and sighed.

Andrew leaned down and kissed the top of Mari's

head. "Maybe her fever has broken. Now we just need for her to get better."

Bethany smoothed a stray curl away from Mari's face, then looked at Andrew. His face was only inches from hers as he bent over his daughter. He was a good father, gentle and caring, and he loved Mari so much.

When he stood up, he glanced at her. "What are you thinking about?"

Andrew's eyes were as dark as Mari's in the shadowed room. "I'm thinking how wonderful it will be when she is healthy again."

He smiled at her. "For sure, it will be *wonderful-gut*." He gazed at Mari. "You're a good mother, Bethany. We are blessed to have you."

As Andrew went back to his room, Bethany shifted Mari into a more comfortable position and let her eyes drift closed, listening to the little girl's deep, even breathing.

When Andrew reached his room, he sat in the chair by the window, the same spot he had occupied all night. He had spent the long hours staring at the moonlit yard, praying for his daughter. And now that she seemed to be getting better, he didn't know what to do. Keep praying? Was her lowered fever a false hope? What would the morning bring?

He stared at the moon. Just past full, it illuminated the barnyard with a silvery light. All through the night he had watched the shadows move across the yard, unable to sleep while Mari was so sick. He had to be strong in front of Bethany and Rose, but deep inside was a dark hole of fear. Fear that Mari would disappear from his life as quickly as Lily had. Death. Life. It made no sense. What purpose was there in a little girl's illness?

Burying his face in his hands, he felt the weariness of the day bearing down on his shoulders. He should lie down on his bed. Try to get some sleep before morning came. Rest, in case he needed to make the trip to fetch the doctor again. His eyes burned, and his joints ached. He never thought he could be this tired, but he was unable to let go of the worry that consumed him.

What had Jonah said? He needed to trust that the Good Lord's ways were right. His head pounded. How could God's ways be right when a baby's life was hanging in the balance?

At least he had Bethany. When he had heard voices from Mari's room, he had feared the worst, but then he found Bethany calmly talking to his daughter, reassuring her, helping her find some way to be comfortable. Bethany might not have given birth to Mari, but she loved her and cared for her as if she had.

And that was the problem. As much as Andrew appreciated Bethany, he couldn't stop thinking that it was wrong. Lily should be the one to be here with Mari. Lily should be the one comforting her in her illness. Was it God's will that Lily's daughter should be raised by a stranger?

Jonah's words took on the rhythm of a trotting horse's hoof beats—*God's ways aren't our ways. God's ways aren't our ways...*

Catching himself as he nearly fell off his chair, he

stumbled to his bed and let sleep finally overtake him. At least for a few hours.

When morning brought the first gray light before dawn, Andrew woke. His eyes were gritty, as if he had been swimming in a murky lake. He poured water into his washbasin and splashed it on his face, rubbing his eyes. He opened his bedroom door quietly, but all he heard was the early morning chorus of birdcalls.

He looked in Mari's room. Bethany was still sitting in the rocking chair, Mari in her arms. His daughter breathed deeply and calmly, untroubled in her sleep, and Bethany looked just as peaceful. He stepped closer and felt Mari's forehead. It was cool and dry.

Smiling, he went down the stairs as quietly as he could. It looked like the crisis was over. He pulled on his boots and went out to the barn to do his chores. Jenny ran up, running in circles around him. He scratched her ears and walked toward the barn, taking stock of the blown-down limbs and other debris left by yesterday's storm. He would have to clean this up this afternoon, after putting in a full day's work in the fields.

Breakfast was quiet. Rose had fixed toast and fried eggs, and was making a soupy combination of bread, hot milk and eggs for Mari.

"What is that?" Andrew asked.

"It's my own special recipe. Now that Mari's fever is gone, she'll need to gain strength," Rose said, sweetening the dish with sugar.

"The doctor said she should have broth." Andrew spread strawberry jam on his toast. "Shouldn't we follow his advice?"

Rose waved away his suggestion. "What does that doctor know about taking care of sick children? This dish will go down as well as broth, and it has more substance."

Andrew watched her sprinkle nutmeg on top of the dish. He had to admit that it looked and smelled delicious, almost like a bread pudding.

Bethany came down to join him after Rose had gone upstairs.

He grinned at her as she rubbed the back of her neck. "Did you end up with a stiff neck this morning after sitting up all night?"

Bethany cracked two eggs into the skillet on the stove. "I'm stiff, for sure, but it doesn't bother me. I fell asleep sometime during the night, after Mari's fever started going down. How about you?"

Andrew nodded. "The same. It was a relief to see her sleeping quietly this morning." He finished his toast. "Will you be able to get more rest today while Rose sits with Mari?"

"I hope so. There is so much work to be done, but Mari comes first. I'll take a nap this afternoon." Bethany turned over her eggs and started toasting a slice of bread. "If you get a chance, would you go over to *Daed*'s house for me? There's a Bible storybook that I'd like to read to Mari to keep her occupied when she's awake. It's going to be hard to keep her in bed once she starts feeling better."

"For sure, I will. I'll go now before I start plowing. Jonah will want to know how Mari is doing."

Whistling for Jenny to come with him, Andrew

headed to Jonah's farm as soon as he finished eating. He found the older man in the barn, supervising John and James as they harnessed the team of workhorses.

"How is Mari?" Jonah asked, as soon as he saw him. He ruffled Jenny's ears.

"Her fever is down and she's sleeping. It looks like the worst has passed."

"We can thank the Good Lord for that."

Andrew kicked at a stone embedded in the barn's dirt floor. With all his praying last night, begging God to spare Mari, he hadn't thought once about giving thanks for His mercy.

"Bethany sent me over to borrow a storybook that she wants to read to Mari to keep her occupied."

"I know which one you mean. It's Bethany's favorite. I'll get it as soon as these boys head out to the field." Jonah helped the boys hitch the horses to the harrow and watched them drive out to the cornfield. "Sometimes I can't believe those two are old enough to do farm work, but they are." He chuckled. "I guess I feel old when I notice how big they're getting."

As they walked toward the house, Jonah matched his stride to Andrew's. "How is Bethany? She must have been pretty worried about Mari last night."

"She's fine. You would think that she's Mari's natural mother." Andrew winced at the bitterness that crept into his voice.

"What is wrong with that? Isn't that what you want for Mari?" Jonah stopped on the porch and faced him.

Andrew shrugged. How could he express what he felt?

"I suppose I missed Lily even more last night than

usual. I kept thinking that if Mari…if Mari didn't make it through this illness, I would have nothing left of Lily. She would be gone forever."

Jonah narrowed his eyes, then opened the kitchen door. "Come in and have some coffee."

Andrew sat at the table, ignoring the coffee Jonah poured for him.

"Is it wrong to miss my wife?"

"Not at all," Jonah said. He poured enough cream into his coffee to turn it nearly white. "When we marry, we expect that it will be for life. When something happens to cut that time short, it's hard for the one left behind."

"Even after you've been married for many years?"

"Sarah and I had been married for twenty-two years when she passed away." Jonah sighed and took a sip of his coffee. "That might seem like a long time to you, but to me it isn't long at all. It feels like we had just begun our lives together when she was taken from me."

"So you know how I feel. Lily is still so much a part of me, I don't know if…" He stopped. He didn't want to admit to Bethany's father that he didn't love her and wouldn't ever love her.

Jonah stared at his coffee for a long minute. "I know you and my daughter didn't love each other when you married. And it sounds like you haven't found a way for it to grow yet."

"How can I love her when I still love Lily?"

"Love isn't a feeling. It's a decision. A choice you make."

Andrew almost laughed. "What do you mean? Love is all about feelings."

"*Ja*, for sure, we feel love." Jonah stroked his beard. "But there are times when it's hard. Love is work when your wife burns your dinner and you have to eat only bread and butter. Or when she gets angry because you've tracked muddy boots across the kitchen floor. Or when you get tired of her talking to you when you're trying to go to sleep."

Andrew smiled. He remembered going through those times with Lily, but he still loved her.

"Those are the times when we need to decide to love our wives, and they must decide to love us. That's why love isn't a feeling. Feelings disappear when troubles come but love never fails."

"Are you telling me that I need to decide to stop loving Lily?"

"I can't do that. I still love Sarah, and I always will. But my love for her has changed. I love the life we had together, and I love the memories of her that I hold close. But those things are in the past. I can't hold on to that love the same way I did when she was with me. I need to live my life. I need to let her go so I can reach forward to what God has for me now."

Andrew took a sip of his coffee.

"You'll always have your memories of Lily, even after Mari has grown and set up housekeeping with her own husband. But you can't let those memories keep you from appreciating and loving the new wife the Good Lord has seen fit to give you." Jonah drained his cup. "Let's go find that book."

Chapter Fourteen

By Thursday, when Dr. Hoover stopped by to check on Mari, her fever was gone.

"The hard part now, Mother, is to keep her quiet as she recovers." He watched Bethany under his bushy white eyebrows and he put his equipment back into his bag. "She won't have a lot of energy, but she'll get tired of being in bed very quickly."

"Can we let her lie on the couch downstairs?" Bethany asked. She bit her lip as she looked at poor Mari, covered with red spots over every inch of her body.

"Anything you can do to keep her resting." Dr. Hoover tapped Mari's nose. "You listen to your mother you'll feel better soon."

Mari giggled at the funny face he made, even though she didn't understand the *Englisch* words he had spoken.

After the doctor left, Bethany sat on the chair next to Mari's bed. "The doctor said you'll feel better soon, but you still need to rest for a few days, and drink a lot of water."

"This spot is brown," Mari said, pointing to one of the spots on her arm.

"*Ja*, for sure. The doctor said the red spots would turn to brown as they fade away."

Bethany tucked the covers closer around Mari's legs. The days since the storm passed had been comfortably warm, but not hot.

"Are you hungry, Mari? It's nearly dinnertime."

"I want *Mammi* Rose's milk soup."

"I'll ask her to make some for you." Bethany kissed the little girl on the top of her head and stood. "Will you be all right until *Mammi* Rose comes up to sit with you?"

Mari lay back on her pillow and gazed out the window. "I don't like to be alone."

Bethany sighed as a single tear made its way down Mari's cheek. "I will come right back as soon as I ask *Mammi* Rose to make some milk soup for you."

"I want *Mamma*." Mari's voice was so quiet that Bethany almost didn't hear her.

She sat down on the edge of the bed again. "I'm here. What do you need?"

Mari turned on her side, facing away from Bethany. "I want *Mamma*. My real *Mamma*."

Bethany had no answer for Mari, nothing she could do to give her what she longed for.

"I know, Mari. I know."

Bethany wanted nothing more than to be held by her own mother, too.

Another tear pooled in the corner of Mari's eye and she squinted to push it out. As her face relaxed into sleep, Bethany gently rubbed her back until her breathing deepened and became regular.

While she waited, her mind went back to when she had tried to comfort James the morning after *Mamm*'s passing. He had been such a little boy and couldn't understand what had happened. Bethany had tried to comfort him, but he had struggled in her arms.

"You're not my *mamm*," he had said. "You'll never be my *mamm*."

He had pushed her away, hitting her with his little fists until his sobbing had finally faded. Then he had let Bethany hold him and comfort him...but she knew. She would always be a poor substitute for *Mamm*, just like she was a poor substitute for Lily. Still the second choice. Still the second best.

When Mari was sound asleep, Bethany looked at the clock on the little table by the bed. It was time for dinner, but she had no energy to think about what to prepare and no time to make anything more than cold sandwiches. A working man needed more than sandwiches to keep him going. A good wife would make sure he had nourishing food at every meal.

As she reached the top of the stairway, Bethany took a deep breath. Fried chicken? When she went downstairs and into the kitchen, Rose was working at the stove, a skillet of chicken sizzling as she turned the pieces one by one.

"That smells delicious," Bethany said. "What can I do to help?"

Rose had a peculiar expression on her face. "Is everything all right upstairs?"

"Mari is sleeping now, but she would like some of your milk soup when she wakes up. Dr. Hoover said she is recovering well. We just need to wait for the spots to go away, and he says they should be gone by next week."

"But everything else is fine?" Rose looked into Bethany's face, waiting. But for what?

"*Ja*, for sure."

"Andrew is pleased with you as his new wife?"

Bethany turned from Rose's penetrating gaze. Some ears of sweet corn were piled on the kitchen counter, waiting to be cleaned. She picked one up and started peeling away the green husk.

"I suppose he is. He hasn't said anything different."

"But is he happy? Do you make him as happy as he was with my Lily?"

Bethany's hands shook. For sure, Andrew wasn't as happy with her as he had been with Lily. Ripping the husks off the ears of corn, she tried to act as if she hadn't heard Rose's question. Once the ears of corn were on the counter, ready to go into the simmering water in the big pot on the stove, Bethany gathered up the husks and silk to take to the refuse pile.

"I'll go see if Andrew is ready to come in. I know you don't want to put the food on the table until he's ready."

Walking toward the refuse pile at the edge of the garden, Bethany found Andrew, clearing weeds from the bed of day lilies.

"They've spread even farther, haven't they?" she said.

She had startled him, and he nearly fell into the stream. When he saw her, he grinned. "They're nearly over the bank of the stream, but they're doing fine."

Bethany turned one orange flower toward her, cupping the blossom between her fingers. They were lovely, but she still remembered that they represented Andrew's love for his first wife. Letting go of the flower, she sighed. There was no use in worrying about it. Lily would always be part of their lives.

"Rose is frying chicken for your dinner, and there's sweet corn, too."

"That sounds good." He pulled one more weed and threw it on the pile. "She's making herself pretty useful around here, isn't she?"

"Rose?" Bethany still trembled. Andrew hadn't heard Rose's hurtful questions. "I suppose so."

"She was a great help when Mari was so sick."

"*Ja*, she was."

Bethany followed Andrew to the pump and worked the handle while he washed up.

"You don't sound like you really agree with me." Andrew splashed water on his face and neck.

"I thought she was only going to live here on a temporary basis, but it seems like she's settling in for good."

Andrew shook the drops of water off his hands. "You're not going to bring that up again, are you? With the drought still going on out west, I can't ask her to go back there." He stepped closer to her. "What is bothering you, Bethany? It isn't only Rose, is it?"

How could she tell him without sounding prideful? Because it was prideful for her to want to be more important than a woman she had never met. A woman that meant more to her husband and his daughter than she ever would.

"It isn't important, and dinner is almost ready. We need to go inside."

Bethany started toward the back door, but Andrew caught her elbow, holding her until she looked at him.

"You aren't sorry you married me, are you?"

She looked beyond his shoulder to the patch of day lilies at the edge of the garden. Was she sorry?

"It doesn't matter whether or not either one of us regrets what we did. What matters is that Mari is happy."

Bethany forced herself to smile, but Andrew frowned.

"I know you, Bethany, and there is something bothering you. What is it?"

She glanced toward the house, mindful that Rose could be watching them. Her fingers twisted themselves into a knot while she tried to keep the words in, but this was Andrew. Her best friend. If she didn't think about the wedding, and the fact that he was supposed to be her husband, she could confide in him the way she used to when she was a girl.

"I'm not enough."

"What do you mean?"

"Mari wants her mother, and Rose wants her daughter. Even you—" she gestured toward the bed of day lilies "—would rather be married to Lily than to me."

His silence was all the answer she needed. She turned and walked away from him, heading toward the barn. Anywhere to get away from Andrew, and especially Rose.

"Bethany, wait." He caught up with her, took her arm and led her to the workbench. "Sit down." He pointed to the stool where he sat when he mended harnesses, then faced her. "You're wrong."

"Admit it, Andrew. You would be happier if Lily had never died and you still lived in Iowa."

He nodded, his shoulders slumped. "But I can't change the past. I can't bring Lily back."

"I'm tired of being the second choice. I expect it from Rose. She didn't choose any of this. And Mari is only a child. But you…" She drew a deep breath, trying to control the awful self-pity that threatened to consume her. "You asked me to be your wife, to step into this role. But everywhere I turn, I only see reminders of the wife you'd rather have. No matter what I do, I'm not enough to take her place." She stood, pushing past him. "I'm going back to *Daed*'s to stay for a while. I need to think about our future, and so do you."

"Bethany, wait. Stop."

She ignored Andrew's calls and stalked down the lane toward home.

Andrew stood in the barn doorway, watching Bethany's retreating back. He knew her moods, and there was nothing he could say to her right now. She would get over it eventually. She always did.

He kicked at a stone. What if she didn't?

The scent of chicken frying reminded him that it was dinnertime, and it had been hours since breakfast. Heading toward the house, he decided to think about what to do about Bethany while he ate.

Rose was alone in the kitchen. Andrew hung his hat on the hook just inside the door.

"How is Mari doing?" He sat at the table.

"Bethany said she was sleeping. I'll take her dinner to her when she wakes up." Rose laid a platter of fried chicken on the table and turned back to the stove to pick ears of corn out of the big kettle. "Where is Bethany? She went out to get you."

Andrew took a drink of water. "She went to visit Jonah."

"Will she be here for dinner?"

"I don't know."

Rose turned to face him. "So, it has happened."

"What has?"

"You married this girl on a whim to spite me, and now that things aren't working out, she's leaving you and Mari on your own."

"You don't know that. She just went to see Jonah."

Rose sat in her chair. "I saw her leave the barn, and I heard you call after her. The two of you had a disagreement, and I'm not surprised."

"That isn't what happened."

"Then why are you letting her go?"

"I'm not letting her go. I'll talk to her after dinner."

"Humph." Rose folded her hands in her lap, ready for the silent prayer. "If there was any love between you, dinner wouldn't matter." She bowed her head.

Andrew's thoughts were in such a turmoil that he couldn't pray. Even when he raised his head and took a chicken leg from the platter, Rose's words still echoed— *if there was any love between you...* Was that the problem? He cared for her, didn't he? Perhaps someday love would grow.

Then Jonah's words came back to him. He had to choose to love Bethany. Hadn't he done that? He had chosen to marry her, hadn't he?

The bite of chicken turned dry in his mouth. Bethany was right. He swallowed the tasteless meat.

She was right. He hadn't let go of his love for Lily. As long as he refused to let Lily fade into the past, he wouldn't be able take hold of what God had given him. And Bethany had suffered for it.

"I need to go." Andrew stood up. Where would he go? To Jonah's house? What would he say to her?

"You haven't eaten your dinner, and I spent all morning fixing it." Rose spread butter on an ear of corn. "Bethany walked away from you, so she should be the one to make the first move."

"I'm going to talk to her. I'll eat after I get back."

Andrew grabbed his hat on the way out the door and jogged down the farm lane. As he passed the kitchen window, he saw Rose watching him. He couldn't tell if she hoped he would bring Bethany home, or if she was happy to see their marriage falter. He pushed away the thoughts. Rose might be difficult, but he had never known her to want harm to happen to anyone.

Jonah and his sons were sitting at the kitchen table when Andrew stepped onto the porch. Jonah met him at the door.

"Bethany came over here a while ago." He opened the screen door, but didn't invite Andrew in. "She didn't even stop by the house but went straight to the barn."

When Andrew glanced toward the barn, Jonah went on.

"I'd leave her to herself for a few minutes. Is Mari all right? And Rose?"

Andrew nodded. "Dr. Hoover stopped by this morning and said Mari is coming along fine." He rubbed the back of his neck and glanced toward the barn again. "Rose is acting a bit odd, but she's been worried about Mari."

"And Bethany?"

"I don't know what started it, but she's pretty unhappy."

Jonah moved out onto the porch, out of earshot of Bethany's brothers.

"She has been very worried about Mari. Did she say anything that might give you a clue?"

Andrew glanced toward the barn again, but there was no sign of Bethany. "She said that she wasn't enough to take Lily's place." He looked at Jonah. "But I never asked her to take Lily's place. I only wanted her to be herself."

Jonah tapped his chin with one finger. "Our actions often outweigh our words. Have you shown her that you appreciate her, and not only the role she has taken? Have you shown her that you want your marriage to be one filled with love?"

"I thought I did. I thought she was content with our life together. Things had improved, and she was even getting along with Rose."

"Then you need to talk to her, tell her how you feel, and then show her how you feel."

"What if she doesn't want to talk to me?"

"Keep trying. Don't give up on her, or yourself."

Jonah went back into the kitchen, letting the screen door close with the soft slap of wood against wood.

Andrew rolled his shoulders and started toward the barn.

Bethany had seen him coming and stood at the edge of the haymow, her hands on her hips.

"I don't want to talk to you, so you may as well go back home."

Andrew stopped on the threshold. "Even if I came to apologize?"

She crossed her arms. "What kind of apology can you give me?"

"What if I told you that you are right?"

Turning away, Bethany walked to the back of the haymow. Andrew climbed up the ladder and followed her. She had sat on the bare floor in the empty mow, her knees drawn up and her hands clasped around them. As he approached, she turned her face away. He squatted down next to her, watching the dust motes swim in a narrow sunbeam.

"You were right. I have clung to Lily's memory. It's been so hard to let go of her, that I'm sure it seems like I'd rather have her here than you."

"It doesn't just seem that way. It's true. You would be happier if she had never died." Bethany's voice was almost a whisper.

"I might want that to be true, but it isn't. Lily is never coming back." Andrew picked up a piece of last year's hay from the floor. "Jonah told me that I need to move on, to leave the past in the past and grasp hold of what God has given me now."

"And what is that?"

"It's you, Bethany. You and Mari, and even Rose. We're a family. I know it isn't easy to get along sometimes, but we have to try."

"It isn't easy most of the time." She sniffed as if she had been crying.

"But if we choose to..." Andrew swallowed. He wasn't sure how Bethany would react if he mentioned love. "If we choose to get along and appreciate each other, things will go a lot better."

Bethany sighed and rested her forehead on her knees.

"You are enough. You are more than enough. And I didn't make a mistake when I asked you to marry me. I don't want you to take Lily's place, I want you to make your own place."

She didn't move.

"Will you come home?"

"I'll be there by suppertime." Her voice was muffled.

Andrew climbed back down the ladder. She might be coming home, but he didn't feel like he had solved anything.

Bethany walked across the road to Andrew's farm just before supper as she had promised him, but nothing had changed.

When she let herself in the kitchen door, Rose was upstairs with Mari, so Bethany started gathering leftovers for supper. The fried chicken from dinner was keeping cool in the springhouse, so she made a chicken salad for sandwiches. By the time she had the salad made and the bread sliced, Rose had come back downstairs.

"So you decided to come back?" Rose avoided looking at her as she started setting the table.

"I was only visiting *Daed*. I told Andrew I'd be home by suppertime."

"Will you be running over there every time you and Andrew have a disagreement?"

Bethany stirred the chicken salad, remembering Andrew's words. They needed to choose to get along.

"Our disagreement was a small one, and easily solved. It isn't anything for you to be concerned about."

Andrew was harder to convince. All through supper, he treated Bethany as if she was a newly laid egg.

"How did Mari do this afternoon?" he asked Rose.

"We played a game and I read to her from that Bible storybook." Rose passed the bowl of chicken salad to Bethany. "She fell asleep about the time Bethany returned home."

He smiled at Bethany. "Did you have a good visit with Jonah?"

Bethany nearly choked on her sandwich. He knew what she was doing this afternoon. "For sure. It was nice to spend time with my brothers, too." She gave him a pointed stare. "They made me feel very welcome."

"I'm glad. You should visit them more often. I know they miss you."

By the time supper was over and the dishes washed, Mari had woken up from her nap. Andrew carried her downstairs to sit in the living room while Rose and Bethany worked on their sewing and Andrew read from the *Budget* newspaper. The evening seemed to last forever, but Bethany kept a smile on her face. Andrew's request to choose to get along seemed to work.

As soon as the room grew dark, Rose put her sewing away.

"I'll see you folks in the morning." She kissed Mari. "Sleep well, little one."

Andrew carried Mari up to her room, then went out to check the barn while Bethany tucked Mari in her bed and stayed until she fell asleep. After she heard Andrew go into his room and close the door, she laid her hand on the little girl's forehead. Cool and dry. Bethany went to her own room and soon fell asleep.

Later that night, Bethany woke to Mari's cries. She was calling for her *mamma* again, and Bethany sighed. She swung her feet onto the floor and walked to Mari's door.

"I'm here, Mari. What do you need?"

"I don't want to be alone."

There was no moon, so the room was dark. Bethany felt for the matches she kept on a shelf and lit the lamp by Mari's bed.

"You're not alone anymore." Smiling, she adjusted Mari's pillow as the little girl struggled to sit up. "Now, why aren't you asleep?"

"I'm not sleepy."

"It's nighttime. You need to sleep."

Mari yawned. "Will you read a story?"

As Bethany picked up the Bible storybook from the bedside table, Mari scooted over in her bed to make room for her. When she sat, leaning against the wall, Mari climbed into her lap.

"Which story do you want to hear?"

Mari opened the book on her lap, turning it until she found the picture she wanted. "The story about the lions."

"You mean Daniel and the lions?"

Mari nodded, then pointed to the other man in the picture, looking into the lion's den. "Who is that?"

"That is the king that put Daniel into the lion's den."

"He's a bad man."

"He was a man who didn't know God. But Daniel knew God."

As Bethany read the story, Mari leaned her head against her shoulder.

"That is a happy story," Mari said when she finished.

"For sure it is. God saved Daniel from the hungry lions."

"I like happy stories, not sad ones." She sat up, turning to look into Bethany's face. "I know a sad story. I was sick."

Bethany nodded. "That is a sad story, but it has a happy ending, because you're getting well now."

"That's good."

Mari leaned against Bethany and was quiet for so long that Bethany thought she had gone to sleep.

"I know another sad story."

"Do you want to tell me?"

Mari nodded. "My *mamma* is gone."

"That is a very sad story."

"What is the happy end?"

What could she say? Lily was gone, and she wasn't coming back. Where was the happy ending?

Mari sat up again. "I know the happy end."

"What is it?"

"God gave me a new *mamma*."

"*Mammi* Rose?"

Mari grinned and shook her head.

"Dinah?"

Mari shook her head again. "You. My own *Mamma* Bethany."

She leaned against Bethany. This time her breathing grew even, and Bethany was sure she was sleeping.

"I'm sorry I'm not your real *mamma*." Bethany kissed the top of Mari's head.

"You are my real *mamma*." Mari sighed. "My new real *mamma*. God gave you to me."

"Who told you that?"

"*Daed* did."

Bethany hugged her, then sat on the edge of the bed, helping Mari snuggle under her sheet. She had to bite her lip to keep the tears from falling.

"Are you sad?" Mari asked, reaching to wipe away a tear that had escaped.

"Not sad. I'm happy. You told me the perfect happy ending to your sad story." She leaned down to kiss Mari's spotted forehead. "I love you, Mari."

Mari yawned again, her eyes closing. "I love you, too, *Mamma*."

"You go to sleep. I'll stay right here, and you won't be alone."

Bethany sat on the chair and turned the lamp down until it was a faint glow. When she did, she thought she heard a soft noise in the hall, but she could see nothing in the dark. She stepped to Mari's doorway to look, but everything was as it should be. Her bedroom door stood open and her window blinds moved in a slight breeze. That must have been what she had heard. Then she heard the soft sound of a door closing behind her. Had Andrew been in the hallway, listening to her conversation with Mari? She hoped so.

Sitting down again, she watched Mari sleep, smiling to herself. That little girl had given her the gift of her love, and Bethany's chest ached with the realization of how precious that gift was. For sure, she thought she had loved Mari with her whole heart since the day she met her, but tonight her love had been returned.

Chapter Fifteen

More than a week after Mari became ill, she was feeling better and it was hard to keep her quiet and in bed. Bethany brought the armchair into the kitchen from the front room in the mornings so Mari could rest comfortably while Bethany and Rose worked. She had also taken Mari's blankets out to the backyard in the afternoons so she could rest in the shade of the big tree by the lane, where Jenny's doghouse stood. The days were long and tedious since Mari wanted to play and be active, but quickly grew tired.

The weather didn't cooperate, either. After the brief respite after the storm the week before, the hot weather increased again until every day was sweltering, and each night was a sweaty, uncomfortable battle to sleep. Meanwhile, Rose and Bethany were working hard to can the garden's produce. They needed to can as much as they could to survive the winter.

Today they were canning green beans, working in the kitchen while Mari sat in her chair, looking at the pictures in her book.

"From Martha's last letter, it sounds like their gardens are doing better this year."

Bethany snapped the end of a green bean and wiped the sweat from her forehead with her sleeve. "Have they gotten rain?"

"She said the community got together and drilled a new well, much deeper than any the farmers had dug. Folks can get water from there for their gardens and homes. She says it's a blessing."

Bethany couldn't imagine the work involved in carrying water from a community well. She was thankful for her kitchen sink and pump. "What would they do if they hadn't dug a deeper well?"

"What we did last year. We made do. I would use water for cooking, then let it cool and use that water for cleaning. Then I would water the plants with it. I tried to make every bucket serve for at least three jobs."

"But you had a good well. Andrew said that some of them were going dry."

Rose nodded. "My neighbor's well gave out. They packed up and moved back east. To Ohio, I think they said. They couldn't sell their farm, so they just left it."

They worked in silence for a few minutes. Mari had fallen asleep, her book still open in her lap.

"Do you think Martha will want to move back here?" Bethany reached for another handful of beans.

"I'm afraid her mother wouldn't be able to make the trip."

"But we have water here, and plenty of food. Even if the garden isn't doing as well as other years, we'll still be able to fill the cellar for the winter. I hate to think of them working so hard."

Rose snapped the remaining beans in her hand and took the last handful from the bowl. "Martha has talked about moving back here, but her mother is crippled and confined to her bed. She hasn't even gone to church services for the last year. Martha is afraid the long train ride might be too much for her."

While Rose examined the canning jars, making sure there were no cracks or chips in them, Bethany poured the green beans into a pot of boiling water. Steam rose around her face, making the hot kitchen even hotter. Bethany watched the clock. The beans needed to cook for five minutes, then they would pack the jars. They needed to work quickly so the jars would stay sterile.

Once the beans were in the jars, Bethany shut the stove dampers and they moved to the shady front porch. Bethany carried Mari, along with her blankets, and set her on the swing, while Rose sat on the old rocker. Bethany sat on the end of the swing next to Mari, moving it gently with her foot.

"I hope *Daed* and the boys are doing all right today."

"Why?" Rose's voice was sharp.

"It's Thursday. You usually make dinner for them on Thursdays, don't you?" Bethany pushed with her foot again. "You missed going over there on Monday, too. Did they do their own laundry?"

Rose shrugged. "It doesn't matter to me. Your father is so stubborn, he could probably make the clothes come clean by just glaring at them."

Bethany had to laugh. She had seen *Daed*'s glare often enough. "I think you're right about that."

"It's nice and cool out here now," Rose said. "Do you think this afternoon will be as hot as yesterday?"

"I think so. It's a hot summer for sure, isn't it?"

"Where did Andrew go so early this morning?"

"He said he had some work to do for the doctor, to pay for his visit here."

Rose was quiet, her head leaning on the back of the rocker. Bethany watched Mari sleep on the swing, then glanced at Rose. The older woman's eyes were closed, too, and she was snoring quietly. Bethany propped her elbow on the end of the swing and leaned her head on her hand. All around her, insects buzzed in the grasses and in the trees. A slight breeze blew, making the shady porch pleasant, but Rose was right. It would soon be so hot they wouldn't want to do any work. Today was the day to clean the upstairs, but Bethany was tempted to let it go this week. No one would notice, especially since they only went upstairs late at night after the rooms had a chance to cool down.

Just as Bethany decided that she must at least change the bedsheets and run the dust mop, *Daed* came up the lane from the road. When Bethany waved, he walked across the grass toward them.

"How is Mari this morning?" *Daed* kept his voice low when he saw her sleeping on the swing, but Rose opened her eyes.

"She's doing much better," Bethany said. "How are you? I haven't seen you since Mari got sick."

Daed put one foot on the porch step and ran his fingers through his beard. "I'd be much better if Aaron wasn't cooking dinner today."

"Aaron?" Bethany wrinkled her nose, remembering the smell of the scorched green beans the last time he had tried to cook.

"No one else volunteered, so we're stuck with him."

Bethany looked from *Daed* to Rose, and then back to *Daed*. Rose stared at the porch railing, ignoring *Daed*. He didn't look at her, either, but went on talking.

"I know the boys have appreciated the meals Rose has fixed for them over the past few weeks. Did you know she makes a creamed chicken dish that we can't get enough of? How many times have the boys asked for that one again?"

This time he looked at Rose, but she only crossed her arms.

"I know John has asked at least three times."

"Humph. It was only twice." Rose still didn't look at him.

"And Nathaniel has already prepared the chicken. He even took the feathers off."

Rose didn't answer. Bethany wondered if she should take Mari into the house and let these two argue without her.

"And James picked the last of the peas and shelled them. Fresh buttered peas is one of his favorites."

"At least he has a roof over his head. A place that is home." Rose sniffed.

Daed shrugged, looking at Bethany. "All I said was that if she planned to stay here in Indiana, she should sell her place in Iowa."

Rose glared at him. "You want me to sell the home where I raised my daughter and the farm my Lemuel loved." She stalked into the house, letting the screen door slam behind her.

Mari rubbed her eyes. "*Datti* Jonah!"

Daed walked over to give Mari a kiss on the top of her curls. "How's my pumpkin today?"

"My throat doesn't hurt."

"That is good."

"But my spots are still here." She bent her elbow and pointed to a few brown spots on her arm. "Will I always have spots?"

Daed shook his head, looking serious, but he winked at Bethany. "Not always. They will fade away and you'll be our bright little pumpkin again."

Mari lay back against her pillow. "Why is *Mammi* Rose angry?"

Daed glanced at Bethany. "She isn't angry at you. She is unhappy with something I said."

"You and Rose don't get along very well, do you?" Bethany ran her fingers through Mari's hair, trying to find some order in the curls.

"Not today." *Daed* sighed. "She's a headstrong woman."

"Did she ask you about living in the *Dawdi Haus*? She might be happier if she had her own place."

"She didn't bring it up, but we can talk about it."

Rose came back out to the porch with a pitcher of water and some glasses. Bethany helped her serve the water.

As Rose handed a glass to *Daed*, she said, "Talk about what?"

"The *Dawdi Haus*. No one is living in it, and it should be used. Bethany was asking why you don't come live there."

"I'm not giving up my home."

"I'm not asking you to give it up. Just change it."

Rose glared at him again and Bethany stood and picked up Mari.

"We're going in. You two can argue all you want, but Mari and I are going to start fixing dinner."

Neither *Daed* nor Rose said anything as Bethany went inside. She got Mari settled on the chair in the kitchen with her book, but the little girl didn't open it. She laid her head down on her pillow, ready to finish her interrupted nap. As she drifted off, Bethany went out to the springhouse to fetch a dozen eggs and some butter and cream. Since the stove was already hot from the canning, she would build up the fire just enough to fix a custard to have with a light dinner of bread and butter. None of them felt like eating, as hot as it was, but they needed to have something nutritious.

Before she mixed up the custard, she thought of the glass of water she had left on the front porch. She had only taken one swallow before she'd brought in Mari, and now she went to get it rather than wasting the water. But as she approached the front screen door, she heard *Daed* and Rose talking. Before she realized she was eavesdropping, she heard them mention her name.

"What does Bethany have to do with it?" *Daed* asked.

"It isn't only Bethany. She's a sweet girl, but…"

"But you still don't like her taking Lily's place?"

Rose sniffed. "We've discussed this before. I can face the fact that my daughter is gone. I still think I'm the one who should raise Mari, and I want to do it in Iowa. That's my home."

"But I'm here, and so is Mari. Why are you so insistent on going back there?"

"I'm an independent woman, Jonah, and I have been for ten years. Why should I give that up?"

Bethany couldn't tear herself away but stepped closer to the door.

"Don't you get lonely sometimes?" *Daed*'s voice was soft, persuasive. "I know I do. God brought us together at this time to be together. To be a couple."

Bethany covered her mouth. *Daed* was in love with Rose?

"We've talked about some tempting possibilities," Rose said. "And if I were to marry again, you would be the one I chose."

Daed chuckled. "We should do it soon, then. I'm tired of standing outside your window at night."

"I didn't say I would marry you. I have a particular way I like to do things. Since I'm not married, there is no one to tell me that I'm doing something the wrong way. No one to complain if I want to leave the lamp lit so I can quilt late at night or go outside to enjoy the night air. I don't even have to worry if someone will dislike my cooking. I'm not sure I want to give up my freedom this late in life, and my home is waiting for me."

"Your very quiet, very lonely home. You've told me

how much you like being around the boys and how they make you feel useful."

Rose didn't answer. Bethany heard the creak of the porch swing as it received *Daed*'s weight.

"What is the real reason you won't marry me?" he asked. "Is it because you don't love me?"

The only sound Bethany heard was the chair's rocker against the wooden porch floor.

Finally, Rose said, "I can't answer that, Jonah. I do love you, but I can't marry you. I don't want to tie myself to any man again. I'll be going home to Iowa as soon as I can."

Bethany heard the squeak of the rocker as Rose stood and hurried back to the kitchen, sorry that she had overheard that conversation. But at least now she knew who the night prowler was. All this time, *Daed* had been courting Rose.

Andrew was milking Dinah when Bethany came into the barn just before supper. He had spent the day at Dr. Hoover's house taking out the rotted porch supports and propping up the roof with the beams the doctor supplied. It had been a long, hot day, and he was ready to rest for the remainder of the evening. All those plans disappeared when Bethany stood by Dinah's shoulder, watching him.

"I found out who our prowler is."

The smile on Bethany's face made him grin.

"Who is it?"

"Daed."

"Jonah?" Andrew stopped milking until Dinah

shifted her feet, reminding him of the job at hand. "What has he been doing?"

"Courting Rose."

He shook his head. "That can't be. Rose doesn't want to get married again."

"That's what she told him, but he still said he wanted to marry her."

Andrew stripped the last of the milk from Dinah's udder and picked up the pail.

"That explains why Jenny didn't bark at him."

Bethany followed him as he took the milk to the springhouse to cool until morning.

Setting the pail in the trough of flowing water, he asked, "How did you find this out?"

"I happened to hear them talking when they were on the front porch this morning."

Andrew closed the springhouse door and faced her. "You were eavesdropping?"

"When I heard what they were talking about, I couldn't help it."

"When are they getting married?"

"They aren't. Rose turned him down." Bethany walked with him toward the house. "She said she wanted to go back to Iowa."

"She can't do that. She can't support herself there."

"She said your mother wrote that the community dug a new, deeper well that they're all sharing."

"But even then, how can anything grow there?" He opened the door for Bethany, then followed her into the house. "I'm putting my foot down. She can't go back."

Rose came out of her bedroom just as they came into the kitchen.

"I want to talk to you." She sat at the table, set for supper with cold chicken, bread and vegetables from the garden. "Mari has gone to bed, and it's time we cleared up a few things."

Andrew sighed. Rose was taking control again.

"I'm going back to Iowa."

"You can't do that."

"Sit down, Andrew. You, too, Bethany."

Andrew didn't sit. "You can't go back to Iowa, at least not until the drought is over."

"The train leaves at noon tomorrow. I want you to drive me to the station."

"I won't let you go."

"Rose," Bethany said. "What happened to make you decide this so suddenly? Is it the disagreement you had with *Daed*?"

Rose fixed her eyes on Andrew. "Sit down, and I'll tell you."

Andrew sat, waiting to hear the excuse she had thought up for this plan.

"I know what you've done." She folded her hands in front of her on the table, not looking at either one of them. "I saw it while Mari was sick, but I didn't want to believe it. Just now, when I put her to bed, I had to face it." She looked at Bethany, then at Andrew. "Your marriage is a lie. You are living separate lives under this roof and aren't building a Christian family for Mari the way you led me to believe. In fact, I don't even think the two of you love each other."

Andrew couldn't look at Bethany. "But we are married. You were there and witnessed the ceremony."

"I can also tell the bishop the other things I've witnessed. Separate bedrooms? That is not the way married couples live." She laid her hands flat on the table. "It isn't too late to have this marriage annulled and bring both of you before the church for discipline."

"You can't do that," Bethany said. "It isn't right."

"I can do that. Mari is my granddaughter, and her welfare is my first concern. I can't let her live in a family based on lies." Rose stood. "I'm bringing this matter to the bishop first thing in the morning."

Andrew buried his face in his hands as she walked out of the room.

"What are we going to do?" Bethany asked.

When he didn't answer, she jostled his shoulder.

"Andrew, what are you going to do? You have to stop her."

"I've never been able to stop her. When she sets her mind to something, it happens. All we can hope is that the bishop won't believe her."

"But she's right. Not that our marriage is a lie, but about—about the rest of it."

"That's no reason to ask for us to be brought up before the church."

Bethany leaned back in her chair, her arms crossed. A fly buzzed around the plate of chicken.

"This all comes back to Lily, doesn't it? You treat her mother as if she's a steam kettle about to blow up because that's the way Lily always treated her. It's time for you to take a stand, Andrew. You need to tell Rose that she can't ruin our lives."

He had to do the hard thing. Bethany was right. Rose had gotten her own way too often.

"I'll talk to her in the morning, before she goes to the bishop. Maybe she'll be thinking more clearly, and I'll be able to reason with her."

Bethany started covering the food, preparing to put it away in the springhouse, but Andrew snatched a piece of cold chicken from the plate first. She might not be hungry, but he was. And he had to fortify himself for his confrontation with Rose in the morning.

When Andrew woke the next day, the sky held the pale gray light that came just before dawn. He dressed and went out to the barn. The time to talk to Rose would come soon enough, after the morning chores were done. She certainly wouldn't try to see the bishop before breakfast.

But when he got to the stalls, only Dandy was there, waiting for his morning hay and oats. Andrew filled both feed boxes, then went through Whiskers' stall to the pasture to call him in. The horse wasn't there. From where he was standing, he couldn't see that the fence was down anywhere, but could Whiskers have jumped the fence? Or perhaps he had pushed through the gate.

It wasn't until Andrew came back into the barn that he saw that the spring wagon was missing. He swallowed down the panic that sought to engulf him. He forced himself to think. Who would take the horse and wagon, and why?

Rose. Would she have driven herself to Bishop's house so early? Or had she gone on to the train station?

He started toward the house, but before he crossed the gravel drive, Bethany appeared at the back door.

"Mari's gone," she called, her voice shrill. "She isn't anywhere, and neither is Rose."

"When I came downstairs and Rose wasn't in the kitchen, I didn't wonder about it. Sometimes she sleeps later than we do." Bethany struggled to talk through her tears. Andrew held her, cradling her head against his shoulder. "But when I went to wake Mari, and she wasn't there, I panicked. Then I saw that her clothes were gone, and her doll."

"I found that Whiskers was gone, and the spring wagon." Andrew held her away from him, so he could see her face. "Did you check? Did Rose take her things?"

Bethany nodded. "Do you think Rose took Mari when she went to talk to the bishop?"

Andrew shook his head, and Bethany's insides turned over. "I think she plans to take Mari to Iowa with her."

"She—she can't do that. Mari isn't completely well yet. What is Rose thinking?"

"She isn't thinking straight, that's for sure." He turned her toward the house. "Get ready to go to town with me. I'm going to borrow Jonah's buggy. We'll stop her at the station before she even gets on the train."

As Bethany started up the porch steps, he stopped her. "It's going to be all right. We'll find them."

"You're sure?"

Andrew nodded. "I'm sure."

He started toward *Daed*'s house at a run while Bethany went inside. She got her bonnet and the bag she carried when she went to town. At the last minute, as she heard the buggy coming up the lane, she put out the fire in the kitchen stove.

When she got out to the buggy, *Daed* was sitting in the driver's seat.

"Andrew remembered that he hadn't milked the cow yet." *Daed*'s face was lined with grief. "But we'll leave as soon as he's done."

"Did Rose give you any idea that she was thinking of doing this?"

He shook his head. "I think I must have pushed her too far when I insisted that she needed to sell the farm in Iowa. I hadn't realized that it meant so much to her."

"I heard you talking to her about marriage yesterday. Were you serious?"

"For sure, I was. Ever since she came, my life has been different. We have our disagreements about some things, but that makes life interesting."

"She isn't anything like *Mamm*."

Daed whooshed out a breath. "You're right about that, except that Rose needs me, just like your mother did. I think we would have a good life together, and she would enjoy living here." *Daed* ran his fingers through his beard. "I even thought that maybe she had feelings for me, too."

Bethany patted *Daed*'s arm. "I think she does. She has been much happier the last few weeks, ever since we noticed that a prowler was coming around our house at night. Now that I know it was you visiting Rose, everything makes sense."

Andrew came out of the barn at a trot and jumped into the buggy next to Bethany. "Now we can go. Should we go to the bishop's house first, or straight to the train depot?"

"We'll go straight to Shipshewana." *Daed* picked up the reins and Melba started off at a trot. "Whether she goes to the bishop or not, we know she's going to end up at the train station. We'll meet her there."

"What if she refuses to come home with us?" Bethany asked. "I know we can keep her from taking Mari, but we can't let Rose get on that train. She belongs here."

Andrew had put one arm along the back of the seat to brace himself, and now he dropped his hand down to Bethany's shoulder. "I thought you wanted her to leave."

"I did, once. But she has changed, or maybe I've changed. We work together now, and what would we have done without her when Mari was so ill? She knew just what to do." Bethany chewed on her lower lip. "And you're right. We can't let her go back to Iowa until the drought is over."

They drove in silence, each caught in their own thoughts. Bethany watched Melba's ears as she trotted along the road. Why had Rose done such a thing? Sneaking away was one thing, but she had taken Mari. Stolen her out of her bed when the little girl was still recovering from the measles. Bethany's hand clenched and unclenched. She longed to have Mari safe in her arms again, safe at home.

It was still early morning and there was no other traffic on the roads. Even the state highway was quiet as *Daed* turned the buggy north, toward town.

"What will we say when we see her?" Bethany asked. "What if she...well, what if she isn't in her right mind?"

"I don't think we need to worry about that. We all know how headstrong Rose is, and she will do almost anything to make things go her way," *Daed* said. "She needs to understand that we won't let her take Mari back to Iowa, and that we want her to stay here, too." He stopped Melba at the stop sign in the middle of town, then drove on to the train depot in the next block. "I'll handle Rose. You two take care of Mari."

The station platform was empty when they drove up, but Whiskers was tied to the hitching rail. The spring wagon was empty.

"Where could she be?" Andrew asked as he jumped out of the buggy, then helped Bethany out.

"Inside the depot, most likely." *Daed*'s face and voice were grim as he strode toward the door of the passenger waiting room.

For sure, there was Rose, sitting on a bench with Mari sleeping on her lap. *Daed* sat beside her, while Andrew led Bethany to the bench facing her. No one else was in the room this early.

"How did you find me?" Rose tucked the blanket around Mari's shoulders.

"You didn't hide where you were going," *Daed* said. "But why did you take Mari?"

"I couldn't bear to leave her." Rose's eyes glistened with tears. One trickled down her cheek. "She's my only grandchild, and all I have left of my dear Lily."

"But she isn't your daughter. She's Andrew's daughter, and Bethany's. She belongs with them."

"I only want the best for her."

"Why isn't being with her father and mother the best?"

The corners of Rose's mouth turned down. "Are you aware that your daughter has been living a lie? That those two don't have a true marriage?"

Daed took Rose's hand. "I know that when Andrew and Bethany got married, they didn't think they loved each other. It was too soon after Lily's passing for Andrew, and four years had gone by since they had been together. But I trust that love will grow." He looked at them and smiled. "I think it's growing before our eyes."

Bethany glanced at Andrew, catching his surprised gaze. Why did *Daed* think they were beginning to love each other?

Daed focused on Rose's hand in his and rubbed the back of it with his thumb. "I told Andrew last week that love isn't a feeling, it's a choice. They can choose to love each other or not, and what they choose will make all the difference in their lives." He cleared his throat. "The same is true for us. We can choose to love each other and pledge our lives to each other, or we can remain as we are, two lonely people trying to forge our own path through life."

"I don't want to give up my past…"

Rose's voice faltered as *Daed* put one arm around her shoulder and drew her closer to him.

"You'll always have memories of your past, but I want

you to decide to spend your future with me. I want to be the one to protect you, to love you and to spoil you."

"And to keep me from doing silly things like sitting in an empty train station?" Rose smiled at him.

"*Ja*, for sure." *Daed* pulled her close and kissed the top of her bonnet. "Come home with me and be my wife and the mother my boys need."

Rose smiled. "Those boys need a lot of mothering."

"They certainly do. And Mari needs a grandmother who loves her dearly."

Mari stirred, rubbing her eyes. "Where's *Mamma*?"

Rose turned the little girl so she could see Andrew. "Your *daed* is right there."

Mari slid off Rose's lap and climbed into Bethany's.

"Are you all right?" Bethany asked.

Mari nodded. "I'm hungry. And my spots are almost gone." She snuggled into Bethany's arms. "Will they come back?"

"I hope not," Bethany said, holding her close.

"Well," *Daed* said, "it's time to go home. Give me your train ticket, Rose, and I'll try to get your money back."

"I don't have a ticket." Rose stood up, brushing her skirt. "The booth isn't open yet."

"It's a good thing we came along when we did," *Daed* said, picking up Rose's bag. "Otherwise you might be on your way back to Iowa."

Rose frowned at him. "You know that I fully intended to travel to Iowa today."

"Why did you let me stop you?"

"I knew that if you really wanted to marry me, you

wouldn't let me get on that train. But if you weren't serious, I was ready to take Mari home and get on with our lives there."

"It's a good thing that I'm a serious man, then." He led the way out to the buggy.

Andrew took Mari and Bethany slipped her hand into his elbow as they walked out. She was happy that Rose and *Daed* were finally settled. But all this talk of love echoed hollowly. No matter what *Daed* said, she knew her marriage to Andrew would always be just a convenient arrangement. He would always hold Lily first in his heart.

Chapter Sixteen

Once Rose and Jonah's wedding was announced at church the next Sunday, Andrew thought he could start to trust his mother-in-law again. But the fear of knowing how easily Rose had taken Mari from him stayed with him. He even found himself waking in the middle of the night and going to Mari's bedroom. He would kiss her forehead, satisfying himself that she had no fever, and that she was safe. The interrupted sleep was taking a toll, though. He had trouble keeping up with his work, especially after dinner.

On Wednesday afternoon, when Bethany had taken Mari upstairs for her nap, he went out to the front porch. He had gone to Shipshewana that morning to finish the work on Dr. Hoover's porch and had brought home the old posts and rails that had rotted at the bottom. The rest of the wood was still usable, though, and Andrew thought he would build a pigsty. Before he started on that project, though, he planned to rest his eyes for a few minutes as he sat in the rocking chair.

He was nearly asleep when he heard the screen door open. Someone walked quietly to the swing and sat on it, and he knew it must be Bethany. He waited for the quiet squeak of the chains as she started swinging, and when he didn't hear it, he opened his eyes. Rose was sitting on the swing as if she was waiting to talk to him.

"I need your help," she said when she saw he was awake.

"For sure. What kind of help? Do you want me to get something for you?"

Rose shook her head. "Not that kind of help." She leaned toward him and lowered her voice. "When Jonah and I wed, then Bethany will be my stepdaughter."

Andrew nodded. "And the boys will be your stepsons."

"But Bethany and I have had a difficult time getting along sometimes, and I've noticed a difference since she found out that I'm marrying her father."

"She says she's happy about it."

Rose smoothed the edge of her apron against her knee. "I think she's happy that Jonah is pleased. I'm not sure she likes the idea of me stepping into her mother's place."

"Just like you didn't like her stepping into Lily's place."

The older woman's eyes widened. "I hadn't thought of that." She pleated the edge of her apron, then smoothed it again. "I treated her rather harshly, didn't I?"

"She knew you were still grieving about Lily's passing."

"That is no excuse for how I acted." Rose sighed. "But I hope you never have to experience losing a child."

Andrew leaned forward. "I nearly thought I had, when you disappeared with Mari."

"Like I did when you brought her here to Indiana."

"It's different. She's your granddaughter, but she's my daughter."

"You knew she was safe with me."

"I thought she was with you, but I didn't know if she was safe or not until I saw her sleeping on your lap in the train station."

"You know I would never hurt my own granddaughter."

Drawing a deep breath, Andrew went on. "But I didn't know that. Mari is my daughter. My responsibility." He leaned closer. "She's my whole life. Think about how you would feel if someone had taken Lily away from you without your permission or knowledge."

Rose blinked back tears. "I never thought of it that way." She drew her hand back. "Lemuel always complained that I was hardheaded and hard-hearted."

"But what does Jonah say?"

A small smile broke through. "He says I'm hardheaded, but that he's worked with mules before and he'll make me behave."

Andrew laughed. "You didn't let that comment go, did you?"

"I told him that he's just as much of a mule as I am, so we should get along fine."

Andrew leaned back in his chair and rocked it a few times. "Were you and Lemuel happy?"

Her eyes widened again. "I've never thought about it. Happy?" She shrugged. "He worked, and I worked.

I raised Lily and he raised corn and wheat." Her chin quivered as she pleated the edge of her apron again. "He could be a hard man sometimes, and I was glad when Lily married you. You are a gentle man, and a good husband and father."

Andrew stood and looked into the front room, making sure Bethany wasn't around to hear what he was going to say next. He sat down on the swing next to Rose.

"I loved Lily, and I still do. When we moved to Iowa and I met Lily, though, the reason why she was attractive to me was that she reminded me of Bethany. If Lily hadn't passed away, we would have continued building our farm and our family, and we would have been very happy." He took a breath. "But if my family had never moved west, I would have married Bethany. I think I loved her once, and I think I might love her again."

Rose drew a breath to answer him, but he stopped her.

"From what Lily told me, I'm not sure you and Lemuel had the kind of loving marriage Lily and I had, and the kind I hope to have with Bethany."

"You don't know what you're talking about."

"Maybe not. But I do know that Jonah will love you with all his heart. Whether your marriage to him is happy or not, and whether Bethany and her brothers accept you as a stepmother or not is up to you. You know you can be difficult, but you can choose not to be. You can choose to be the loving wife and mother Jonah and his family deserve."

"It isn't that easy."

"I know that. It takes practice. But isn't it worth trying for Jonah's sake?"

Rose nodded. "You've given me a lot to think about." She looked at him with a thoughtful expression on her face. "I wouldn't be surprised if God called you to be a minister someday."

Andrew shook his head. "Not me. I'm not the minister type."

"You never know. God's ways are not our ways."

On Thursday morning, Mari climbed the stairs ahead of Bethany, carrying the dust mop.

"I mop, right, *Mamma*?"

"That's right." Bethany smiled as she helped Mari lift the long mop high enough to clear the last step at the top. It was good to see Mari bright and cheerful again.

"Which room should we clean first?" she asked.

"*Mamma*'s room." Mari pulled the dust mop down the hall.

As Mari tackled the floor, Bethany dusted the window frames, her blanket chest and the table next to her bed. Mari knew the routine, and they soon had the sheets off the bed and replaced with clean ones.

"I like working," Mari said as they went to her room next.

"I like working with you," Bethany said.

"Is it fun?" Mari grinned at her.

"For sure, it's the best fun there is." Bethany gave Mari a hug.

By the time they finished, it was time to start dinner. Rose was in the kitchen, humming as she peeled some boiled eggs.

"I thought you were making dinner for *Daed* and the

boys today," Bethany said as she and Mari put the dust mop and rags away.

"I finished their dinner early and put it in the cellar to cool. As warm as it is today, I knew no one would want a hot dinner."

Rose cracked another egg and Bethany picked one up to help her. Rose hesitated before she started peeling the egg.

"I wanted to ask for your forgiveness." Her voice was quiet and ended in a quaver.

Bethany shrugged. "There's nothing you've done that needs my forgiveness."

"I treated you terribly when I first met you. I resented you taking my daughter's place, and I was wrong."

Rose had rushed through her words, but when she got to the last one, she glanced at Bethany, as if she was afraid.

Bethany's first thought was to brush it off. Rose's treatment of her had hurt, but it was in the past. Then she saw the older woman's quivering chin. She needed Bethany to forgive her.

"Now that you're marrying my *daed*, I think I know how you felt. It's hard to think of someone taking *Mamm*'s place."

"Especially someone you dislike?" Rose concentrated on peeling the egg in her hand.

"I don't dislike you."

"You did. I know you asked Andrew to send me home."

"That was weeks ago. Now I'm glad he refused. What would we have done without you when Mari was sick?" Bethany finished one egg and picked up another.

"Besides, no matter how I feel about you moving into *Mamm*'s place in our family, you make *Daed* happy. I haven't seen him smile so much in years."

"But you still resent me marrying him."

Bethany shrugged, glancing sideways. "I'll get used to it." She nudged Rose with her elbow. "And Mari won't know any different. You'll always be her *Mammi* Rose and *Datti* Jonah."

Rose looked at her with a genuine smile. "I think we'll all be just fine, don't you?"

"For sure, I do."

After a cold dinner, Andrew asked Bethany to come with him for a walk.

"Aren't you going to take a nap?" Bethany asked.

"I don't take naps. I just rest my eyes."

"I take naps," Mari said. "I like naps. I make up happy ending stories."

Rose started clearing the table. "You two take your walk. Mari and I will rest together in the front room."

Bethany followed Andrew out the kitchen door and toward the barn as Jenny met them and fell into step with them.

"What are you going to show me?"

"I've been working on something and I wanted to show it to you."

She followed him down the steps to the cellar. He turned away from the dairy to the other end of the cellar. Before they reached the corner, Bethany could smell a telltale odor.

"You got a pig?"

Andrew leaned over and scratched the pig's back.

"Jonah gave her to us. She's due to farrow soon, so we'll have our own ham and bacon by winter."

"That will be delicious," Bethany said, looking at the sow with more interest, wondering when the piglets would be born. As much as she disliked hogs, she had enjoyed playing with the baby pigs when she was a girl. Mari would love them, too. Then she looked more closely at the sty. "Is the fence made out of porch rails?"

He grinned. "For sure. I replaced Dr. Hoover's porch posts and rails, and he gave me the old ones. There was plenty of usable wood to build the sty."

"That was convenient." She scratched the sow's hairy back. "Now that I've seen her, can we find some fresh air?"

Andrew led her out through the dairy and the pasture gate to the garden. Bethany stared at it, trying to figure out why the orderly rows of plants looked so different.

"The lilies are gone?" She turned to Andrew. "What happened to them?"

"I took them out." He led the way to the springhouse, where a stone bench sat in the cool shade.

"Why did you do that? I thought you wanted to keep them."

"I took them out because they reminded me of Lily and my old life."

"Wasn't that why you wanted to keep them?"

"I have a new life now, and it's time to put the past behind me."

Bethany sat on her hands, wiggling her toes in the black dirt. "Why are you telling me this?"

"Nearly losing Mari has woken me up to some things."

"Like what?"

"Like how important it is to hold loved ones close."
Bethany nodded.

Andrew leaned his forearms on his knees and tented his fingers together. Bethany watched a black ant climb over her toe and back down onto the path. The minutes stretched as she listened to the insects hidden in the grasses and the bird calls in the woods.

"Custard," Andrew said, startling her. "That's your favorite pie. And blue is your favorite color. You like frogs and snakes, but you don't like bugs."

Bethany stared at him.

"You like fresh-baked bread and watching the stars at night. And your favorite flowers are purple lilacs."

He glanced at her.

"You like a clean house, but you don't like scrubbing the floors. You like to watch the fireflies in the evening." He scooted closer to her. "And you like babies."

She felt her face heat in a blush at that and looked down at her toes again.

"I know you, Bethany. We've been friends our entire lives, and I realized recently that I love you. I've loved you for a long time."

When she dared to look at him again, he took her hand and held it.

"You are not my second choice for a wife. You are my first choice. You've always been my first choice."

"But you married Lily."

He nodded. "When I thought you had married Peter. I thought you had forgotten all about me."

"I would never forget about you. How could I?"

Andrew squeezed her hand. "I'd like to start our marriage again, and this time as a real marriage." He put his arm around her and drew her close. "But I have to know. Dave told me he thought there was another man you had feelings for, and that's why you turned down all those marriage proposals. I have to know who it is."

Bethany laid her hand along the side of his face, looking into his eyes. "It was you. It's always been only you."

When he kissed her, Bethany realized that a kiss on the cheek would never be enough again.

The hot summer days gave way to September and even though the days could still reach sweltering temperatures, the nights brought a fresh coolness. Rose and Jonah planned their wedding for the second Tuesday of the month, and the couple looked forward to the day with the excitement of teenagers. But Andrew still wondered if older folks could be as happy as he and Bethany were.

He paused in his afternoon milking as he thought of the depth of the love that had grown between the two of them, but Dinah didn't let his mind wander very long. She swung her tail at him until he remembered his task.

As he covered the milk pail and put it in the springhouse, he heard Jenny barking. The postman had come, and Andrew jogged out to the mailbox to see what he had brought. There was only one envelope. A letter from *Mamm* in Iowa. He took it into the house, ready for his supper.

Mari ran to greet him at the door, and he scooped her up in a bear hug, then sat at the table with her on his knee.

"A letter came from *Mamm*," he said, slitting the envelope open.

Rose and Bethany turned to watch him as he unfolded the letter.

"It's addressed to all of us." Andrew read the first few lines to himself. "She says *Grossmutti* has passed on."

Bethany sank into the chair beside Andrew while Rose turned to the window.

"Such sad news." Rose sniffed and wiped her eyes with the corner of her apron. "What will Martha do now?"

"She says she thought of moving in with my brother, Noah. But he and his wife live with her parents on their farm and are barely making a go of it."

"Then she must come here," Bethany said in the firm voice that told him her mind was made up. "We can make room for Martha or build a *Dawdi Haus* for her. She belongs here. This is her home."

Andrew frowned, watching the envelope in his hand. "Are you sure?"

"We will find a place for her."

"Rose," Andrew said as she sat in the chair across from them. "What do you think?"

"Bethany is right. She belongs here. I think I have an idea." Rose tapped the table with her forefinger as she considered it. "I'll need to see what Jonah thinks, but what if he and I went to Iowa? We can help her pack her things and sell her farm, and I can put my farm up for sale at the same time."

"I thought you didn't want to do that," said Bethany. "You were adamant about keeping it."

Rose raised her eyebrows. "I was wrong. It's time to sell the place. Or try to sell it. My home is here, with all of you."

"Would you go now? The wedding is only a week away." Bethany took Mari into her lap as her daughter tried to get her attention.

"We won't travel before the wedding. We can make it our wedding trip." Rose smiled at the thought.

"*Mamma*, who is coming here?"

"We're going to ask *Mammi* Martha to come," Andrew said. "Would you like that?"

"Two *mammis* are best." Mari held up three fingers. Ever since her birthday in August, three fingers had represented every number.

"I'll talk to Jonah about the trip right away," Rose said, rising from the table. "As soon as he agrees, we'll send a letter telling her our plans."

Bethany couldn't help laughing at Rose's enthusiasm. "What if Martha doesn't want to come?"

"She will." Rose went to her room for her cloak and bonnet. When she came out, she was tying her bonnet ribbons under her chin. "Martha is a sensible woman, and she always agrees with my plans."

After Rose left, Bethany and Andrew looked at each other and burst out laughing.

"What is funny?" Mari asked, looking from Bethany to Andrew.

"Not funny." Bethany hugged Mari. "Just fun. We like to see *Mammi* Rose when she's happy."

"She left before she could eat her supper," Andrew said. "Do you mind if we go ahead and eat? I'm starving."

"For sure we can."

Bethany set the table with Mari's help as Andrew read the letter again. *Mamm* sounded sad, but relieved at the same time. Her mother had been very ill for a long time, and in much pain for most of that time. *Grossdatti* had passed away only months after *Daed*. *Mamm* would need a nice, quiet place to live where she could be taken care of instead of being the one to care for sick loved ones.

"I think *Mamm* should have her own home, rather than living here with us."

Bethany opened the oven door to take out the casserole she had made for their supper.

"You don't think she'll want to live in this house? It was hers for so many years."

Andrew shook his head. "She writes that even though she misses her mother, she is enjoying the peace and quiet of living on her own, without needing to be responsible for anyone else."

Bethany lifted Mari onto her stool, then sat in her chair. They bowed their heads for the silent prayer, then Andrew scooped a spoonful of the chicken and noodles onto his plate.

"Where would Martha live if she didn't move in with us?" Bethany asked.

"The *Dawdi Haus* on Jonah's farm is still empty, isn't it?"

"Not for long. Aaron and Katie are moving into it after they get married."

Andrew set down his fork. "When is that going to happen?"

"In November, I think. I heard Aaron talking to *Daed* about getting the *Dawdi Haus* ready for them."

"Then we'll have to build one here."

"I'm surprised that there isn't one already."

"There has never been a need for one until now." Andrew helped himself to more noodles. "Where do you think we should build it?"

"There isn't very much level ground, except out in the fields." Bethany helped Mari cut her noodles into smaller pieces. "We could build it into the hill, like this one was."

"Maybe on the other side of the lane, just past the big tree. My grandfather used to have a sheepfold there."

Bethany nodded. "It's a pleasant spot, yet close enough to the house so she can come over whenever she wants."

"Or enjoy the company of her granddaughter."

Bethany grinned. "I'm looking forward to having her here. I hope she agrees to the plan."

"We'll find out soon. I'll write to her as soon as Rose tells us what Jonah said about her idea of traveling out there."

"If I know Rose and *Daed*, they will be going."

Andrew caught Bethany's gaze and smiled. He caught her hand in his and squeezed it. "You are a wonderful wife. You know that, don't you?"

"I know you think so, and that is enough for me."

She smiled back at him with no trace of discontent. He was truly blessed.

Epilogue

In November, it was time to celebrate Aaron's wedding.

Andrew had helped Aaron make repairs to the *Dawdi Haus*, and Bethany had helped Rose and Martha with the finishing touches. By the time they were done, the little house looked fresh and new. Aaron had wanted it to be a surprise for Katie, and Bethany could hardly wait to see what she thought of it.

The wedding was going to be held at the Miller home, and Bethany helped with the preparations along with the other women in the church, but on the day of the wedding itself, she had no responsibilities and could enjoy the day.

She and Mari sat next to Lovina and Rachel in the back rows of benches during the worship service. When the time for the wedding vows came, Bethany held Mari on her lap, reliving the moment when she made her own promises to God and to Andrew. Promises that she no longer wondered if she would regret.

After the wedding, Lovina made Bethany sit at a table with Mari and little Rachel. "You need to take things easy. I'm sure you've worked much too hard already today."

"Not that hard, but you're right. It will feel good to sit down for a while."

Lovina frowned at her. "You haven't told Andrew yet, have you?"

Bethany held a finger up to her lips. "Not yet. Not until I'm sure."

"It's been three months. I think you are as sure as you can be."

"I'll tell him tonight, after we're home."

Mari tugged on her skirt. "Tell him what?"

Lovina went back to the kitchen, leaving Bethany to answer Mari's question.

"I'm going to tell your *daed* how much I love him."

"I love him, too. Can I tell him?"

"You can tell him any time you like." Bethany kissed the top of Mari's *kapp*.

She gave the girls a handkerchief to play with. Mari hadn't been able to make a handkerchief baby yet, but she insisted on trying until she mastered the skill. Bethany showed her how to twist the handkerchief just so until the poor cotton cloth was a damp, wrinkled mess. Rachel, curious about everything Mari did, looked on.

By the end of the afternoon, Bethany was exhausted. She hadn't gotten tired of watching Aaron's and Katie's faces, though. She didn't think she had ever seen a happier couple.

The young men started cleaning up as people left, loading the benches into the church wagon. Chore time was approaching, and folks had to get home.

Lovina gathered up Rachel after the dishes had all been washed.

"I'll see you on Sunday?" she asked.

"I'm looking forward to it."

Andrew was ready to go soon after that, and Bethany got into the new buggy with Martha and Mari for the ride home.

"That was a lovely wedding," Martha said. "I wish I had been here for yours, but it couldn't be helped."

"I'm glad I was there," Bethany said, "but I was so nervous that I hardly remember anything about it."

"Did you remember that you invited your brothers to spend the night with us tonight?" Andrew asked.

"For sure, I did. They're coming over for supper, and they'll stay until chore time in the morning."

"The last time they were at our place, John and James stayed up all night."

"Not this time." Bethany was determined they wouldn't pull that stunt again. "This time, I'm deciding when they go to bed, not Nathaniel."

By the time Mari was in bed and asleep that night, though, Bethany was having second thoughts. Martha had gone to bed the same time as Mari, but Nathaniel had brought up the subject of whether the Plain people should use tractors, and Andrew was caught in the debate. John had joined in the discussion, which was lasting far past the younger boys' bedtimes.

She finally convinced John and James to go to sleep in her old bedroom over the porch, leaving Andrew and Nathaniel to fend for themselves. After making sure her brothers were putting themselves to bed, she wandered down the hall to her bedroom to check the clock on Andrew's side of the bed. It was nearly eleven o'clock.

"Andrew, come to bed," she groaned to herself, but she was determined to stay awake until he came upstairs.

Bethany brushed her hair and braided it for the night, then went back to the head of the stairs. Andrew and Nathaniel were still talking, their voices drifting up the staircase. She peeked in Mari's door to check on her. The room was dim, but enough light filtered in the window that she could make out the form of her daughter sleeping peacefully under the quilt Rose had made. She leaned against the door frame, thinking of how blessed her life was, and how full of love.

She heard Andrew on the steps, but didn't move until he came up behind her, peering over her shoulder at their daughter.

Bethany leaned her head against Andrew's cheek. "You and Nathaniel talked for a long time."

Andrew put an arm around her and drew her close. "Did we keep you awake?"

"I wanted to talk to you."

"You should have gone to bed instead of waiting for me."

"But I have something to tell you."

The clouds that had been blocking the moon drifted away and the light filtered through the window onto Mari's face. Bethany reached up and tugged at Andrew's beard.

"I thought you'd like to know that you need to finish the *Dawdi Haus*. We'll want to use that other bedroom soon."

"Did you want to move into the downstairs bedroom?"

"We'll need to."

"What is wrong with our room?"

"Someone else needs to use it."

Andrew stilled, then caressed her cheek with one finger. "Someone small?"

She nodded. "And probably hungry."

"Do I need to make a cot?"

"And I need to make diapers."

"That is the happiest news of all." He leaned closer and kissed her.

* * * * *

If you enjoyed this Amish romance,
be sure to pick up these other Amish historical
romances from Jan Drexler:

The Prodigal Son Returns
A Mother for His Children
An Amish Courtship
The Amish Nanny's Sweetheart

Find more great reads at
www.LoveInspired.com

Dear Reader,

This story was inspired by an incident in my grandmother's life.

Before any of us were born, Grandma had a sweetheart. Sometime during their college years, they lost touch. He married and raised a family.

Meanwhile, Grandma married and raised a family of her own.

Fifty years later, now both widowed, Grandma and her sweetheart attended the same wedding. His request—"Do you mind if I write to you?"—led to a renewal of their romance. Their marriage lasted ten years, until Grandma's sweetheart passed away.

Andrew and Bethany's story grew out of the question "What if they had been reunited sooner?" What if?

But as we know, God's ways are not our ways. Grandma's story happened just as it should have.

I love to hear from my readers! You can contact me through my website, www.JanDrexler.com, or on Facebook at www.Facebook.com/JanDrexlerAuthor.

May God bless you,
Jan Drexler

"I wanted to talk to you about a project I'm getting started on. I'm opening a bakery."

"You are?" Annie couldn't keep the surprise out of her voice.

"Ja," Caleb said. "I stopped by to see if you'd be interested in working for me."

"You want to hire me? To work in your bakery?"

"I've had some success selling bread and baked goods at the farmers market in Salem. Having a shop will allow me to sell year-round, but I can't be there every day and do my work at the farm. My sister, Miriam, told me you'd do a *gut* job for me."

"It sounds intriguing," Annie said. "What would you expect me to do?"

"Tend the shop and handle customers. There would be some light cleaning. I may need you to help with baking sometimes."

"Ja," I'd be interested in the job."

"Then it's yours. If you've got time now, I'll give you a tour of the bakery, and we can talk more about what I'd need you to do."